BILLY the GOAT'S Big Breakfast

Jez Alborough

DOUBLEDAY

To Adele

 *Billy's Breakfast Song* can be heard
and downloaded, along with the sheet
music, from **jezalborough.com/billythegoat**

BILLY THE GOAT'S BIG BREAKFAST
A DOUBLEDAY BOOK
978 0 857 53036 3

Published in Great Britain by Doubleday, an imprint of Random House Children's Publishers UK
A Random House Group Company

This edition published 2013

1 3 5 7 9 10 8 6 4 2
Copyright © Jez Alborough, 2013
Billy's Breakfast Song © Jez Alborough, 2013

With thanks to Philippa and Dave for help with the musical notation.

RANDOM HOUSE CHILDREN'S PUBLISHERS UK
61–63 Uxbridge Road, London W5 5SA

www.randomhousechildrens.co.uk
www.randomhouse.co.uk

Addresses for companies within The Random House Group Limited can be found at:
www.randomhouse.co.uk/offices.htm

THE RANDOM HOUSE GROUP Limited Reg. No. 954009

A CIP catalogue record for this book is available from the British Library.

Printed in China

Nat the Cat made a breakfast to share
with her friends Billy Goat and Hugo Hare.
She was going to make a breakfast treat,
with some lovely homemade bread to eat.

Nat mixed up water, flour and stuff
until it was stretchy and springy enough,

then left it to rise in a small gooey ball –
that's when the doorbell rang in the hall.

'Hi, Billy,' said Nat, 'come in, take a seat.'
'I'm ever so hungry,' said Billy, 'let's eat!'

He ran to the kitchen and down he sat.
'We can't start breakfast yet,' cried Nat.

'You've come too early – the food isn't made,
the juice isn't juiced and the table's not laid.
And Hugo Hare won't be here until eight,
we can't start without him – you'll just have to wait.'

Billy Goat sighed and stared at the bread,
'I'm not very good at waiting,' he said.
'Why don't you lay the table?' said Nat.
'You'll have waited a lot by the time you've done that.'

So Billy brought butter, jam and three mugs,
some knives and plates and the juice in a jug.

He slowly laid out the cups, knives and plates
then ran out of things to do – except wait.

But the food made waiting harder because
his tummy kept saying how hungry he was.
The juice in the jug looked zingy and yummy,
'I want some of that,' cried Billy Goat's tummy.

Billy thought that he'd take just a couple of sips
as he lifted the jug to his slobbery lips.
He gulped and he glugged then he took a big slurp,
put down the jug, then burped a big **BURP**.

Billy's tum was still hungry, it wanted some more,
he looked round the kitchen and guess what he saw?

There, on the stove, sat the mix for the bread.
'Have a nibble on that,' his tummy said.

Billy tried to resist,
he knew that he should,
but he felt so hungry,
the bread looked so good.
He closed both his eyes
and gave up the fight,
as his mouth opened wide
and he took a big bite.

'**YUCK!**' thought Billy. 'This bread is too chewy!
It should be all crumbly, not squishy and gooey.'
Just then someone called his name from outside,
'Hi, Billy! It's Hugo – I'm here,' he cried.

Billy tried to answer, but what could he do?
His mouth was full of a big lump of goo!

He just couldn't speak, he felt such a chump,
so with one great, big **GULP**

he swallowed
the lump.

'Hello,' said Billy, as his friends bustled in,
but Nat saw beyond Billy's big, sticky grin.

The juice was all gone, to the very last drop
and the mix had a bite-sized hole in the top.

Nat turned on the oven and put in the mix,
but then she was left with a problem to fix –

now there's not enough food to get them all fed.
'I'm just popping out for a minute,' she said.

'Oh, Hugo,' said Billy, with a lump in his throat.
'I've been such a naughty, greedy goat.
I knew it was wrong and I knew it was rude,
but before you came in I ate half the food.
The horrible bread made my tummy rumble
and now it's started to gurgle and grumble.'

His tummy did something else as well –
as it mumbled and rumbled it started to swell.
Hugo could hardly believe what he saw.
It was twice the size that it had been before!

'I'm back,' cried Nat – Billy wanted to run,
he didn't want Nat to know what he'd done.
But Hugo stepped in, he grabbed a big coat
and threw it right over his friend Billy Goat.

'Why are you all covered up?' asked Nat.

'He's cold,' said Hugo – Nat soon fixed that.

'Come sit by the stove and get warm,' she said,

'and soon you can eat my freshly baked bread.'

So rumbling, grumbling under a coat
sat a bloated and ever so hot little goat.
But worse was the feeling growing inside
of the secret which Billy was struggling to hide.

RUMBLE

GRUMBLE

GURGLE

'I'm not cold, I'm **HOT**,'
blurted out Billy Goat,
'and I've got a big tummy
beneath this coat.

I swallowed a lump of your bread and soon,
my tummy swelled up like a great big balloon!
Now I feel horrible deep down inside.
I'm ever so sorry, Nat,' he cried.

'Oh, Billy,' said Nat, 'that bread was still raw.
That's why it made your tummy so sore.

It had to be baked and the mix had to rise.
That's when it blows up to double the size.'

She took out the loaf and it smelled so good,
just like a freshly baked loaf really should.

'But there's no juice,' said Billy, 'and the loaf is too small.
It's my fault there isn't enough for us all.'

But Nat said, 'That's why I popped out before.
I bought us some muffins and juice from the store.'

They all sat down with a knife and a plate
and this time nobody needed to wait.
They ate muffins and jam and butter all spread,
on Nat's crusty, crumbly homemade bread.

They swallowed and slurped it all down and by then
Billy Goat's tummy was happy again.
When the breakfast was finished Nat made up a song
and both of her friends started singing along.

♩ = 162

What's in Bil-ly's tum-my? A big lump of goo.

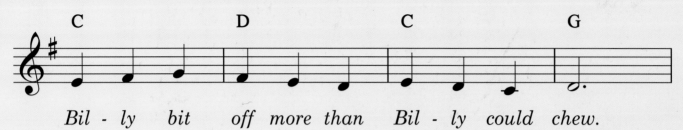

Bil - ly bit off more than Bil - ly could chew.

He thought it was bread but in - stead it was dough and

in - side his tum - my it star - ted to grow.

Oh no! Sil - ly Bil - ly, you made a mis - take. Be -

fore you can eat it the dough has to bake. So

if you don't want a bal - loon in your tum...

Next time just wait___ for Hu - go to come.

They'd eaten the food and drank the juice dry
and now it was time to be saying goodbye.
With so much fun to share between three
what a splendid big breakfast it turned out to be.

THE SWORD AND THE SCALPEL

Harry Brand fails medical school in 1935 and takes himself off to Ethiopia, to serve as a medical orderly with a Red Cross unit, serving with the army of Haile Selassie. There he gains first-hand knowledge of the horrors of war, as well as meeting a woman who is to have a profound effect on his life. Harry soon finds himself engaged in a greater war, against Nazi Germany. Harry's instincts are for saving lives, but now he must learn to kill to survive ...

THE SWORD AND THE SCALPEL

'The condition of man is a condition of war, of everyone against everyone.'

Thomas Hobbes
Leviathan

The Sword And The Scalpel

by
Alan Savage

Magna Large Print Books
Long Preston, North Yorkshire,
England.

British Library Cataloguing in Publication Data.

Savage, Alan
    The sword and the scalpel.

    A catalogue record for this book is
    available from the British Library

    ISBN 0-7505-1414-0

First published in Great Britain by Severn House Publishers
Ltd., 1996

Copyright © 1996 by Alan Savage

Cover illustration © Len Thurston by arrangement with
P.W.A. International Ltd.

The moral right of the author has been asserted

Published in Large Print 1999 by arrangement with Severn
House Publishers Ltd.

Magna Large Print is an imprint of
Library Magna Books Ltd.
Printed and bound in Great Britain by
T.J. International Ltd., Cornwall, PL28 8RW.

Contents

Contents

Part One

The Call to Arms

'As long as war is regarded as wicked, it will always have its fascination. When it is looked upon as vulgar, it will cease to be popular.'

Oscar Wilde
The Critic as Artist

Chapter One

Bombs in the Desert

The aircraft swooped low out of the cloudless sky. Single-engined biplanes, each flew behind a stuttering red pattern, from which a leaden hail sent dust scattering to left and right along thin pathways of death. But the bullets were avoidable. More deadly were the little bombs fastened under the lower wing, close to the thick green, white and red stripes, to be released at the touch of a lever. When these came plummeting downwards, bits of earth and rock flew skywards in response, and bits of men and animals too, where the bombs had struck their targets.

The Ethiopian tribesmen galloped to and fro, firing their rifles into the air at the marauding squadron, shrieking their defiance even as they died. Standing outside the medical tent, Harry Brand waved a huge white flag with a red cross to and fro, while sweat poured down his cheeks and soaked his shirt, but the perspiration was caused more by angry frustration and heat than by fear.

'I thought the Italians invented the Red Cross,' he shouted.

'Actually, it was a Swiss,' Andrews pointed out. 'Although it was as a result of an Italian war, to be sure.'

'So now they ignore it,' Harry said.

'By no means,' Andrews said equably. 'They would point out, if asked, that they have not actually dropped a bomb on us.' He nodded towards the approaching tribesmen. 'Customers.' He knocked out his pipe, which he invariably lit in moments of stress, while he watched the group of men approaching, carrying those hit by the bombs or the exploding rocks. But he was more interested in the young man who was now laying down the flag.

Harry Brand was, he felt, a clear case of the weight of family history threatening to bury a man in the sand. Harry himself looked the epitome of the best in English manhood. Twenty-two years old, over six feet tall, powerfully built, good looking in a rugged fashion, with wavy dark hair and an engaging smile, he was well-educated, well-read, and no doubt could perform elegantly on a dance floor. Then what was he doing in this particular part of the hell that was Ethiopia in the spring of 1936, taking part in a war the world condemned but seemed unable to do anything about? Simply because his father and grandfather,

12

and probably his great-grandfather as well, had all been soldiers. There had been no other profession acceptable to a Brand of Lower Cheviston. Some of those earlier Brands had been army surgeons, thus providing an alternative for those like Harry, civilized enough to prefer saving life to taking it, providing, of course, that one still wore uniform. But Harry had dropped out. Andrews wondered how many men had failed medical school and yet made sensible and worthwhile careers for themselves? He had known quite a few. But for Harry Brand, failure had been absolute zero. Thus he was here, working as a glorified medical orderly, expiating that failure in the most ghastly fashion.

'God curse all white men,' growled Sheikh Bairan in Amharic, as his men were laid on the ground before the tent. 'With the exception of yourself, Doctor sahib.'

'And Brand sahib, I hope,' Andrews remarked, also using the national language, and kneeling beside the first wounded man. Harry was at his shoulder, and Andrews heard the young man swallow. He had not been out here very long, and had arrived in the midst of a prolonged lull in the fighting, as the Italians, surprised at the vigour of the Ethiopian resistance, had ceased their offensive in the previous December, and only resumed it a week ago, at the beginning of this April, 1936. Thus this was the first bombing raid Harry Brand had experienced, and whatever he had learned at Edinburgh, he would never have seen a shrapnel wound before, in the flesh, as it were. 'Morphine,' Andrews said, for the man was recovering from the numbing shock of having been hit, and was beginning to moan. A moment later he began to scream, but by then Harry was administering the drug, and gradually the shrieks became moans again.

'There's not much left,' Harry muttered.

'There's not much of anything left,' Andrews pointed out, 'including us.' He spoke rapidly in Amharic, and two of the women who acted as nurses hurried forward to clean the wound, while the doctor moved on to the second man.

Harry remained with the first, watching the women. They had become experts, stripping away the bloodstained clothing to get at the wound; the flying steel fragment had torn the inside of his thigh open from just above the knee to beside his genitals. The women chattered as they swabbed at the blood and muck, giggling. They were long past feeling any disgust at what they had to do. Or perhaps they never had felt disgust at sights and smells that would have turned the stomach of any untrained Englishwoman.

14

'This man is dead,' Andrews told the sheikh. 'Take him outside.' He returned to the wounded man. 'Good girls,' he said.

'What exactly are they gabbling about?' Harry asked; he had picked up only a few words of Amharic thus far.

'They are wishing he was one of the Italian airmen, so that they could cut it off,' Andrews translated, and glanced at his junior. 'They would too, you know.'

They ate their dinner for fear a fire would reveal their camp. As if the Italians did not know exactly where they were, Harry thought. The wounded had been removed some distance away, to lie with the other sick, close to the sluggish river that was the main reason for the field hospital having been installed here. The water meant they could be given the precious liquid whenever their throats grew too dry, even if they would remain under guard all night, just in case a hungry crocodile emerged from the turgid depths in search of a meal. The guards chattered incessantly, their voices drifting on the slight breeze, and to a certain extent obscuring the groans and occasional shrieks of their suffering comrades.

And even in the dark insects hummed; they also were a concomitant of being too close to water. But they had to be close to water, which was why the Italians knew where to find then. Just as the Ethiopian company, or body of men—Harry did not suppose the Ethiopian army actually had such things as companies or platoons—were also camped close to the water, an offshoot of those who remained loyal to Haile Selassie and the concept of their country. He slapped mosquitos. 'What's it all about?' he asked.

Andrews shrugged, and filled his pipe. 'Mussolini needs an empire to impress his people. Dictators often find themselves in that predicament.'

'Well, as he seems to be getting his empire, it can't be that much of a predicament. Why don't we smash him, doctor?'

'You should ask Stanley Baldwin that, not me. Nobody wants a war, I suppose.' He glanced at Harry. 'What does your old man think about it?'

Harry grinned. 'He thinks we should bomb Rome, and the hell with the Vatican.'

'Do you share that view?'

'Not about bombing Rome. I think we should send the Home Fleet to the Med and tell Musso we'll sink any of his ships we don't like the look of if he doesn't pull out of Africa. This part of Africa, anyway.'

16

'I imagine you and your dad are in a minority. Does the Brigadier know you're here?'

'He does by now.'

'You don't suppose there are going to be a few fireworks when you get home?'

Harry finished his coffee. '*If* I get home, once he gets over the ranting and raving and going red in the face bit, I think he'll be rather pleased.'

'And you're footloose and fancy-free,' Andrews mused. 'Oh, to be twenty-two again. You mean there's no one bewailing your absence?'

'Well, of course, my mother and my sister. I've some cousins I'm rather fond of ...'

'I wasn't thinking of incest.'

'Well ... ' Harry refilled his cup. 'There was a broad Scots lass in Edinburgh. But she wanted both to be a virgin when she married and to be married to a GP. When I dropped out, so did she.'

'Don't you ever have the urge?'

'For one of these?' Harry gave a brief laugh. 'They terrify me. And I'm damned sure they don't fuck right. Now tell me I'm a racist.'

'I think you're being bloody sensible, for whatever reason. You're probably wrong about the fucking part. But for the rest, that's a whole can of worms. And not only

17

as regards family customs, blood laws, or just an itinerant boy friend. Most of them have the clap.'

Harry frowned. 'Yet you have them handling wounded men?'

'Bring me a nice starched English nurse, or preferably half-a-dozen, and I'll make a few changes. Good evening, Bairan. Is all well?'

The sheikh made an obeisance; he had the highest respect for the English doctor. 'People come.'

'Eh? Shit!' Andrews was on his feet. 'Eyeties?'

'We do not think so. These people are on foot, with one camel. You wish us to shoot them?'

'If they're not Eyeties, I think we had better find out what they want.'

Harry was also on his feet. Now he went into his tent and picked up his revolver. 'Put it back,' Andrews commanded.

'We don't know who these people are.'

'It doesn't matter who they are, Harry my boy. We are non-combatants, and if you don't want to wind up against a wall smoking a last cigarette, you make damned sure that you remain a non-combatant at all times. If it comes to shooting, Bairan's boys will take care of it.'

Harry bit his lip, and returned the revolver to its holster, then went outside again. Andrews was on his feet, gazing into the darkness, at the group of people approaching. Several of them were members of Bairan's force, but there were three people walking in the midst of the soldiers, with their camel. One of the newcomers was also Ethiopian, and carrying a pile of belongings. The other two were Caucasian, and Harry frowned into the gloom. The man was tall and thin and wore a straggling grey beard; behind it could be seen a dog collar. His clothes were rumpled and dusty, and his shoes cracked. His companion was a woman, and her divided skirt and blouse were in hardly better shape, but she herself looked far less exhausted. She too was tall, only a few inches shorter than the man, and strongly built. She was also less than half his age, Harry estimated. She wore her yellow hair short, but it still straggled out from beneath her sun helmet. Her features were too bold ever to be described as pretty, but were most attractive.

He glanced at Andrews, recalling their conversation of a few minutes before; neither of them had seen a white woman for several months. Andrews went forward. 'Welcome. Had trouble?'

'Just the Eyeties getting too close,' the man replied in English. 'Carlton Shafter.' He held out his hand, which Andrews shook. 'My wife, Marion.'

'Jim Andrews. This is my assistant, Harry Brand.'

Harry shook hands, drinking in the woman, who even exuded a faint whiff of perfume together with sweat. To his gratification, she also seemed to like what she was looking at. 'We had to abandon the Mission,' she explained. 'We've been travelling for two days. Then we heard there was an English doctor here.'

'You look as though you could do with a drink,' Andrews said. 'Brandy?'

'Lead me to it,' Shafter agreed. 'But ... you have brandy?'

'Some. It's not Hine Antique, but it's drinkable.'

'And food?'

'Oh, indeed. Come and sit down.' He gave rapid orders to the Ethiopian women, who had gathered to look at the newcomers, and they began preparing a late supper.

'God-damned wogs,' Shafter remarked. 'Do you reckon they'll poison us?'

Andrews and Harry exchanged glances. This man was a missionary? 'They haven't managed it so far,' Andrews said.

Marion Shafter sank into the offered chair with a sigh. 'I'm not sure how many of the bones in my body are still actually connected. What I would really like is a bath. Is that at all possible?'

'Of course,' Andrews said. 'But we can't offer you a tub. And I think you should wait until daybreak. There are occasional nasties in that river.'

Harry was up as usual at dawn, scanning the sky with his binoculars, and then climbing up the hill to do the same at the ridge. He was a bit put out that he had done this yesterday as well, and yet had not seen the Shafters approaching; they had to have been out there, somewhere, but his eyes had not yet become sufficiently accustomed to the unending vista of plain and hill and ravine to pick out everything that moved. On the other hand, he was delighted to have the company. And what company! He returned down the hill to join Andrews for breakfast. 'No sign of our guests?'

'Sleeping like the dead, I'd say,' Andrews suggested.

'Know them?'

'Heard the name. What do you reckon?'

'That she's a looker. How the devil did she come to be married to someone like Shafter?'

'He must have hidden depths. Or maybe she's genuinely religious. Ah ...'

Harry turned, because there she was, standing behind him in a thick cotton nightdress with a towel draped over her shoulder. 'You said I could have a bath, this morning.'

'Oh. Right,' Andrews agreed. 'I'll put you in charge of that, Harry; I have work to do. And Harry, keep an eye on things.' He grinned at Marion. 'I didn't mean on you, specifically, Mrs Shafter.'

'Only on any nasties which may be about,' Marion agreed. 'Lead on, Mr ... I'm sorry. I've a terrible head for names.'

'Brand,' Harry said. 'Harry Brand.'

'Harry,' she repeated.

He strapped on his revolver holster, and led her down to the water. Those of the wounded who could move sat up to look at them. Some of the women were washing clothes, squatting on the bank and beating them with flat stones. 'How long have you been in East Africa?' he asked, as Marion showed no great interest in what the women were doing; or, indeed, in the wounded. Presumably she figured a field hospital in the middle of a war had to have sick and wounded scattered about.

'Too long.' She turned to her left to walk upstream of the watchers, rounded an outcrop of rock to leave them out of sight, and surveyed the brown water flowing past her feet. 'When you said nasties, what did you mean?'

'Crocodiles.'

'Oh, them. Right. What I would like you to do, therefore, Harry, is go upstream, about fifty yards, and keep your eyes open. I'll give you a shout as soon as I'm finished.'

'Suppose there's one already within fifty yards?' he asked, somewhat offended by the calm way she had taken control of the situation.

'I'm sure you'll spot it, and drive it off with your little gun. And Harry, I'd be obliged if you didn't turn round until I call.'

He walked away from her, watching the water as he did so, as well as the mud banks on the far side of the river, where the big reptiles liked to bask. But there was nothing there; with the sun only just clearing the horizon, there were unlikely to be any very active as yet—as crocodiles draw their energy from the sun's heat rather their own cold blood, they are creatures of the day, not the night. And in any event, his thoughts were definitely not on reptiles. Perhaps if he had met a woman like Marion Shafter in London he would have thought nothing of her. But out here ... she was so calm and relaxed about her situation. Indeed, she was so in *command* of her situation. She made him feel like a very young boy, although he did not think she was all that much older than he was. He squatted and then sat, on a projecting rock, watching the water. As was always the case, once the sun was a couple of feet above the horizon it was suddenly very hot. The air was clear and there was no wind. There would be wind, later on, as the land heated up, but for the moment all was still. 'Hello there.'

Harry turned, and gulped. Had she called him too soon? He watched Marion step from the water and drop her nightdress over her shoulders. For a few unforgettable seconds she had been naked to his gaze, a big woman, at breast and buttock and thigh, but all very clearly delineated and quite beautiful to look at. While the dripping wet patch at her groin ... She smoothed her nightdress into place; clinging to her wet body it did very little to eliminate from his memory what he had just seen. 'And not a croc in sight,' she remarked. 'I think you were pulling my leg, Harry.'

'Now, that would be a pleasure,' he said, without thinking, and flushed.

'Do you like pulling women's legs, Harry?'

He was not going to be put down. 'Only if they're worth pulling, Marion.' She laughed.

'We saw quite a few people as we came

24

in,' Carlton Shafter remarked, eating a late breakfast. 'Moving down river. They seem to have a sizeable force around here.'

'If you're thinking of a European-style troop concentration, forget it,' Andrews said. 'There are a fair number of groups, as you saw, and I understand they are gathering further down the river, with a counter-attack in mind. Here, until yesterday, they reckoned they were beyond the reach of the Eyetie aircraft, and they need to be near to water. So they get as close to the river as they can. But that idea seems to have gone out of the window.'

'They're just fuzzy-wuzzies, really,' Shafter agreed, and watched his wife and Harry emerging from behind the rocks leading down to the river. 'Bloody menaces. Why can't they lie down and accept defeat? They don't have a hope.'

'They're fighting for Ethiopia, home and beauty, Mr Shafter,' Andrews remonstrated. 'They have as much right to do that as we have to defend England.'

'Wogs,' Shafter commented. 'What has he been doing,' he called, 'scrubbing your back?'

'Mr Brand has been a perfect gentleman,' Marian retorted.

'What a character,' Andrews remarked, and gave instructions in Amharic. His patient reluctantly bent over to allow the boil to be lanced.

'How long will they be staying?' Harry asked, swabbing the wound as the pus came pouring out. The Ethiopian boy had given a little yelp as the scalpel had broken the skin, but was now maintaining a stoic silence.

'God knows. What does a missionary do when he's run out of his mission? Beats me why he didn't stay, as it seems he actually prefers the Eyeties to these people.'

'Probably afraid for his wife's virtue,' Harry agreed, washing his hands before opening the door of the tent for the next patient, a young woman who was hardly inside the flap than she was retailing a long string of complaints. Harry looked past her to where Marion was seated at the table, apparently writing up her diary. There was no sign of Shafter.

'Take a break,' Andrews suggested. 'This is going to be a long one. She's looking for psychological rather than medical help.'

Harry nodded and stepped outside, past the dozen people who were patiently waiting for the doctor's attention, and walked across to the table. Marion looked up. 'Well, hi. How are the sick?'

'Sick.' Harry sat down. 'Where's your husband?'

'God knows. Literally. He's probably

converting someone.'

'One of the Ethiopians? I got the impression he didn't like them.'

'He doesn't. They're a cross he feels we need to bear. May I ask, what's a nice boy like you doing in a dump like this?'

'The answer would bore you.'

'Try me.' She closed her diary and leaned back, and once again Harry was impressed by the way she could look so cool and chic, in a clean open-necked shirt, unbuttoned just far enough to be interesting, and another divided skirt. Even her boots didn't look really scuffed. And she had just walked, or ridden on a camel, for two days? Not that he was really interested in how she had managed that; his mind was too full of memories of what lay beneath the skirt and shirt.

'If you'll tell me what a nice girl like *you* is doing in a dump like this?'

She made a moue. 'I'm married. Do you want to ask another question?'

'Yes. But it would be impolite.'

'Try me,' she said again.

He decided to accept her challenge. 'You strike a purely outside view as being an odd couple.'

'Most couples are, to outside views. Shafter's doing a great job, according to his beliefs. I admire him. As for living here, well, it's an adventure. Or it was,

27

before this war started. But it can't last forever. And as missionaries, well ... I suppose we're reasonably protected, from the worst of it.'

'Yet you abandoned your mission when the Eyeties came too close.'

'Not really for that reason. They bombed us and blew up our windmill. All we had was a well, you see. Very deep. So we needed the windmill to raise the water. And then, all our congregation packed up and left. So we had a choice of sitting there all by ourselves and dying of thirst, or moving on to where there was water. What decision would you have made?'

'I apologize. I think you're a very courageous woman. Not in just what you're being forced to do, the way you're having to live, but the way in which you seem able to take it all in your stride.'

'Maybe believing in God helps,' she suggested. 'Now it's your turn.'

'There's nothing remotely noble about me,' Harry said. 'I'm a failed medical student. But my family has a long tradition of medicine. Military medicine. So I found me a war and volunteered for the Red Cross.'

'I would have thought that was intensely noble,' Marion remarked. 'Tell me, when last did you see a white woman.'

'Is it that obvious?'

She smiled. 'It's in your eyes, every time you look at me.'

'And I'm looking at you all the time. I apologize again. I'd better get on with it.'

He stood up, and she caught his hand. 'I didn't say I objected, did I?'

'But you're married.'

'True. Now you can ask me, when last did I see a white man, under forty?'

She was galloping where he would have preferred a trot. He was old-fashioned, that was his trouble. But she could be reined in. 'Then we're even,' he said. 'I really must get back.' She made another moue, and released his hand. As she did so, there came a shout from the hill. The man was speaking Amharic, but Harry had been in the country long enough to know what he meant. And a moment later he saw three biplanes, flying wingtip to wingtip as they came up the valley; they could have been the same ones as yesterday. 'Take shelter,' he snapped, seizing her hand again to pull her to her feet.

Andrews appeared in the tent doorway. 'Shit,' he commented. 'This time they're coming for us. Can't they see the cross?'

'Where's Shafter?' Marion asked, in some alarm. Surprisingly so, Harry thought, in view of their conversation.

'As you said, probably converting some-one.' Harry seized her wrist, dragging her towards the shelter of the rocks, to which most of the patients and the Ethiopian nurses had already fled, as they heard the first explosions. They reached the rocks and threw themselves to the ground as there came another series of crumps and crashes. But these were accompanied by renewed shrieks of terror, so loud that Marion's sudden little moan was unheard.

Andrews had remained standing in front of the tent. Now he let out a yell as he realized what was happening. 'Gas!' he bawled. 'Take action! Gas!'

'Oh, my God,' Marion moaned, raising her face from the dirt into which Harry had hurled her. 'They can't! They just can't!' She gazed at Harry, and bit her lip, at the same time reaching for her thighs with a quizzical expression.

Harry pulled off his bush jacket, seized her wrist again. 'Come on!' The planes were circling for another run. Harry threw himself down the slope towards the river, the woman tumbling behind him. To their right the wounded were wailing in fear as the planes lined up again. Harry fell over the edge of the bank into the water. Marion fell beside him with a gigantic splash, and they crouched against the bank. Harry had retained hold of his bush jacket, and this was now soaked with water. 'In here,' he gasped, and dropped the jacket over both their heads.

They clung to each other. Breathing through the water-soaked jacket was difficult, but what air they were getting was relatively clean. Above them and around them the explosions continued, accompanied by the shrieks of the dead and dying.

'The bastards,' Marion moaned. 'Oh, the bastards. They knew ... ' she subsided. Her face was against his, as her body was against his. They had been thrust into the most utter intimacy by the attack. He could almost feel her heartbeat against his. 'Harry,' she whispered. 'I'm hit.'

Harry was still holding her close, and kneeling, they were in water up to their shoulders. He slid his hand down her back, rounded her left buttock, and she gave a little moan; when he brought his hand round in front, his fingers were red. 'Jesus,' he muttered.

'I don't think it's serious,' she said. 'But God it hurts.'

Harry sought the wound again, and she gave a little murmur; he could not tell whether it was of satisfaction or pain. He listened. The sound of the explosions had stopped; so had much of the shouting. He could still hear the roar of the aeroplane

31

engines, but now these too died, and there was nothing but silence. Save for a movement of the water close at hand. He reached for his revolver, having to thrust his hand between their bodies to draw the weapon. 'What are you doing?' she whispered.

'Don't move,' he told her. 'There's something out there.' He drew a deep breath, ducked out from beneath the bush jacket, and let it down again. Holding his breath, he looked left and right, and saw, not a crocodile, but one of the Ethiopian women, feebly beating the water as she tried to keep her face above the surface. But even as he watched, she disappeared. If the crocs were able to survive the gas, he thought, they would dine well tonight.

He ducked back beneath the shirt, took several deep gulps of air. 'Nothing,' he said, and blinked in the gloom. While he had been outside she had taken off her own shirt, dropped her divided skirts, and wrapped the shirt round her left thigh and buttock, where she had been hit. He gulped, because she was again against him. 'How is it?'

'Sore, but I think I've checked the bleeding. Shafter,' she said. 'Dr Andrews ...'

'Stay put,' he told her. 'They know the drill. Andrews does, anyway. Haven't you

32

been gas-bombed before?'

'No.' She huddled close.

'Not Shafter?'

'I shouldn't think so. Do you think he's all right? God, if anything has happened to him ...'

'We'll look after you.'

They gazed at each other in the gloom of the shirt. Harry considered kissing her, but now was neither the time nor the place. 'How long must we stay here?' she asked.

'Another half-an-hour. There's a bit of a breeze. That'll blow the gas away.'

She sighed. 'Those bastards. Half-an-hour, while people are dying.'

'We can't help them if we're dying ourselves,' he pointed out. 'You said something about them knowing something. What did you mean?'

'I don't know what I meant. I was gabbling, I suppose.' She rested her head on his shoulder.

'Supposing we survive, where will you go?' he asked.

'That depends on where Shafter goes.'

'You love him, right?'

She raised her head. 'Oh, no,' she said. 'But he's my husband.' This time he did kiss her. It was long and slow and deep. As he did so, her hands wandered up and down his chest, sifting the hair and stroking his nipples. He did the same to her, save that there was no hair. Then for several seconds they tore at each other's clothes, hands driven by a combination of fear and hysteria. She unbuckled his belt to put her hands inside his pants and hold him; he slid his hands down the inside of her skirt to discover she wore no underclothes. And now he did find hair. They moaned, and sought each other ...

'Marion! Marion, where are you? Marion, speak to me.' Their heads sprang apart, as they sought buttons, their own buttons this time; Marion pulled up her skirt. Then they stood up together, panting, as Harry lifted his shirt over their heads.

'Marion!' The voice was from the encampment.

'Lend it to me,' she gasped. Harry gave her his shirt, and she dropped it over her shoulders; it was so large it drooped past the bandage under the skirt. 'Here, Shafter! Here.' Marion did not look at Harry as she scrambled up the bank, dripping water.

'Marion! Oh, my darling!' Shafter stumbled down the bank towards them, and a moment later Marion was in his arms.

Harry clambered up more slowly. 'Harry saved my life,' Marion was saying. 'He took me in the water and put his shirt over my head so that I could breathe.'

'Then I thank you, sir,' Shafter said.

Harry made no reply. There was nothing he could say. And besides, now he was looking at the row of wounded tribesmen, flung to and fro by their efforts to breathe air where there was none. There were several dead women, too, half in and half out of the water. He felt sick, and then remembered. 'Andrews!'

'He is up there,' Shafter said.

Harry ran up the slope to where the camp had been pitched. The tents had been blown down, by the blast from a bomb which had landed very close to them; the crater was deep and within a few feet of the collapsed canvas. Here two more of the women, those who had been acting as nurses, were dead. And in front of them, by the table which miraculously still stood, there lay Andrews. Harry knelt beside him. At least his boss had died from the impact of a shell splinter and not from the gas. But the stench of the gas still hung on the air, mingling with so many other stenches, making breathing difficult.

Someone said something, in Amharic Harry raised his head, and then stood up. 'Sheikh Bairan!' The chieftain was accompanied by half a dozen men. They looked dazed and shaken. Could these be the only survivors of the attack? Bairan continued to address him, at the same time pointing and gesticulating. Harry could only understand the word death. 'I'm sorry,' he said.

'He asks do you wish him to bury Dr Andrews for you,' Shafter said.

Harry looked past him at Marion. Her face was expressionless, but there were pink spots in her cheeks. 'I would be grateful,' Harry said. 'Would you say a prayer, Reverend?'

'Of course.' Shafter spoke to Bairan, while Harry looked at Marion again. He knew nothing but guilt, that he should have been virtually raping another man's wife while the man he respected more than any other had been dying. But she had wanted what had happened. That was a fact which could not be dismissed as long as they remained together.

Bairan and his men fell to work, using the bomb crater beside the tents as a starting point; it was to be a mass grave and in the looming heat of the day it had to be done immediately; already there were insect clusters seeking space on the bodies. Harry picked through the tents, at least partly to occupy himself. But there was a good deal to be rescued. Even some bottled medicines had survived the blast, and there was a litter of surgical instruments, earth-crusted pieces of steel with which he was so familiar, but which he had never been allowed to use, professionally. 'You will have to be the doctor, now.' Marion knelt beside him.

He glanced at her. 'I wouldn't know how to begin.'

'Of course you do. You are as well-trained as any doctor. What is an exam?'

He began placing things in a haversack. 'And who am I supposed to doctor?'

'Me, for a start.'

He sprang to his feet. 'My God, I'd forgotten. Are you in pain?'

She made a moue. 'A little. I have staunched the bleeding. But I think there is something in there, and in any event, in this country there is always the risk of infection. Will you attend me, doctor?'

'About just now ...' he began.

'At least I know you are a gentle man,' Marion said.

Chapter Two

The Fascists

'Your wife is hit, Reverend Shafter,' Harry said.

'What? What did you say?' Shafter was watching the surviving men of Bairan's command dragging the corpses out of the gullies and from beneath the rocks where they had optimistically taken shelter, and carrying them up the slope to the mass grave beside the field hospital. There seemed an awful lot of them. 'Where is she?' the missionary demanded.

'Over there.' Harry led Shafter to where he had left Marion. She was lying on her face, her head pillowed on her arms. Now even her skirt, worn over the shirt wrapped around her thigh, was stained with blood.

'My God!' Shafter knelt beside his wife. Marion's face was pale, but she managed a smile.

'She is sure there is something in the wound,' Harry told him. 'I am going to have to take it out.'

'You? You aren't a doctor.'

'There isn't a doctor, any more, Mr Shafter. And I at least have *some* medical training.'

'We have to get out of here,' Shafter muttered. 'Those bastards may come back. In any event, there is nothing here now.'

'Mr Shafter,' Harry said, as earnestly as he could. 'Your wife cannot travel as she is. She is losing blood. We could bind up the wound as it is and stop the bleeding, but if there is a foreign matter in there, infection, or even blood-poisoning, could set in.'

Shafter glared at him, and Marion squeezed his hand. 'I want him to do it, Shafter. It's my life, isn't it?'

Shafter looked left and right. 'We can't expose her before these nignogs.'

Who probably know more about medicine in this part of the world than any of us, Harry thought regretfully. But he did not consider this was the time for argument. 'Then if you will carry her to some place private, I will get some gear together.'

He went back to the remnants of the field hospital and his haversack. He really did not know how much he was going to have to do, so he selected a scalpel and a roll of bandages; the only antiseptic was iodine, which had made even the stoic Ethiopian warriors shriek with pain. He also found a bottle of morphine capsules and a phial of anti-tetanus serum. But all the catgut was gone. Well, he reflected, he probably wouldn't make a very good job of stitching her up, anyway. And maybe it wouldn't be necessary. He gesticulated at Bairan in an attempt to indicate that he did not wish Andrews to be buried until he could return, but he wasn't sure he got through; Bairan and his men kept looking at the sky, and it was obvious they were in a hurry to be away before the Italian bombers returned.

Then he followed Shafter behind a clump of rocks. The missionary had laid his wife on a groundsheet on the earth, and was kneeling beside her. 'What are you going to do?' he asked.

'See what needs to be done,' Harry told him, and also knelt beside the woman. 'We have to take these down.'

Shafter grunted, and unfastened the waistband of Marion's skirt. Then he eased the material down past her thighs. He did not seem surprised at the absence of drawers or knickers. 'Do you want them right off?' he asked.

'We will need that, yes.'

Shafter grunted again as he eased the divided skirt over Marion's ankles. Marion's eyes had been closed but now they opened, as Harry gently removed the shirt from round her thigh and buttock. It was soaked in blood. 'How bad is it?' she asked.

'I haven't found out yet. I am going to have to turn you over. Would you like some morphine?'

'No.'

'I think you should have some,' Shafter recommended. Harry couldn't be sure whether he was more concerned about any pain, or about her remembering what was being done to her, and by whom. Marion made a face, but she took the

40

pill and swallowed it. 'Now this.' Shafter produced a small flask of brandy, which he must have had all the time, Harry realized. While guzzling their limited supply!

Marion pulled another face. 'You are going to lay me out,' she complained.

'Drink it. It'll make the morphine act more quickly.' Shafter held the liquor to her lips, and she obeyed.

'Over we go,' Harry said, rolling her on to her face. Marion gave a little sigh, and seemed to subside. Harry peered at the wound, which was in the fleshy part of the back of the thigh, about three inches down from her buttocks.

'Is it serious?' Shafter knelt beside him.

'Any wound is serious in this climate.' The flesh was jaggedly torn, and was again seeping blood. His inability to stomach an excess of blood had been one of the reasons for his failure at Edinburgh. He swallowed, and used his tweezers to pull the lips of the cut apart. I should be wearing gloves, he thought, and should have washed my hands in antiseptic. Instead his hands were coated in dust, and Shafter was waving away the flies which were seeking to intrude. He picked up the scalpel, drew a deep breath, and penetrated the throbbing redness. But to his enormous relief almost the first careful thrust touched something metallic. A moment later he had extracted the sliver of metal which had slashed into the soft flesh.

'What have you got?' Shafter asked. Marion did not move; the morphine together with the alcohol had rendered her unconscious.

'I only have iodine.'

'Iodine? My God, man ...'

'It works,' Harry told him. 'And she is unconscious.' Very carefully he poured some of the red-brown liquid into the wound, watched it coagulate into a crust. Even in her unconsciousness, Marion moaned and stirred.

'She needs stitches,' Shafter said.

'I know she does. But I have nothing to stitch her with. So she'll have to live with a scar. The important thing is to limit the bleeding. Help me part her legs.'

Between them they eased her legs apart. Shafter watched him with smouldering eyes, but Harry ignored him and deftly placed lint, again soaked in iodine, over the gash—this was something he had practised a hundred times since coming to Ethiopia—unwound his bandage roll, and passed the thin material round and round Marion's thigh until he was satisfied. Then he split the cloth and tied it tightly. 'Will she be all right?' Shafter asked.

'I am going to give her an anti-tetanus

shot,' Harry said, loading his hypodermic needle.

'Is that sterilized?'

'No.' Harry punctured Marion's buttock, and thrust the serum in.

'But my God, man ...'

'His help is necessary, to be sure,' Harry said, more calmly than he felt. 'I am doing the best I can. Has she no underclothes?'

'All our gear was destroyed by a bomb. Those bastards ...'

'Had no idea she was here. So this will have to do.' Harry didn't know what made him make the irrelevant remark, but as he did so, he looked up, seeking Shafter's help in easing the divided skirt back up the woman's legs, and was surprised at the expression on the missionary's face. But he was too busy to deduce what it meant.

Not only had Andrews been thrown into the pit by the time Harry regained the encampment, but Bairan's men were busy filling it in again. Harry knew there was no point in remonstrating with them. He went back to Shafter. 'Would you say a prayer?' The missionary muttered something under his breath, but he returned up the slope to the encampment and did his duty. Bairan and his men seemed impressed; like most Ethiopians, they practised at least a version of Christianity.

It then turned out that Harry had a good deal to do, as Marion was not the only one to have been hit and survived. The men, and a couple of women, lined up to be treated by the 'doctor'; they knew nothing about degrees—or lack of them. Harry did the best he could with his very limited supplies. Fortunately, most of the wounds were superficial; perhaps the Ethiopians had tougher skins than the missionary's wife, and the flying fragments of metal and rock had found it more difficult to penetrate. One of the men, however, had broken his arm, and this needed to be set. Harry offered him one of the precious morphine tablets, but he refused, and gritted his teeth while Harry, anxiously watched by the others, manipulated the bone back into what he hoped was the right place, and then splinted it with lengths of broken tent pole.

Then he felt like some of Shafter's brandy himself, but decided he had better not. The missionary had watched the proceedings impatiently. 'Now let's get the hell out of here,' he said, when Harry was done.

'We need a litter for your wife,' Harry reminded him.

Shafter began negotiating with Bairan, while Harry returned to where Marion lay. She was still quite out, breathing

44

heavily but evenly. He knelt beside her and took her pulse, which was certainly faster than he liked, but that seemed obvious. He had rescued a thermometer, and this he put under her arm, having to open her shirt to do so. Once again he was overwhelmed by the femininity of her. A fine specimen of a doctor you are, he told himself, you'd be struck off in ten seconds, if you were a doctor. He was just buttoning her shirt again when Shafter returned. 'What the hell is going on?' the missionary demanded.

'I was taking her temperature. Under her arm seemed the most sensible place to do it, although there are others.' Shafter glared at him. 'And she does have a temperature,' Harry added. 'Nothing dramatic at the moment, but we'll have to watch it.'

'The wogs are prepared to carry her,' Shafter said. 'But they're going downstream. Seems this fellow Bairan knows where there is an Ethiopian concentration, and he wants to join up with them.'

'Makes sense to me,' Harry agreed.

'Downstream is towards the Italians,' Shafter said. 'I think we should go upstream, towards the mountains and away from the fighting.'

'And just how do you propose to do that?'

'We don't have to go with them. We can

stay here until Marion is a bit better, and then put her on the camel. They've found the animals, and most of them are alive. They can spare us one.'

'There are one or two difficulties regarding that plan,' Harry said.

'Oh, yes?'

'In the first place, what do you suggest we use for food? These people have been supplying us.'

'They can leave us some.'

'For how long? Because, you see, while Marion *may* be fit to travel on her own in a couple of days—and I wouldn't bet on it—she is certainly not going to be able to *sit* on a camel, without a considerable amount of pain and a probable reopening of the wound.' Shafter gave him another of his glares. 'So I think,' Harry said, 'if you'll pardon the expression, Reverend: needs must where the devil drives.'

He had another hunt through the destroyed field hospital, but found little more of any value; even their bottle of medicinal brandy had been shattered. He would probably after all have to requisition Shafter's; he had no idea what they were going to have to face before they joined the larger body of troops.

At least Bairan had assured Shafter that there were doctors and medicines with the army, and that they were doing the best thing for Marion. His men also concocted a litter, using what was left of the canvas slung between two poles, and in this the wounded woman was placed. She had regained consciousness by the time they were ready to move, but was very groggy and obviously didn't know where she was. 'The best thing is to let her rest as much as she can,' Harry advised Shafter.

It was just on dusk when they set off, following the river; they were now reduced to a force of twenty, of whom most, including Marion, were wounded, and if Marion was the only stretcher case, more than half of the others were hurt in some way or another, the most serious being the man with the broken arm. They had all inhaled some of the gas and were subject to spells of coughing. 'I don't think they're up to fighting anybody at this moment,' Harry remarked to Shafter.

Bairan understood this as well as anyone, and it was his intention to walk all night, so as to avoid being seen by the Italian planes. This made very good military sense, but it increased the difficulties of the journey, and Marion several times cried out in pain as her bearers stumbled over unseen obstacles and on one occasion fell into a shallow ravine, carrying her with them. After that

Harry stayed by her side. 'I can give you another dose of morphine,' he said. 'But frankly, I'd rather not if you can possibly bear it.'

'Afraid I'll turn into an addict?'

'No. Afraid I may have a more urgent need for it when next we encounter the Eyeties.' She shivered.

By morning Marion's temperature had risen again. They camped by the water, in the shelter of some stunted acacias, and Harry spent most of his time, in between exhausted naps, placing water-soaked handkerchiefs, his and Shafter's, on her forehead in an attempt to keep her cool. She was restless and in some pain; that she didn't feel like eating much was reasonable and all to the good, he thought; they were existing on a diet of snakes and very scrawny crows, brought down by the rifles of their escort. But he gave her lots of water to drink. As this came from the river, downstream of the massacre, he didn't know if he was poisoning her or not but as it was all any of them had to drink he reckoned they'd all go down with cholera together, and that would be that. It was also, of course, necessary to uncover her wound and re-dress it. He didn't like the look of it at all, but recalled that pus was actually a good thing. He cleaned it up again and then peered at her. 'Would you like some more of that morphine, now?'

'I thought you said I couldn't.'

'We can't afford to waste it. But I have to put some more iodine on your wound.'

'Oh, God! Must you?'

'We can't take any chances on infection.'

She made a moue. 'Supposing you didn't have iodine?'

'Then I'd have to cauterize it.'

'Bring on the iodine. But don't waste the morphine. Hold me instead if I lose control.'

Harry cast a glance at Shafter, who was keeping guard; they had made the Ethiopians withdraw some distance from the virtually naked woman. Then he applied the iodine. Her entire body seemed to tense, and she gave a series of little whimpers. He put his arms round her shoulders and she buried her face in his chest, while the pain slowly wore off. Then she raised her head. 'Four days ago I didn't know you existed.'

'Snap.'

'Now ...'

He kissed her on the forehead. 'We'll both have a few memories. If we're around to indulge them.'

It was a time for reflection in a big way. Harry supposed that he, as much as any of the Ethiopians, or Marion Shafter for that matter, was suffering from shock. They were in a war, but none of them had any experience of modern warfare. Bombing was something else again, and gas-bombing separate even to that. He supposed he was best off, because at least his father had told him of the horrors of the Great War—which was how he had been able to cope with the gas—but he had never actually expected to experience them himself. Besides, basically, a medical unit should not be exposed to the actual rigours of warfare. He had come to Ethiopia expecting to face some pretty grim experiences, but passively, as it were. Now ... he was aware of anger. It was a somewhat selfish anger. Some thirty people had been killed in the attack but he was interested in only one of them. Jim Andrews had regarded him with some reservation when he had first arrived, a reservation which had grown as he had learned that the young man was one of the famous Brand family, without a member of which, present and correct, someone had once written, no British Army was ever complete.

And this had been a failed member of that illustrious breed. Yet they had become friends, in their few weeks together. Jim

50

had appreciated Harry's total commitment to his job, his willingness to undertake any task, no matter how menial or unpleasant, and his anxiety to learn. 'We'll make you into a GP yet,' he had promised. Now he was dead.

Then there was Marion. The other side of the coin. Harry did not know if she was going to die or not. He did know that he had fallen for her, desperately. So the emotion was not only illegal and immoral, it was also absurd. She was merely the first white woman he had seen for too long, and their circumstances had made her more compelling than she should have been. But that did not alter the fact that he wanted her with a quite desperate yearning, compounded by the knowledge that she would respond—he was quite certain of that. But the very idea was absurd.

By nightfall, when Bairan was ready to resume their march, Marion's temperature had shot up again, and she was delirious, even muttering from time to time in Italian! Shafter and the sheikh thereupon had a vigorous argument. 'This bloody wog won't stop,' Shafter complained to Harry. 'Says we must keep moving, no matter how sick my wife may be.'

'He's probably right,' Harry said.

'Oh, you don't give a damn. She's just

51

another lump of flesh to you.'

'She's my patient, Reverend. And that makes her important. But if the three of us stay here by ourselves we're done.'

Most of the Ethiopians had by now begun to recover from their injuries and the damage to their lungs—at least in the short term—and Bairan was able to revert to some kind of military organization. He was actually a very efficient soldier, given his lack of training and his even more important lack of modern weapons. Now he sent out an advance party of three men, who ranged wide from the river. And this was just as well, because just before dawn they returned to say there were Italians in front of them, camped about a mile from the water. Shafter did the translating, as usual. 'This bloody wog wants to attack them,' he complained to Harry.

'What kind of force is it?'

'Oh, a patrol. But they've penetrated almost to the river, and this bothers him. He wants to find out how many more Italians are in the vicinity.'

'That seems to make military sense.'

'With Marion along? Anyway, it may only be a patrol, but it may well have radio, and a machine-gun. These bloody wogs don't know how to fight a war.'

'I would say they're doing the best they can, given their lack of fire-power,' Harry said. 'So what's his plan?'

'That we stay here with the women while he takes the men out and does his stuff.'

'Musn't complain. The break will do Marion good.' He sat beside her, took her temperature. She was awake and lucid, thus he could use her mouth. And to his great relief the fever seemed to have broken; she was a degree lower than the previous evening.

She had also been listening. 'What happens if they get beaten?'

He grinned. 'We surrender to the Eyeties, I guess. You scared of that?'

She gave him an odd look. 'No. I'm not scared of that.'

'That's my girl. They may pinch your bottom, and that could be painful.'

Now she frowned. 'Aren't you scared?'

'As a matter of fact, yes. But if I can start talking before they start shooting, I may do quite well. I've spent several holidays in Italy, and always got on very well with the people.'

She continued to frown. 'You mean you speak the language?'

'Don't you?' He remembered her delirium.

'Yes,' she said thoughtfully.

Bairan mustered his men and they crept into the darkness, leaving the three white

53

people and the six women, as well as the man with the broken arm. The Ethiopian women were actually just as warlike as their men, and just as anxious for vengeance, too. They only had two rifles, but each was armed with a long and very sinister-looking knife. 'I would say we're pretty protected,' Harry suggested, although he checked the bullets in his revolver just to be sure. Jim Andrews might have warned him not to become involved, but he wanted to become involved; he was in the avenging business too.

'Female wogs,' Shafter commented.

He wandered off to sit by himself and watch the dawn. Harry returned to be with Marion. 'I know I've mentioned this before,' he said, 'but it really does amaze me that your husband chooses to live here when he hates these people so much.'

'He doesn't hate them,' Marion said. 'He despises them.'

'And how do you feel about it?'

'Don't let's quarrel, Harry. Please. I don't ever want to quarrel with you.'

He squeezed her hand, and she brought his hand up against her breast and held it there. 'When do you think I'm going to be well again?' she asked.

'Well now that the fever has broken, you could recover at a rate of knots.'

She kissed his fingers. 'When I do,

I have an awful lot to be grateful to you for.'

They stared at each other; it was now quite light enough for them to see each other. But then, it was quite light enough for others to see *them*. 'I'll look forward to that,' he said, his voice thick with desire. 'But right now, the more you rest, the quicker you'll be back on your feet.' As he spoke, the Ethiopian women, squatting only a few yards away as they cooked what they regarded as breakfast, began to mutter together, and one or two stood up. Harry stood also. Their ears were much sharper than his, but now he too could hear the distant rattle of gunfire. 'It's happening,' he told Marion.

'Oh, Harry.' she said. 'Hold me close.' Regardless of the women, or of the likely imminent reappearance of Shafter, he held her against him, while he listened to the distant shooting. But it could not be all that distant, he estimated. After a few minutes the noise ceased. 'Who do you think won?' she asked.

'We'll have to wait and see. Just relax.' He laid her down again, and climbed up the little rise, where Shafter and the Ethiopian women were gathered, chattering at each other. Shafter had Harry's binoculars. 'See anything?' Harry asked.

'Dust. Men. Coming here.' Shafter

continued to peer through the glasses. Harry itched to take them away from him and see for himself, but he felt he had already taken too much away from this unfortunate man. 'They're the wogs,' Shafter said. 'With ... shit, two prisoners.'

The women were asking agitated questions, and he replied brusquely, which made them more agitated yet. Now Harry did take the glasses, and studied the approaching group. Nine men had accompanied Bairan to attack the Italians. Now he counted just nine Ethiopians. They had lost a man. But, as Shafter had said, they had two prisoners, unhappy-looking men in torn uniforms, staggering along before the prods of their captors, their hands tied behind their backs. He glanced at the women, a trifle anxiously. The men were close enough for them also to make identifications, and they were becoming quite excited. 'Look at the way they're treating those poor devils,' Shafter grumbled.

'Well, those poor devils haven't been gassed yet, at any rate,' Harry said. 'However, I think you'd better prepare to take charge, Padre.'

Shafter glanced at him, then went down the hillside to greet the victorious Ethiopians. Bairan immediately began shouting at him, as did the two Italians. Harry could understand them. They were saying, 'Help us, signor, for the love of God. These men mean to murder us.'

He went forward as well, followed by the women, who were showing the greatest interest in the prisoners, although for the time being held away by their menfolk. Bairan and Shafter were still arguing as they gained the shelter of the trees, where the Italians were allowed to drop to their knees. One of them looked at Harry. 'Water, signor, please, water.'

Harry went to the stream and dipped his tin mug, brought it back. As he stretched out his hand, one of the Ethiopians caught his wrist. Harry raised his head. 'Let go of my arm, old chap, or I'll break your arm.'

The man did not understand him, but he could understand the menace in Harry's tone and he released the wrist. Harry held the mug to the Italian's lips and he drank greedily. Then he went back to the stream to refill the cup for his companion. Bairan asked a question. 'The sheikh wants to know why you are doing that?' Shafter inquired.

'I would have thought that was fairly obvious,' Harry remarked.

'He thinks it's a waste of water.'

'Well, right this minute, we've some to spare.'

'You don't understand,' Shafter said.

'The sheikh wants us to ask these chaps some questions. And if they won't answer, he's going to kill them.'

'I have an idea they'll answer a lot more readily if their tongues aren't stuck to the roofs of their mouths,' Harry said, and gave the second Italian a drink. 'Now, what does the sheikh want to know?'

Shafter had another discussion with Bairan, then knelt beside the prisoners. 'The sheikh wishes to know where your main body is, and how many men does it contain,' he said, in good Italian.

'My name is Andrea Violetti, my rank is sergeant, and my number is one seven zero nine four six,' the soldier said.

Shafter looked at Harry. 'That is absolutely correct procedure,' Harry said.

'Listen,' Shafter told Sergeant Violetti, 'if you do not tell the sheikh what he wants to know, you are going to die. Unpleasantly.'

'By the laws of war, signor, I have to give you my name and number. Nothing else.'

'Listen,' Shafter said. 'These wogs don't believe in the rules of war, and even if they did, they reckon you broke the laws when you gas-bombed their encampment.'

'I know nothing of that,' the sergeant said.

'Can't you get through to him?' Shafter asked Harry.

'Listen,' Harry said. 'I know you are obeying the rules of war. But this is not a European war. As the reverend says, if you don't cough up these people are going to take you apart. And what difference can it make? You people have all the power. Knowing where your main body is or how big it is cannot possibly give these men any advantage.'

'It is a matter of honour,' the Italian explained.

Bairan had by now joined them, and spoke to Shafter. 'He says we must move on and join the main body. We have no time to waste,' Shafter interpreted.

'I thought he didn't want to move in daylight?'

'He means to, now he knows there are Italians about.'

'Sounds backward to me,' Harry said. 'So let's move. These two can do some walking.'

Shafter spoke to Bairan, who replied contemptuously. Shafter swallowed. 'The sheikh does not intend to take the prisoners with him. Unless they tell him what he wants to know.'

'Well, they're obviously not going to. And it's a bit risky, leaving them here.'

'He's going to give them to the women,' Shafter said.

Harry gulped, and then turned back

to the Italian. 'For God's sake tell the sheikh what he wants to know,' he said. 'Otherwise the women are going to cut you up.'

'We are prisoners of war,' the sergeant said. 'The Geneva Convention ...'

'Is something these chaps have never heard of. And if they had heard of it, they might just recall that it outlaws the use of poison gas. So you have just the one chance to save your skins, and that chance must be taken now. Speak up.'

The private had been listening, and rolling his eyes. 'Yes,' he said. 'I will tell you ...'

'You will tell them nothing, Antonio,' the sergeant snapped. 'We are soldiers of Il Duce. We swore an oath. If we must die, then we must die. We must not break our oath.'

Harry scratched his head and looked at Shafter, who looked at Bairan. But the sheikh did not need an interpreter to understand the Italian's refusal. He spoke brusquely, and the women clapped their hands and came forward to seize the sergeant. He preserved a stoical silence as they stretched him on the ground, while their menfolk gathered round to watch. Harry went to Marion's litter. 'I don't think you should look at this,' he recommended.

'They're not going to ... I don't believe it,' she said. The women had pulled off the sergeant's pants and drawers to expose his genitals. Now they were cackling at each other in amusement as he reacted to their touch and they drew their knives. 'No!' Marion shouted. 'You must stop them. Shafter!'

Her husband looked at her, watched her turn away from the castration to bury her head in Harry's shirt. Harry held her close and found that he was holding his breath. The sergeant gasped and then screamed as one of the women held his shaft away from his body while another sliced at the flesh; his scream became almost animal-like in its self-horror, as the actual pain had not yet reached him. The private started to yell as well, gabbling information in Italian at the top of his lungs.

'God,' Marion muttered against Harry's chest. 'Is it done?'

'No,' Harry said. For the women were reaching for the private as well.

The Ethiopians were full of spirits as they moved out into the bright morning sunlight; the women especially were on a high. The three Europeans were less ebullient. Shafter did not look at his wife as he trudged along, shoulders hunched. Marion seemed to curl in her litter, not wishing to look at the men who took turns to carry her. Harry walked beside her, but he didn't really want to look at anyone either. He had felt nothing but loathing for men who could drop gas bombs on relatively helpless people, but no doubt the airmen had been simply obeying orders, and as the sergeant had claimed, they had known nothing of it. Now he thought of the two bodies lying beneath the trees, wrists and ankles bound together behind them, severed genitals crammed into their mouths—he could only hope that they had died quickly, before the ants and the hyenas got to them. What did one think about when reduced to such an extremity? Nothing his father had told him of the Great War remotely approached savagery at this level.

They stopped just before noon, when they reached a clump of trees growing beside the water. They had left the last of the hills now, and the river had dwindled to a stream dissipating itself in a large bog. Now it was hot and the air was filled with insects while to every side the plain seemed to stretch forever, shimmering and throwing up mirages. But of people, whether Ethiopian or Italian, there was no sign. 'The wog says we will move on again this evening,' Shafter told Marion and Harry. 'Right now it is too hot.'

'You'd better get some rest,' Harry said.

'Don't leave me, Harry.' Harry looked at Shafter, who snorted, and then walked away to choose a place to sleep beneath one of the trees. The bearers had also wandered off, and the women were making a fire to cook the birds they had shot along the way. 'I just hope they don't offer me anything,' Marion said.

Harry sat beside the litter. 'How do you feel?'

'Sort of ... fey, I suppose. How do you feel? Those were *men.*'

'Don't remind me. I suppose fey just about sums it up.'

'Harry!' She held his hand. 'I want to have sex with you.'

'Snap. Maybe, when this is over, when we can get back to some kind of civilization ...'

'Now, Harry. Before ...' she bit her lip.

'I don't think they mean to cut my balls off, darling,' he said.

'Look,' she said. 'Four days ago we didn't know each other existed. Three days ago your friend Andrews was confidently talking about what he was going to do when he went home. Two days ago I had no more idea I was going to have my bum torn open than I supposed I would ever have wings. Last night, those

63

two poor Italians were probably having a drink together and reminiscing about their girls back home. Can you dare suppose what might have happened by this time tomorrow?'

He hadn't thought about it that way. But of course she was right. But just to have sex ... in the open air, and with her husband not fifty yards away! Marion might have been able to read his thoughts. 'Shafter is fast asleep. Anyway ...' she made a moue. 'We have an arrangement.'

He wasn't sure that was encouraging. 'And the Ethiopians?'

'If any of them notice, they'll probably cheer.' She began to unbutton his shirt.

He unbuttoned her shirt in turn, slipped his hand inside. He had wanted to caress these breasts from the moment he had seen her. Now they were his, and she was turning her mouth up to be kissed. It was not until he slipped her skirt down and touched the bandage that he remembered

'Your wound!'

'Bugger my wound,' she said, and smiled. 'No, don't do that. I want you inside me.'

Insects buzzed in his ears and attacked his naked shoulders as he satisfied her, but he hardly noticed them. He thought he had been waiting all his life, for this woman, this moment. 'I love you,' he muttered. 'I adore you. Oh, Marion, when this is over, I'll talk to Shafter ...'

'Let's wait till it's over,' she said.

It seemed impossible that their companions did not know what they had done, but no one looked any different when Bairan clapped his hands for them to continue. By then the sun had started to droop towards the mountains to the west. They ate a hasty meal—even Marion had regained her appetite—and then her bearers lifted the litter and they set off. Shafter as usual walked some distance away, and Harry stayed by the litter. His head was in a spin, and his shoulders itched where the insects had attacked him. Whenever he closed his eyes he saw, and heard, those two Italians. Yet he had to be the happiest man in the world. He would speak to Shafter as soon as they reached the army, and a divorce would be arranged. There would not be the slightest problem, because Shafter was so patently disinterested in whatever happened to his wife. As for what Dad and Mum would say when he came home with a wife they had never met ... but he would not be the first Brand of Lower Cheviston who had broken a few rules to obtain the woman he wanted.

The litter bearers stopped so suddenly

he all but bumped into them. Bairan had held up his hand, and now they listened. 'Engines,' Shafter said. 'By all that's holy ...'

Bairan gave orders, and the litter was unceremoniously dropped to the ground. Harry gave Marion his hand to help her up, and she leaned against him as they peered into the gathering gloom to the east. 'There!' Shafter yelled.

The Ethiopians also shouted at each other, and unslung their rifles. But they had no chance: coming towards them across the plain was a squadron of armoured cars, eight automobiles, each containing four men and a machine-gun. 'Down!' Harry snapped, and threw Marion to the ground, rolling beside her into a shallow ravine as the cars began to spit red.

The Ethiopians screamed their defiance and returned fire, but their rifles were no match for the machine-guns, and several of them were hit in the first few seconds. The rest sought shelter, but there was very little, and the cars advanced inexorably. Harry lay on top of Marion and kept both their heads down. He no longer wanted any part of this war, on either side. 'Thank God,' Marion muttered. 'Thank God!' Having run away from the Italian advance once, she seemed to have chosen her side, very definitely.

'Up, up,' a voice barked above them, in Italian.

Harry pushed himself up, and had the revolver plucked from his holster. He raised his hands. 'English.' he said.

Marion also stood up. 'This is an English doctor,' she explained.

'Signora Shafter!' The major commanding the Italians had already greeted Shafter, now he came forward to kiss Marion's hands. 'Thank God you are unhurt.'

'Only in a manner of speaking,' Marion told him. 'Your bombs wounded me.'

'But that is terrible. You will come with us, and we will take you to a doctor.'

'This doctor has already seen to me,' Marion said.

The major saluted Harry. 'I congratulate you. Now, I will send you back to our headquarters in one of my cars, and you will be repatriated to England. A car is also available for you and Reverend Shafter, Mrs Shafter. I myself cannot come with you at this time, as I must obtain information from these people.' Eight of the Ethiopians were grouped together, surrendered; five of them were women.

'Do you think you will be able to do that?'

The major grinned. 'My men will enjoy

67

their work. Do you not find some of these Ethiopian women very attractive?'

Harry picked up his small bag of remaining medical stores and walked away. Marion followed. 'And so it goes, Harry. That is what war is all about. Mistreatment of the individual. You must know that, as you come from a family of soldiers.'

'I still don't enjoy seeing it in the flesh. How come that officer knew who you were?'

'Shafter is actually quite well-known. That man must have met us somewhere.'

It didn't seem important. Harry looked at Shafter, waiting by one of the two armoured cars designated for their use. 'What are you going to say to him?'

'Nothing. I told you, we have an arrangement.'

'Well, that should make obtaining a divorce simpler.'

She frowned. 'Divorce?'

'Darling,' he said. 'I want to marry you. I love you.'

'Oh, Harry!' She kissed him on the cheek. 'That is very sweet of you. But ... we had an adventure. Now it is over. I am sure we are both glad of that. Take care. I shall always remember you.'

He could not believe his ears. 'You mean ... just like that? After ...'

68

She kissed him again. 'After one of the best fucks of my life. But I am married to Shafter. Remember me, Harry.'

She walked towards her husband.

Chapter Three

A Green and Pleasant Land

'Oh, good shot, Harry' Jocelyn Brand cried. 'Now you get to croquet him. Right into the next garden.' She stuck out her tongue at her husband.

Hector Brand merely waggled his eyebrows as his cousin lined up for the shot, one foot firmly planted on his own ball. Only two years older than Harry, Hector had followed the family tradition; he was a captain in the Shetland Light Infantry. Being on leave he was in mufti this afternoon, but his every movement depicted the soldier. 'Here I go,' he remarked, as Harry sent his ball across the big lawn almost into the rhododendrons. 'Back next week.'

But he grinned as he spoke. Like most of the Brand family, he felt sorry for Harry. Failure at any level was anathema to the Brands, and then that Abyssinian business

... no one knew for sure what had happened out there—save perhaps the Brigadier—but whatever it was it had affected Harry seriously. Hector remembered a very jolly boy from their school holidays together before he had gone to Sandhurst. Since his return from East Africa Harry seldom smiled, and did a lot of staring into space.

Hector duly returned his ball to where his partner, Harry's sister Louise, could make use of it. But Harry and Jocelyn had gained too great an advantage, and the game soon ended. 'Lemonade all round,' Louise said, producing a laden tray. She was two years younger than Harry, and was another who had noticed the change in her brother since his return from the Ethiopian War. But then, so had everyone else in the family. As now, when Harry slouched off into the house.

Hector sat in a deck chair beside his uncle. 'How's Harry enjoying life in the City?'

Brigadier George Brand, DSO, MC and bar, snorted. At forty-nine he had very little hope of advancing further in the present state of affairs. His career had set off at a great pace when he had become one of the youngest colonels in the British Army, before the age of thirty during the Great War, but since 1918 an Army career had been nothing but frustration. In his heart he could not blame his son for opting out of that tradition, but it was still disappointing. And now ... 'He loathes it. Sitting on a high stool behind a desk from nine to five every weekday was never a Brand pastime.' Like all the Brands George was big and powerful and forthright, as well as handsome.

'Have you talked to him about what happened out there?'

'It was a filthy war, like all colonial wars,' George said.

'What about our next one?' Hector asked, giving his uncle a sidelong glance. His own father and this man had been very close before William Brand, head of the Scottish branch of the family, had been killed in 1917. Since then, although Hector had succeeded his father, he had looked upon George Brand as head of the clan.

'What next one?' George demanded. 'If we didn't fight for Czechoslovakia, when we could have licked Hitler, we're not likely to fight for Poland, now he's ten times stronger.'

'That would mean Chamberlain breaking his word,' Hector argued. 'He's not that sort.'

'It's academic,' George said. 'Hitler isn't going to have a go at Poland; he's too afraid of what Russia might do.' He grinned.

71

'So you'll have to wait a while for your majority. As for Harry, God knows. There was a woman.'

'Eh? An Ethiopian?' Hector was scandalised.

'Good God, no. He's odd, but not that odd. Some missionary's wife.'

'Let me get this straight,' Hector said, even more scandalized. 'Harry has had an affair with a missionary's wife? In Ethiopia?'

'I don't know all the facts of the case,' George confessed. 'He's been somewhat reticent. But I would say he definitely fell in love with this woman. And she stood him up.'

'I'm not surprised.'

'Yes, well ... he really has some problems. I was wondering if you and Joss could sort him out. Heaven knows, Helen and I have tried.'

'What about Louise?'

'Louise doesn't know anything about it.'

'She knows Harry isn't the happiest man in the world, right now. What he needs is a new woman to take the first off his mind. Surely Louise can find someone from amongst her set?'

'I am sure she can. Trouble is, Harry regards Louise's set as a bunch of over-sexed kids. I'm not sure he isn't right.'

Hector accepted some lemonade from the subject under discussion while he considered the matter. 'All right,' he said. 'Leave it with me. With Joss, anyway. I'll have to put her completely in the picture.'

'Do so. And I'd be grateful if you could sort something out, old man.'

'It's hard to imagine Harry in bed with anybody,' Jocelyn Brand remarked. It was after dinner, and they had drunk their port and played a few rubbers of bridge.

Now she stood at the window of their bedroom and looked out at the garden, and the rain; she reflected that they had been very lucky to get in their game of croquet—they were calling this spring of 1939 the wettest this century.

Hector stood behind her and put his arms round her waist. Even after three years of marriage and knowing that she was pregnant he still loved the feel of her. Now he nuzzled her neck as he slid his hands up and down the satin nightdress. 'That's because you don't know him.' Harry had already left for East Africa when they had got married. 'He used to be quite a livewire.'

'And now he's doting on some illegal love.' She turned in his arms.

'I suspect there's more to it than that.

73

The Ethiopian War seems to have been an especially dirty one, on both sides. Come on, now, consider.'

Jocelyn kissed him on the chin, and went to the bathroom, red-brown hair floating behind her. Hector didn't suppose she was truly beautiful—except to him—because of her freckled complexion and somewhat blunt features, but she exuded femininity, with her heavy breasts and strong thighs. A real Brand woman, even if she had been a Macartney before her marriage. He lay on the bed and waited for her to return. When she did so he could tell from her expression that she had completed her mental process. 'Constance.'

'Eh?' He sat up. 'Not Constance Lloyd?'

She sat beside him. 'Who else?'

'My dear Joss, Connie Lloyd is the most stuck-up, arrogant bitch in London.'

'Ah! That's because you don't know her very well. She's really a bundle of nerves. Her façade is a defence mechanism. And you must admit she's a looker.'

Hector had to accept that his wife was probably right, in general terms. Constance Lloyd was tall and willowy, with straight black hair which she wore unfashionably long, and extremely attractive features if one could overlook the expression of contempt with which she surveyed most of mankind. The fact that she was willowy put her out of court as far as he was concerned; he liked his women to have things he could hang on to, like Joss. But ... 'Do you really think a woman like Constance would ever look twice at Harry?'

'Why not? He's handsome, well-connected, will one day be wealthy ... and he's all mixed up. Now there's a challenge. Tell me how we do it.'

'A quiet little supper party ...'

'It'll have to be a restaurant. To have it here would be too, well, family-ish. Probably put him off.'

'The problem will be to get him to come, and then to play ball when he gets there. You going to put Constance in the picture?'

Jocelyn switched off the light. 'Only up to a point, or she might not want to play ball either.'

'Ethiopia,' Constance Lloyd remarked, elegantly dangling her martini from two fingers without actually spilling any of it. 'How unutterably ghastly. I thought it was called Abyssinia.'

'The locals prefer Ethiopia,' Harry explained, and took a deep gulp of his gin and tonic.

'It still sounds the most ghastly place on earth,' Constance remarked. 'I say, let the Italians have it, if they're that desperate.'

Hector exchanged a panic-stricken glance with his wife; he would not have said things were going according to plan. But Jocelyn looked contented enough: the ill-assorted couple were certainly striking sparks, but Harry had not yet thrown his drink over her. 'It is ghastly,' Harry agreed. 'On the other hand, it does belong to the Ethiopians. Or it did before Musso took it over.'

'Well, I suppose he felt they needed civilizing.'

'The Ethiopians were civilized, at least after a fashion, possibly at the same time as the Romans,' Harry argued.

Constance was not given to losing arguments. 'After a fashion as you say. I mean, they do all sorts of terrible things. Why, I read that ... ' she paused with an air of surprise that she had got that far.

'They do,' Harry said. 'I've seen them at it.'

Constance's open mouth closed with a snap. 'I think we're being called in,' Hector said, waving at the *maitre d'hotel*.

Dinner was a subdued affair, as Hector and Jocelyn had to do most of the talking, and although there was an orchestra, no one danced. But Jocelyn was even less inclined to lose an argument than Constance, and when the meal was over, the moment

76

Hector had settled the bill, she announced that she and Hector had promised to pay a late visit to a sick friend. 'What sick friend?' Constance demanded.

Jocelyn kissed her on the cheek. 'No one you know, darling. Harry will see you home. But by all means hang on here for a while if you wish. Why not have a whirl around the floor.'

'Well,' Constance remarked, as she watched her friends disappearing. 'This must be awfully inconvenient for you, Mr Brand.'

'It isn't,' Harry assured her. 'And why not call me Harry?'

He wondered why he found her so attractive, while at the same time he instinctively disliked her. Perhaps he was a glutton for punishment. The fact was that she was the first woman he had dated in the three years since returning from East Africa. He simply had not wanted to get too close to anyone in a skirt after Marion. Did he still love her? He still adored her, dreamt of her every night. He had not been a virgin—there had been the odd one-night stand in Edinburgh—but she had certainly put any other experience he had had right out of court. He knew the atmosphere, the combination of revulsion and titillation at what had happened to the Italians, the fact that her wound had meant he had been messing about with her pubic area for some time already, had all combined to bring them both to a climax at the same time, psychologically as well as physiologically. But she had never sought anything more than that. He was the muggins who had supposed that because two people had shared such an experience they would both necessarily want to repeat the mutual orgasm as often as possible. Instead she had swanned away into the evening. He did not suppose he would ever see her again.

So then, in addition to loving her, to wanting her quite desperately, he also hated her, and the hatred had extended to the entire female sex. There was a psychological mess. Thus he wanted to make this girl, carelessly thrown into his path by his cousin-in-law, suffer? That could well be it. On the other hand, Constance Lloyd was undeniably beautiful, even if she could have done with a bit more meat on her bones. And equally she was undoubtedly a young woman wandering around begging to be hit, just as hard as anyone could.

Am I a cad? he wondered. Or can I claim circumstances have made me so?

'Shall we dance?' he asked.

To his surprise, she agreed. They drifted around the dance floor to the slow numbers, rubbing shoulders and hips with other couples, rubbing their own chests and pubes as they held each other conventionally close. 'Did you really see ... well ...' her cheek was against his, and he could feel the heat.

'Every last cut,' he whispered into her ear.

'How did you feel?' she asked.

Almost as if it had happened to him personally, and she were a doctor. But perhaps it *had* happened to him, personally. At least psychologically. 'Very randy,' he said into her ear. She started to move away from him; and he held her close, his hand firmly in the centre of her back. 'I mean, I thought, Harry, old son, while you've got 'em, you had better use them. Don't you agree?'

Now she did get some space between them. 'I'm sure it's a point of view. Will you take me home, now, please?'

'Do leave the light on,' Constance told the taxi driver, and gave Harry a nervous smile. 'I hate driving in the dark, don't you?'

'Actually, I hate driving in the light,' Harry said. 'But you're the boss.' He was continuing his policy of behaving like an utter cad, hating himself for it, and yet also perversely enjoying it; he had never played this role before.

They drove for a while in silence; her parents' house was in Hampstead. 'Are you going to join the Army?' she asked.

'What on earth for?'

'Well, your family are Army people, aren't they?'

'It's a tradition.' He reached across the seat for her hand. 'I'd far rather marry and settle down.'

'Oh,' she said, but she didn't pull her hand away.

'What do you reckon?' he asked.

'What do I reckon about what?'

'You and me, Constance. I'm asking you to marry me.'

Now she did pull her hand away. 'We've only just met.'

'Don't you believe in love at first sight?'

'No,' she said. 'Well ... yes. But it didn't happen.'

'That's because you don't know me very well.'

'Really?' She gave a sigh of relief as the taxi stopped outside the house. 'Actually, one never really knows one very well at a first meeting, does one? It's been a great fun evening, Mr Brand ...'

'You were going to call me Harry.'

'Very well, Harry. Thanks ever so. But I know you have a long way to go ...'

He eased her out of the taxi and on to

80

the pavement. 'Can't I call another taxi from your house, later?'

'Oh, well ...' Constance hesitated and Harry paid the fare. The taxi-driver touched his cap and drove away.

'Abandoned,' Harry said. 'In darkest Hampstead.'

Constance peered at him. 'You're not drunk, are you?'

'Absolutely. Drunk on your perfume. Your beauty. Your sexuality.'

Constance gave a hasty glance up and down the street; he had been speaking quite loudly. 'You'd better come in,' she said, 'and call for that other taxi.' He had, Harry reckoned, scored a total personal triumph, in that her attitude of dismissive arrogance had quite disappeared. She was now merely a nervous young woman with a problem: him. The misbehaving cousin of her very good friends, the Hector Brands. He followed her up the garden path, inhaling her perfume; it actually was delightful. 'Do be quiet,' she suggested and indicated the window above the door; behind the curtain there was a faint glow.

'Is that your brother?' he asked. 'Or your sister? Or your lover?'

'My parents, idiot.' She inserted her key and turned the latch. 'The telephone is at the end of the corridor.'

'If I had intended to use the telephone

81

immediately,' he pointed out. 'I would have kept the taxi.'

She peered at him. 'You *are* drunk.'

'Only with ...'

'Do stop that.' They were in the front hall now, and he was easing the door shut behind him. 'What do you want?'

'A glass of brandy, and you.'

Her eyebrows shot up. 'I'm not sure what you mean.'

'I,' Harry said, very deliberately, 'would like to fuck you, screw you, lie with you, go to bed with you, share my all with you, and have three dots with you, whichever turns you on.'

Her eyebrows couldn't go any higher. 'I'll get you the brandy,' she said.

'And one for yourself.'

She switched on the lights in the drawing-room, poured brandy into two goblets from the decanter on the sideboard. 'If you'd stop pulling my leg for a moment,' she said, 'you'd be quite an interesting man.'

'Who said I was pulling your leg?' He sat on the settee, and tried to catch her wrist when she gave him his brandy goblet, but she evaded him with a quick slither and sat in a chair opposite, knees crossed.

'Because no one could be quite so ... I don't know the word. I mean, you come from a long line of officers and gentlemen.

I know you're not one yourself ...' she realized she had stepped off the edge and hastily back-tracked. 'I mean, you're not an officer in the family tradition, and ...'

'You were right the first time: I am definitely not a gentleman.' He slipped off the settee on to his knees, and crawled across the room towards her, carrying the brandy goblet in one hand. She watched his approach with a mixture of apprehension and amusement. 'When I said I'd like to fuck you,' he said, arriving at her knees. 'I meant in wedlock. How about it?'

'Oh, really, Harry, I told you: we've only just met.'

'What's that got to do with it? All the best marriages are between strangers.'

Constance lost her nerve; she had never been approached like this before. And she had certainly not expected it from her old friend Jocelyn's cousin-in-law. 'I thought you were already suited,' she said. 'Some woman you met in Abyssinia.'

His stare was so intense she drew up her knees even further, when to her consternation he emptied his brandy goblet into her lap, against her stomach. She gasped, and attempted to stand up, and he pushed her back into her chair. 'You ...' she gave a gasp as the liquid soaked through her dress and attacked her petticoat and beyond. 'You bastard!'

'I'll lick you dry, shall I?'

He pushed her skirt up to her thighs. Whatever the shortcomings of the rest of her body, she had very good legs. And apparently very good muscles; she swung her hand and caught him on the side of the head, with such force that he tumbled to the floor. Alarmed at what she had done, and his possible reaction, she scrambled to her feet and backed round the chair. But as Harry regained his knees, the door opened. 'What the devil is going on?' James Lloyd demanded. His heavy frame was wrapped in a dressing-gown.

Constance bit her lip. Harry got to his feet. 'I was asking your daughter to marry me, sir.'

'To ...' Lloyd peered at the somewhat dishevelled young man. 'Do I know you?'

'I don't think we've met,' Harry acknowledged.

'Harry is Brigadier George Brand's son, Daddy,' Constance explained.

'George Brand. You're not in uniform, young fellow.'

'Well, actually, sir, I'm not in the Army.'

'Not in the Army? What's that smell?'

'We spilt some brandy,' Constance explained, keeping as far from her father as the size of the room would allow, just in case he deduced where the brandy had been spilt.

84

James Lloyd poured a goblet for himself. 'What do you do, young Brand?' he asked.

'Well, actually, sir, I have a job in the City.'

'Ah. More sensible than the Army, to be sure. Stockbroking, is it?'

'No, sir. Banking.'

'Ah. There's a future in banking. Baring's, is it?'

'Well, no, sir. Midland.'

Lloyd had been inhaling his brandy before drinking it. Now he put down the goblet with a thump which all but cracked the glass. 'Midland? What position?'

'I'm a teller, sir. You know ... I work in one of those cage things. Shovelling sovereigns.'

'Good God!' Lloyd sat down.

'You never told me that,' Constance pointed out. 'Neither did Joss.'

'Well I suppose she was trying to give me a good press, as it were,' Harry pointed out. 'After all, it's not what a chap does that matters. It's what a chap is.'

Lloyd had got his breath back. 'George Brand's son, working behind a counter?' he demanded. 'Amazing. And you want to marry my daughter? My God, sir, you must be out of your tiny mind.'

'Daddy ...' Constance begged.

'I'll hear nothing more of it. Out of my

85

house, young fellow. Out. And don't let me see you here again.'

'Jimmy Lloyd,' George Brand said thoughtfully. 'Of course I know the fellow. Stockbroking. And you say he ordered you out of his house? By God, I wonder if I should break out the old horsewhip.' He glanced at his son. 'You hadn't been improper?'

'I merely asked his daughter to marry me.'

'Good God. I didn't even know you knew the girl.'

'I met her last night for the first time,' Harry explained.

George gave him a very old-fashioned look. 'What are you trying to do, break the family record for irregular relationships with women?'

'I think you behaved quite absurdly,' Helen Brand remarked. 'Lloyd was quite right to get shirty. Really, Harry, what are we going to do with you?'

'Well, Mother ...'

'Post!' Louise dumped a handful of letters and circulars on the breakfast table.

Jocelyn entered in front of Hector. 'I have just had Constance Lloyd on the telephone,' she announced.

'I can imagine,' Helen said grimly.

'Really, Harry,' Jocelyn said severely.

86

'How could you behave like that?'

'Here's something for you, Hector.' George had been sorting through the post. Now he opened a letter addressed to himself. 'Good God!'

'Something the matter, dear?' inquired his wife.

'We have all to go down to the school to collect gas masks,' George said. 'These must be carried at all times,' he added.

'Gas masks?' Louise demanded.

'I suppose I *was* tight,' Harry said. 'But thanks to you, Joss, she reminded me of something I was trying to forget.'

No one paid him any attention, as there was another epithet from Hector. 'Leave cancelled, must report to barracks. Of all the nonsense ...' he looked at his uncle, who had also been reading an official letter.

'They want me at the War Office,' George said. 'I do believe the balloon is going up.'

'But there's been no crisis on the news?' Helen protested.

'If we're virtually being mobilized, something must be happening, Aunt Helen,' Hector said. 'I'm terribly sorry, but we'll have to leave immediately.'

'Oh, darling!' Jocelyn held his hand, her eyes suddenly damp.

'Now, old girl, it isn't going to take

us more than a month or two to crush Hitler.'

'That's what they said the last time,' Helen muttered.

'I'm going to join the ATS. You said I could, Pa, if there was a war,' Louise said.

'There isn't a war, yet,' George said, and looked at Harry.

As did everyone else. 'I've seen a war,' Harry said.

His father snorted. 'I imagine this one will be different to Ethiopia,' Hector suggested, mildly.

'England, home and beauty, and all that jazz,' Harry said, and left the room to go upstairs. A few minutes later there was a knock on the door. 'It's open.'

Louise closed the door behind her, wandered about the room, fingering things. 'Did you really propose marriage after just meeting the Lloyd woman?'

Harry sat down and began filling his pipe. He had only taken up smoking since returning to England, perhaps in memory of Jim Andrews. 'It seemed a good idea at the time.'

'Because you were drunk. I wonder she didn't slap your face.'

'She did.'

'Good lord. Whatever did you do?'

'Poured brandy into her crotch.'

'Oh, *Harry!* Be serious.'

'I am serious.'

She sat on the bed opposite him. 'You'll be the outcast of London when that story gets about.'

'Sounds attractive.'

'Did you love her that much?'

'I don't love her at all. I was looking for a reaction.'

'I'm not talking about Connie Lloyd. I'm talking about this missionary woman.'

He struck a match, and began puffing. 'You ever been in love, Lou?'

'Oh, yes. Dozens of times. At least four.'

'I hope you always kept your knickers on.'

'I wish you didn't find it necessary to be vulgar all the time.' She got up. 'It would make Dad the happiest man in the world if you'd volunteer.'

Harry's pipe went out.

'So it was all awful,' Louise said. 'But as Hector said, this is different. If it happens. I mean, I don't suppose I'd be able to keep my knickers on if the Nazis occupied London.'

Harry got up and took her in his arms. 'And we can't ever put you in that position, can we?' he asked, as he kissed her forehead.

89

'Brand!' remarked the recruiting major. 'Not the Brigadier's son?'

'His one and only, sir.'

'But ... why are you here?'

'I wish to join up, sir.'

'You mean you're not in the Army?'

'No, sir.'

'Good God!' The major frowned. 'You'll have to take a medical, you know. It's nothing serious, is it?'

'I am perfectly fit, sir. I should explain, I opted for medicine.'

'Ah. Right. There'll be no problem there.'

'But I didn't make it,' Harry said. The major leaned back in his chair. 'So I went to Ethiopia.' The major leaned forward again. 'As a medical orderly,' Harry explained.

'Just what one would have expected, of a Brand,' the major said. 'OTC at school?'

'Yes, sir.'

'Right. There'll be some training, you understand. When can you start?'

'Now.'

'That's the spirit.' He pushed various papers across his desk. 'Just sign where I've marked. I'll try to have you commissioned into your family regiment, but I can't guarantee there's a vacancy.'

'That's not important, sir.'

'A Brand,' the major said severely. 'An

English Brand, must serve with the Royal Wessex, if it is at all possible. Leave that with me. Attention!' Harry stood up and to attention. 'Done like a soldier,' the major said admiringly. 'You're in the Army now, Brand.'

'Oh, Harry! I'm so proud,' Helen said, hugging him.

'Harry!' Louise squealed jumping up and down.

George Brand clasped his son's hand. 'I knew you had it in you, boy. If you make the Wessex, you'll be in my brigade.'

Harry wasn't sure that would be a good thing. He wasn't at all sure that he'd done the right thing, even now. It seemed to suggest a weakness of character, to have submitted to family pressure so easily. It wasn't that he was a pacifist; he had meant what he had intimated to Louise, that he would kill without compunction any man who ever attempted to rape his sister; no doubt it made a lot of sense to reckon on killing any prospective raper first, and in France or Germany rather than waiting until after he had got to England. And he would not accept that what he had seen in Ethiopia had rendered him psychologically unfit to be a soldier. It was just that the whole thing seemed so terribly pointless,

91

such an interruption to the life of the nation.

Not that he personally had anything very important in his life to *be* interrupted, he reflected somewhat ruefully.

The change from banking to soldiering was actually a pleasure, and Harry found many aspects of his new life both enjoyable and interesting. Having been steeped in military tradition all his life he found officer's training camp far less arduous than most. For that reason his new peers at first regarded him with some suspicion, which was shared by the drill sergeants. But they found it difficult to fault him, and his fellow cadets soon realized that he had no side, while the knowledge that he had fought against the Italians in Ethiopia—no one accepted that he had merely been a volunteer medical orderly and nothing more—also helped to raise his stock. He was in any event some years the oldest, as well as the biggest, of them.

His CO was of course delighted to have a scion of so famous a military family under his command, and showed him every favour.

'I served under your father, Brand,' Colonel Hammond told him. 'Great days. Oh, great days.'

Meanwhile the situation in Europe deteriorated. Harry never found out what had caused the scare in July, but it had to have been something to do with intelligence reports coming out of Germany, and as the summer wore on it became very plain that Hitler was considering another expansive move. The question was where? Poland seemed the obvious choice when the Nazi dictator denounced the non-aggression pact between the two countries, but those in authority or in the know in Britain—and these included Brigadier George Brand—were certain that such a move would bring the Soviet Union in on the Allied side, and they did not see how Hitler could contemplate taking on virtually all of Europe at one go. 'What about Musso?' Harry asked on one of his weekend passes.

'Load of old rubbish. It took him a couple of years to beat the Ethiopians. You were there, Harry. You saw their capability.'

Harry didn't reply to that. He recalled that it had taken a British Army, in which Hector's father had served for a while, twenty years to win a war against the so-called Mad Mullah in Somaliland, such was the nature of the terrain in East Africa. And that war had only ended when the Mullah had died; Haile Selassie was still very much alive.

93

Harry was called into Colonel Hammond's office on a morning in late August. 'Sit down,' Hammond invited. Harry obeyed, wondering what on earth was happening. 'You won't have heard the news,' Hammond said. 'It came in late last night. Germany and Russia have signed a non-aggression treaty.'

'Nazis and Communists, sir? I thought they hated each other.'

'Perhaps they hate us more. What is most likely is that they are both hoping to gain more than they lose from such an unholy alliance. The important thing is that this frees Hitler's hand. Our intelligence is quite certain that he intends to move on Poland, now that the Russians have in effect given him the go ahead. When it will happen, we don't know. Military logic would suggest next spring, rather than this autumn and winter, with the attendant threat of bad weather. But we don't know what the Germans have up their sleeves. The point is that we need every capable soldier in uniform just as quickly as possible. This class is not due to be passed out for another three months. But you are so clearly streets ahead of everyone else, and you have some experience of actual warfare. I have therefore obtained permission to commission you now. I'm afraid there won't be any formal ceremony. As of this moment you are Second Lieutenant Brand.' Harry swallowed. He hadn't expected anything so sudden. 'I'm also afraid that there is not yet a vacancy in the Wessex, so you will go to the South Midlands. They're a good regiment. I know their CO, Jimmy Dempster. You'll get on well with him. So ...' he stood up. 'Have a good future.'

'Thank you, sir.' Harry also stood, put on his cap, and saluted.

'Oh, by the way,' Hammond added. 'You have three days' leave before reporting to the South Midlands. Enjoy yourself.'

Harry returned to the barracks. The squad had already been turned out and was in the gym. He packed up his few belongings while he tried to gather his bearings. He had made no real friends during his brief sojourn here; although there had been the odd drunken night out, he was too different to his brother cadets, and there was that age difference. But part of their training had been intended to instill a sense of comradeship, and now he suddenly felt sorry to be leaving. A figure loomed in the doorway. 'Congratulations, sir.'

Harry raised his eyebrows. 'You knew about this, Sergeant?'

Drill Sergeant Wilkinson stood to attention. 'I was informed in confidence, sir, yes.'

'I imagine you think it's a bit premature.'

'No, sir. You're a born soldier. Well, you ought to be. You'll be a general, like your Dad.'

'He isn't quite one, yet, Sergeant. What do you reckon? Will there be a war?'

'Lord, sir, I hope so. It's been too long since the last one. And what has all this training been for, I'd like to know, if we're never going to use it?'

'It's a point of view,' Harry agreed.

He took the train up to London, rather than to Cheviston. If he once went home, quite apart from the inevitable hugs and kisses and congratulations, enormous pressure would be brought on him to stay the entire three days. If he called from London, his presence in the city already a *fait accompli,* he could say that he'd stop at home on the way to his new regiment. That way he'd have two days to himself. To do what? he wondered. Mainly to think.

Talk about *faits accompli!* Even when he had joined, up, he had not considered that an inevitable roadway to killing his fellow man. He had in fact been heartily glad to get out of the bank, and at last to be doing something of which the family could

96

approve. He had not believed anyone could be so crazy as again to start a European War, when the horror of the last one was still so fresh in the minds of everyone over twenty-five. Or indeed, even to those, like himself, who had only just attained that age, but had fathers who could remember. And from what he had seen in Ethiopia, if there was another one it was going to be just as bad, if not worse.

But now it seemed it was going to happen. And he was going to be in the middle of it. He wished he could be absolutely certain of his emotions. So why was he going to London? He knew the city well, but he also knew that it could be the loneliest place on earth. There were people on whom he could call, whom he could telephone, but none of them could be described as friends. He wanted something to happen. He wanted a dream to come true, before he set off into the unknown.

He had read somewhere that if one stood on one of the corners surrounding Piccadilly Circus long enough one would surely see a friend, or at least an acquaintance, go by. That was presuming one possessed a very large circle of friends and acquaintances, he supposed. As his circle was limited it would hardly apply to him. But in fact, he only sought a circle

97

of one. He went to Gieves first, to have his new uniform fitted, and emerged an hour later in the deep khaki tunic over the lighter khaki pants of an officer in the South Midlands, with his single pip on each shoulder glowing in the morning sunlight. Gieves seemed able to fit anyone out in a matter of minutes, certainly if the anyone wanted a uniform.

They would send the rest of his new gear down to Cheviston to be picked up on his way to his regiment. Then, as Savile Row was only a short distance from the Circus, he strolled along. It was, for a brief change, a lovely, warm, late summer's day, which made the emergence of people with gas masks banging on their hips, and the workmen busily putting up mounds of sandbags against all the more prominent building fronts, utterly incongruous. There was also a large number of men in uniform, and Harry had to get into the habit of saluting those who were his superiors, and returning the salute of those who were his inferiors. Obviously, standing on the corner of Shaftesbury Avenue was going to be an exhausting business. But he had an instinct that she might pass by today. He couldn't say why he felt that; it was simply that it was now three years since he had last seen her, that he wanted her quite as desperately now as he did then, even if he remained angry at the way she had walked away from him, and because with everything else happening, this just had to happen as well.

And in fact, he had not been standing there more than ten minutes when he realized that there was actually a woman standing on the far pavement, looking at him. But it wasn't Marion Shafter; it was Constance Lloyd.

Chapter Four

The Call to Arms

Harry crossed the road.

'Well, hello.'

'Hello,' Constance said. 'Gosh, you look different in uniform.'

'Would you call it an improvement?'

'Oh, yes. Very much so.'

'In that case ... lunch?'

'Well ...' her eyes flickered. 'Are you going to pour brandy over me?'

'I never drink brandy for lunch.'

'Oh. Well, then ...'

'There's a neat little place just along here.'

They faced each other, while the waiter arranged cutlery and crockery. 'I had you down as a pacifist,' Constance confessed.

'I probably agreed with you, then.'

'But now the chips are down ...'

'You mean, now the family are all gathered, staring at you.'

'I can imagine. I understand Joss and Hector have gone back to Scotland.'

'Summoned to the colours.'

She peered at him past her martini glass. 'I'm never sure when you're pulling my leg or not.'

'I'd love to pull your leg. I mean, literally.'

'There you go again. I can't imagine why I agreed to lunch with you.'

'I was hoping you'd say, because you'd like me to pull your leg. Somewhere private.'

'For Heaven's sake, how do we always get into these absurd conversations?'

'As we always do, don't you suppose it might be something ordained by heaven.'

Another long look. 'I'm afraid Daddy would never agree.'

'Not even now I'm a wholly respectable officer of the Crown? Commissioned yesterday.'

'Were you? Good lord! Your family must be awfully excited.'

'They don't know yet. You are the very

first person I've told.'

'Oh!' She flushed. 'Then I'm awfully flattered. But that was pure chance.'

'I was waiting for you.'

'For me? How did you know I was going to be there?'

'Instinct.'

'Do you seriously expect me to believe that?'

'No,' he admitted. 'But it would be awfully nice if you did. Finish that and we'll have a bottle of champagne.'

'What, for lunch?'

'Why not?' He ordered.

'Lobster?' she asked. 'Isn't that frightfully expensive?'

'You must have lobster, if you are going to drink champagne with a meal,' he explained. 'Now tell me your plans?'

'I haven't actually made any, yet. Daddy still thinks this is all a storm in a teacup, and will soon blow over, like the Czech crisis.'

'The Czech crisis never actually blew over,' Harry pointed out. 'It just receded for a while, like the tide. But I really was asking about your plans for this afternoon.'

'Well I was going to finish my shopping, after a sandwich lunch ...' she watched the waiter filling their glasses with champagne at the same time as the plates of mussels were placed before them. 'And then, go

101

home, I suppose.'

'Well, the sandwich lunch plan has been changed. How about the going home plans?'

'What did you have in mind?'

'Well, I thought I'd spend a day or two in London, and I haven't yet got a place to stay. You could help me choose one.'

They gazed at each other, and the lobster arrived. 'I hope you don't think I was born yesterday,' Constance remarked, as she cracked a claw.

'I can tell that you weren't, just by looking at you.'

She sighed. 'This is only the second time we have met.'

'I was thinking of love at second sight.'

'That's even more rare than love at first,' she pointed out. 'One has had time to think.'

'You mean one has been thinking about me? I'm flattered.'

Constance found herself flushing. 'This is delicious lobster.'

'Lobster often is.' He nodded to the waiter to refill her glass. 'How about it?'

'Why should I?'

'I will skip the bit about us being made for each other. But aren't you excited, apprehensive? Isn't your adrenalin flowing while you're scared stiff? Don't you feel you may be living your last few days, or even hours, on earth, and just know you have to fill those hours to the brim?'

'I think you should be a poet rather than a soldier. Is that how *you* feel?'

'As a matter of fact, yes. I don't think your Dad is at all right. I feel we're on the verge of something very big.'

She licked her lips, finished her lobster, and drank some more champagne. 'Where were you thinking of looking for a room?'

'The Ritz.'

'The Ritz?!'

'My family always use the Ritz when they're in town.'

'The Ritz won't accept you without any luggage.'

'I have luggage. At my club. We'll pick it up on the way.'

Harry signed the register while Constance wandered around the concessionary windows. Harry paused at her side while the bellboy took his bags to the service elevator, and the under-manager waited patiently with the key. 'That was quick,' she said.

'As I said, the name is known.'

'Lucky you. Well ...' she held out her hand. 'I'll wish you a pleasant stay, and a good war. If there is one.'

'But you're coming up.'

'To your room? You must be joking.'

'There's champagne up there. And we have things to talk about.'

'Do we?'

But she was already full of champagne, and allowed herself to be guided to the lift. The under-manager bowed as they rose. 'My congratulations, Mrs Brand.'

'Your ...' Constance gazed at Harry with her mouth open, then instinctively looked down at her hand. But as she hadn't taken off her gloves no one could tell she wasn't wearing a wedding ring.

'My wife still isn't used to the idea,' Harry explained. Constance shut her mouth again. But how long she would keep it shut he couldn't be sure. The lift halted and they were escorted along a corridor to the door where the bellboy was already waiting with the bag. The under-manager opened the door and fussed happily, illustrating the various services. The bellboy placed the suitcase on the rack and waited patiently. Constance stood by the window looking out, pensively. Harry tipped both bellboy and under-manager, and the door was closed. 'Alone at last.'

Constance turned back from the window. 'What exactly did you sign in the register?'

'Mr and Mrs Harry Brand. I told them we had just got married and were having a brief honeymoon before I joined my regiment.'

'You have got to be about the most absurd human being I have ever even heard of, much less met.'

Harry was uncorking the champagne waiting in the ice bucket on the coffee table. Now he held out her glass. 'Here's to us.'

'Are you trying to get me drunk?'

'I don't want you to get drunk. Just relaxed.'

'I must go.'

'They'll think it very odd.'

She hesitated, then accepted the glass. 'They're bound to find out.'

'By then, I shall be in the Army, and you will have disappeared. However, any time you feel like making it permanent, you just have to shout. Or even whisper.'

She sighed and sat down, one shapely leg draped across the other. 'I suppose I must be mad, too.'

He knelt beside her. 'I am about to be the most terrible cad.' He took her face between his hands and kissed her on the mouth. 'But when it comes to making depositions, my defence will be that I have twice asked you to marry me, and that each time you didn't actually say no.'

'This will be your defence to the charge of rape,' she murmured, when she got her breath back.

'I am not going to rape you,' Harry said.

'Cad, yes. Villain, no. I thought you might like to go along with the idea.'

'What on earth makes you think that?' But she hadn't moved.

He rested his hand on the silk of her stockinged calf and slipped it up to her knee, beneath her skirt. Her breathing quickened as she gazed at him. 'I fell in love with you at first sight,' he lied. 'And ever since then I have wanted to make love with you.' Which, oddly, was not a lie. 'And I have an idea you have felt the same way about me,' he suggested.

His hand was past her knee, now, and she was breathing more heavily than ever. But she still hadn't moved. 'You *are* a cad,' she said. 'Filling me with champagne ... oh, Harry!'

For his hand had slid up to her thigh and her garterbelt. Suddenly she slipped forward, and was kneeling on the floor against him. Her kiss was almost savage, and she clawed so violently at the back of his tunic he thought she might tear even that thick material. But by now they were both past the point of no return. Now he gathered her dress to lift it past her waist; he didn't know much about women's clothes. She smiled into his mouth. 'That won't work.' And released him to unfasten belts and buttons. 'Now try,' she suggested.

He lifted the dress over her head and threw it on to the chair. He entered a world of silk, but now too he was close to a world of throbbing pink and white flesh. Her hat came off, and the wonderland was even more wonderfully shrouded in cascading midnight hair. She stood up to step out of her camiknickers, leaving him free to kiss her thighs and her pubes, burying his face in the black curls. Then she gasped; no one had ever done that to her before, and she had not really expected it of him. But then, never having been alone in a bedroom with a man before, she had not really known *what* to expect. And now she was naked, save for her garter-belt, stockings and shoes, and Harry was realizing that she really did have the most splendid legs, and her breasts, if perhaps small, were none the less perfectly shaped.

She sat down again to take off her stockings, gazing at him. She didn't know how to say it, but she wanted it as badly as he did. He stood up and undressed as quickly as he could. They actually finished together. She looked down at him, flushed, and looked up again. 'Don't you have a brother?' he asked. She shook her head. He put one arm round her shoulder and the other under her knees to lift her from the floor and lay her on the bed. 'Then I *am* a cad.'

'Just be a cad, with me, only,' she begged.

She sat on the edge of the bed, shoulders hunched. Her back was just as attractive as her front. Harry drew his fingers gently through her by now somewhat tangled hair, straightening it as it fell past her shoulders. He found it difficult to believe it had actually happened. Whereas from the moment he had laid eyes on Marion Shafter, he had known they were going to get together, because she was that sort of woman, he had never ever expected to get together with Constance Lloyd—because she was *that* sort of woman. Nor did the fact that she had let him seize her virginity, as evidenced by both her obvious suffering and the stained sheets, alter her essential chastity in his mind. They had both been too full of champagne to think rationally, and he had introduced a mood of *Götterdämmerung* into their relationship.

But now both the champagne and the passion had dwindled, although no doubt the pain remained. He stroked his finger down the fine line of her backbone. 'Let's talk about the wedding.'

She half-turned her head, then looked away again. 'Do you really want to?'

'I want to a lot more now than an hour ago.'

Now she did turn her head, to smile at him, but it was a sad smile. 'Determined to prove you're an officer and a gentleman? As well as a Brand, of course.'

'Realizing that when I said I loved you, I meant it.' Did he? He wished he could be sure.

She got up, went into the bathroom, and he heard water running. She came back into the room. 'It's a very big step.'

'So is, well ... losing one's virginity.'

'Yes,' she agreed. 'It is. But marriage lasts longer.'

He sat up, unable to believe his ears. 'You mean you *don't* want to? Now?'

'I never did want to, Harry. You sort of forced the issue.'

She went back into the bathroom and switched off the taps. A moment later he heard the faint splash as she got in. He hesitated; he had never looked at a woman sitting in a bath. He had never been *in* a bathroom with a woman. But having already shared their bodies ... He went into the bathroom. She had scooped her hair on to the top of her head and secured it with a ribbon, and was now idly soaping one arm. She looked up as he came in, but did not appear embarrassed. 'That tub is big enough for both of us,' he said. 'Would you mind?'

'It might be fun.'

109

He got in, facing her. She brought her legs inside his, so that the soles of her feet were resting on his genitals. 'Are you sure you don't want to marry me?' he asked.

'I want to think about it.'

He considered that, while he lifted one of her feet and soaped the toes; she seemed to like that. But he decided the best way to play it was by a succession of *faits accompli.* 'It's still early,' he said, 'Shall we go out and buy you a nightdress? Or don't you use them?'

She frowned at him. 'I can't stay here the night.'

'It might help to make up your mind.'

'Daddy and Mummy would go spare.'

He hadn't thought of that. 'Well, why don't I take you home, and ...'

'That would also drive them spare. Daddy anyway.'

'What, even now I've given up banking in favour of King and Country, and am about to have my head blown off?'

'I wasn't aware anyone's head was about to be blown off,' she said. 'What was your plan?'

'Simply that if you then decided to have an early night, and when you were sure the coast was clear, slide down a drainpipe or whatever ...'

'How far did you get in school?' she asked. 'Was it Upper or Lower Fourth?'

'So how would you do it?'

'Do I want to do it?'

'Having checked in with wife, I am going to look pretty silly going out for the evening and returning here *sans* wife, don't you think?'

'That was your idea.' She stood up to soap the important parts of her, leaving him looking up at forever.

'You are the most beautiful thing I have ever seen,' he said.

She looked down at him. 'It's very nice of you to say so, but I think your big problem is that I am not a thing.'

He stood up as well, took her in his arms. 'How are you going to do it?' he asked.

He was left totally amazed at the deviousness, as well as the simplicity, of the female mind, once it had determined to have something happen. Constance merely telephoned a friend of hers who actually had a husband who had been called up, and gave her certain instructions. That done she returned to bed with Harry for another hour, which she seemed to enjoy much more, as did he, because the initial passion having been spent there was so much more he could do to her—and there was so much more he wanted to do—before having another bath. Then she

111

took a cab out to Hampstead.

'There's no need for you to come,' she told Harry. 'I'll be home in an hour and settle down with the folks before the wireless, telling them what a busy day I have had, shopping. Lois will call just after six, and tell me how she's having all kinds of psychological problems since Bill went away, and could I spend the night. She's done that before, just after he went, and Mummy and Daddy raised no objections. So I'll come back here, with some things. Including a satin nightdress, if that's what you'd like.'

'You are just magnificent. And tomorrow ...'

'Tomorrow we'll see.'

He wasn't about to argue with that. He'd never had such an afternoon, had never really supposed such a night might be possible. Constance returned as she had promised, with an overnight bag. They dined in the room, in candlelit seclusion, served by an eager floor waiter. There was more champagne, and a bouquet of red roses. 'Are you sure you can afford all this?' she asked. 'On a subaltern's pay?'

'Actually, no. I reckon that by tomorrow morning I'll have blown the lot. But I have a ticket down to Lower Cheviston. I'll have to ask you to pay your own fare until I can borrow some money off Mum.'

'My own fare, where?'

'Well ... you are coming down to Cheviston with me, aren't you? To meet Mum and Lou. Dad isn't there at the moment, I'm afraid. Although that may not, be a bad thing. But you'll love Mum and Lou. And they'll love you.'

'You're jumping the gun again.'

'But ...'

'I am spending the night with you. That's what you wanted, isn't it?'

'Of course.'

'Then let's concentrate on the job in hand.'

In a matter of hours it seemed she had really got into sex. So she had to love him, he reckoned. If he had any sense he'd just take what she had to offer and run. But that wasn't the Brand way.

She was up early to have a bath, and he joined her. 'This could grow on me,' he said, soaping her feet. 'Just the way you did.'

'It is fun, isn't it?'

'But I'm not growing on *you*, is that it?'

'You are growing on me enormously, Harry. I don't know when I've enjoyed a night more.'

'I would hope, never.'

'I'm sure you're right.' She got out, dried herself. 'Don't move. I want to remember you, sitting right there like that.'

'You're talking as if this were goodbye, forever.'

'That's up to you.'

'You mean ...'

'I mean, you have to go off and do your little soldiering thing. And I want you to do that. Then, when next you have leave, if you feel like it, give me a call, and ... well, we could talk about things.'

She left the bathroom, so he got out and dried himself, with the same towel, before following her into the bedroom. 'It could be some time. Before I have leave again.'

'I think that's a very good thing.'

He watched her dress. He wanted to remember every moment of her. 'And what will you do until I call again?'

'Exactly what I have been doing so far, since I became an adult.'

'You mean, if you're dated, you'll go.'

'Depends who invites me. But the answer is probably yes.'

Wearing her stockings and camiknickers she sat on the dressing stool to apply make-up. Harry lay on the bed. Was he being stood-up again? But dammit, she had been a virgin, he kept reminding himself. 'And if you do date, and the fellow, well ...'

'I will slap his face.' She smiled at him in the mirror. 'As I did yours, remember.'

'And suppose he is as persistent as me?'

'I don't think there is a man alive who is as persistent as you. However, should he be, I will have to make a choice, won't I?'

'That will involve confessions, won't it?'

'And that is my business, isn't it? It certainly won't be his.' She kissed him, and left.

As his experience of women was decidedly limited. Harry began to wonder if they were all like Marion and Constance? But for the moment he was on cloud seven. As Helen and Louise immediately recognized, although they quite misinterpreted the reason. 'Oh, I am so *proud* of you,' Helen cried.

'It's not the Wessex,' Harry apologized. 'No vacancies.'

'But the South Midlands are a fine regiment,' Helen said.

'And Jimmy Dempster is an old friend of the family. You'll do well. Oh, you'll do well.'

'I wonder if you could lend me a little,'

Harry confided. 'I'm absolutely bust.' She raised her eyebrows. 'Well ... the lads and I ... we felt we had to celebrate last night. So we painted the town red.' He supposed that Constance could be described as a lad, loosely.

Helen smiled. 'Of course I'll lend you whatever you need. I'm only happy you weren't arrested.'

Louise was even more excited. 'Now I'm definitely going to join the ATS,' she declared.

Colonel James Dempster was a Scot, although he was currently commanding an English regiment. Red-haired and bristling, as Helen had prognosticated, he was delighted with his new subaltern. 'Welcome,' he said, shaking hands. 'This is an honour. How are George and Helen?'

'In the pink, sir.'

'Excellent. I'm assigning you to B Company. Do you know Price?'

'No, sir.'

'Good man. Nelson is his first. Good man. Settle in. I don't know how long we'll be here.'

'Yes, sir. Is there any information?'

Dempster raised his eyebrows. 'None at all, Harry. But as I said, I don't think we'll be here that much longer.'

Tom Price was no older than Harry himself, but he had been through Sandhurst immediately on leaving school and now had a dozen years' seniority. He was a tall, thin, rather lugubrious looking man, an appearance which was relieved whenever he ventured his flashing smile. As he did now. 'I understand you've seen some active service already,' he remarked.

'In a manner of speaking. I wasn't actually allowed to shoot any Eyeties, however often I felt like it.'

'I can imagine.' He introduced Lieutenant Bobby Nelson. Nelson was only twenty, but he too was out of Sandhurst and had three years' seniority.

'Things move fast when there's a flap on,' he explained. 'And there seems to have been a flap on ever since I can remember.' Harry began to wonder where he had spent the past four years.

B Company consisted of eighty-nine NCOs and enlisted men, and three officers; it was not quite up to strength. But the men were fit and keen, and if they were inclined to exchange glances behind Harry's back at this apparently famous new officer who had only been in the Army a few weeks, they very rapidly realized that he was a born soldier, as they square-bashed, and route marched, and practised musketry and machine-gun drill. While his batman,

117

Harry Pope, was the proudest private in the battalion.

Harry had the same reception in the mess, but here his path was made even easier by Colonel Dempster's obvious respect, and the fact that his captain and senior lieutenant had also quickly gathered they had accumulated a good man.

The first week simply flew by, so much so that Harry had the time neither to write to Constance nor attempt to phone her. He wondered if there was any chance of getting a pass for the weekend, if only for a few hours, but it was on the Friday afternoon that he, and all the officers, were called into the mess by Dempster, who looked over their faces with a grim expression. 'Gentlemen,' the Colonel said. 'I have to inform you that at dawn this morning Germany invaded Poland.' There was absolute silence. 'There was always a risk that this would happen,' Dempster went on. 'Once the non-aggression pact with Russia was signed. Now, I understand that negotiations are underway to have the Germans withdraw, but of course these are unlikely to succeed. In this regard an ultimatum is about to be issued. It is unlikely this will have much effect either. It is therefore reasonably certain that within forty-eight hours we shall be at war. As of this moment, therefore, all leave is cancelled and this battalion is placed on a war footing. A new guard roster has been drawn up and will go into effect immediately. You will acquaint your companies with the situation and prepare them for embarkation. Where and when and for where we will embark I have not yet been informed, but I can tell you our ultimate destination will be France. We are a designated part of the Field Force, which will now again be known as the British Expeditionary Force. Any questions?'

To Harry's great relief someone else asked the vital question. 'Are we allowed to make any telephone calls, sir?'

'I have to try to be fair to everyone, as I have to balance the requirements of national security,' Dempster said. 'Every man in my command will be allowed to make one call out, and he may receive one call in. All calls, in or out, will be made through the adjutant's office, and in the presence of Major Harris or another officer, and they will have the right to terminate any conversation should anything be said which might jeopardize the security of this battalion or of the realm. I hope that is understood.' He glanced over their faces. 'Very good. Calls will be made in alphabetical order, commencing now.'

'I'd stick around, if I were you, Harry,' Price recommended. 'You're going to be pretty well at the head of the list.'

Harry was happy to accept the recommendation; the question was, upon whom should he spend his one available call? It came down to a matter of logic. He wanted to call Constance; but it had been her decision that he had no hold upon her, or responsibility to her, other than having slept with her. He should call his mother. On the other hand, Constance was not likely to attempt to call him, whereas Mother, who had been through all of this before, would almost certainly do so. And in any event, Mother would have been kept up to date on events by Father.

When his turn arrived—he was sixteenth —he called the Lloyd residence. It was now past six, and there was every probability that she would be home. In fact, she answered the phone. 'Hello,' he said.

There was a moment's hesitation. Then she said, 'Harry?'

'Can you speak?'

'Not really. Is something the matter?'

Harry glanced at Lieutenant Lee, standing in for the adjutant, and sitting on the far side of the desk. Lee was equipped with an extension, so that he could hear both sides of the conversation. 'Every possible thing,' Harry said.

'Oh,' she said. 'There was a rumour ...'

'Always believe rumours,' Harry said.

'Oh,' she said again.

'Have you been having a busy time?'

'Not very,' she said.

'May I say I'm glad about that?'

'You may. Have you any idea when you'll be back in town?'

'None at all. Nor do I have any idea when I'll be able to call again. I'd like to write to you.'

'Please,' she said.

'Well, then ... I'll say goodbye for the time being.'

'Goodbye,' she said.

'Listen. I love you, very, very much.'

'Do please write, whenever you can,' she said.

The phone went dead. Harry looked at Lee, and Lee looked at Harry. But Lee had been trained to keep his face from making any comment. Harry went outside.

Presumably she had been unable to respond as he would have wished because either her mother, or father, or both, had been within earshot. On the other hand, he couldn't escape a nagging feeling that he might have wasted a call.

'Brand!'

He checked as he went down the steps from the adjutant's office, looked at the Medical Officer, Captain Gregory. 'Sir?'

'A chat,' Gregory suggested. They walked

121

together, away from the queue of patient soldiers, and officers, waiting to use the phone. 'You were at Edinburgh,' Gregory remarked. 'Failed surgery.'

'Yes,' Harry acknowledged.

'And then served in Ethiopia. What were conditions like?'

'Foul.'

'I can imagine. You were a medic, weren't you?'

'I assisted Dr Andrews, until he was killed. Then I was captured by the Italians, and sent home.'

'When you say, assisted, what do you mean?'

Harry grinned. 'I think you could describe me as a medical orderly, sir.'

'You didn't practise at all?'

'Well, after Dr Andrews was killed, I was the only one around with any medical knowledge, so I had to do certain necessary things. I performed a minor operation, set a broken arm, dished out some drugs ... I know it wasn't correct, but there was no one else.'

'I'm not criticizing. I think you did exactly the right thing. The point is, Brand, that I am supposed to have an assistant, and he's never actually turned up. I imagine other battalions have made more noise for the available men. Well, it really didn't seem too important as long as we were in barracks here. If we're going on active service, that is another matter. I've been on to Brigade, and they say there is no one immediately available, and that pending the arrival of a qualified assistant I must make do with what I can. It seems to me that in these circumstances you could be the answer to this maiden's prayer.'

'I'm not qualified, sir.'

'Understood. But you would at all times be acting under my direct supervision, just like any other of my orderlies.'

'What about B Company, sir?'

'Brand, the entire battalion is not quite up to roster. We are six officers short. As with my assistant, they are promised, and will no doubt be joining in due course. Until they do, it is a matter of deciding priorities. In my book, having a totally manned and efficient medical unit is more important than any one company being left short.'

'Do you suppose Captain Price will also hold that order of priorities, sir?'

'I have already spoken to Captain Price, which is why I am now speaking to you. He gave me the go-ahead.' Harry hesitated. His inclination was still in the direction of saving life rather than taking it. But he felt he had fitted in well to B Company, and besides, if he opted out now, wouldn't some of them think he

123

was funking? Gregory was watching his expression. 'I may add,' he said, 'that should you measure up, and I have no doubt that you will, the moment we *are* up to strength, I will give you two choices. One would be to return to B Company as their subaltern. The other would be to return to England on secondment to whichever medical establishment can take you, in order to qualify as a doctor. In the RAMC, of course.' He grinned, and held out his hand. 'Welcome aboard, Senior Medical Orderly Brand!'

As Gregory had promised, both Price and Nelson were entirely understanding. 'It'll be a treat having you carve me up should I get hit,' Nelson grinned.

But Harry decided against telling his mother, when, predictably, she telephoned. Presumably the news would filter through to Father eventually, but by then he supposed quite a lot might have happened; his replacement might even have arrived. For the time being, he moved his gear into the hospital, hardly more than a hut, although very clean and with a surprising amount of equipment. This meant abandoning a most disappointed Pope, as the medical orderlies did for their officers. 'No nurses?' he asked Gregory.

'We're a field unit,' the captain said.

'We deal with our people on the spot, but anything serious goes back to the main hospital. That is when we're actually in the field, of course. The nurses don't get down to our level. We make do with Croom and Gibbons.' The two orderlies saluted.

Sick parade was less attended than Harry had expected, certainly going on what he had observed during his brief stay with B Company. But it seemed that even the habitual malingerers were fired up with the idea of going to war. On the other hand, Colonel Dempster required his MO to hold a special foot inspection. The battalion's feet were inspected once a week anyway, but this was an extra. 'No one knows how much marching we will have to do when we get to France. But we certainly need to be prepared to do a good deal.'

But even the feet were in good nick; Harry was actually very impressed with the health of the battalion. While his secret fears, that to return to the medical world would bring back the nightmares of the war in Ethiopia, vanished in this aseptic atmosphere of modern methods and equipment. On the other hand, he reminded himself, none of these men had been in action as yet, and been brought in bleeding and moaning. On the *other* hand, no matter what happened, none of these men was ever likely to have to endure castration, either.

But it was a salutary thought that he was one of only a handful of men in the battalion, and the *only* officer save for Dempster and Major Harris—both Great War veterans—ever to have been under fire.

Having been forewarned, Colonel Dempster had the loudspeakers relay Prime Minister Chamberlain's speech at eleven o'clock on Sunday morning. The Prime Minister himself spoke in sombre, and indeed, sorrowful tones, of his disappointment at the failure of his self-appointed mission to keep the peace in Europe, but when he had finished, and the National Anthem had been played, there was only a brief silence before someone in the ranks shouted out, 'We're off to beat old Hitler. Hip, hip, hoorah!'

The officers turned to discover who the culprit might be, but Dempster assessed the mood of his men and himself, shouted, 'For King and Country! Hip, hip, hoorah.'

Everyone started to shake hands, as if they had just won a victory instead of not yet having fought a battle, Harry thought. But his own adrenalin was flowing. How he wished Constance could be here to see him. And even more, Marion, and realize what a mistake she had made. 'Five bob says I'm the first man in the battalion to bag a Jerry,' Nelson said.

'Done,' Price agreed. 'I don't suppose you'll have much opportunity, Harry.'

'Am I allowed to?' Harry asked Gregory. 'In Ethiopia, Jim Andrews wouldn't let me pot any Eyeties, much as I wanted to.'

'Because you were officially neutral. You're not neutral now,' Gregory said. 'And if any Jerry pushes his head into our field hospital, you have my permission to blow him in two. Of course,' he added, 'we'll see if we can sew him up, afterwards.'

Did you wind up in Upper or Lower Fourth, Constance had asked, contemptuously. Harry supposed they were all of them fourth formers, at this moment. But that was the way they had to be, if they were going to fight and survive. Time to look on the serious side of life, when they had survived. So, he resolved, no more women. He was engaged in man's business. That same afternoon the trucks arrived to take them down to Folkestone, for embarkation.

Part Two

Ever Backwards

'The essence of war is violence, and moderation in war is imbecility.'
Macaulay quoting John Hampden.

Chapter Five

Of Men and Women

The BEF now entered a period of what Harry had to consider ordered chaos. But the order became more evident as they crossed the Channel, although this transportation did not begin for another six days, and was then undertaken at night, because of the threat from German aircraft as well as submarines. As there were well over a hundred thousand men to be shipped, together with their arms and their trucks and their guns, the operation took over a month.

For those long weeks the various battalions were confined to their encampments along the south coast, close to their appointed embarkation points, unable to communicate with their families or even to fraternize with the locals, for fear of leaking information, as if the Germans did not already know that the British would transfer an army to France immediately war broke out, and by the shortest possible route. The South Midlands were already in place before the commanding general was announced: he was to be Field Marshal Lord Gort, who held a VC gained in the Great War, and who, rather oddly, had until now been Chief of the Imperial General Staff, the highest position in the Army. Thus this appointment could be taken either as a demotion, or a measure of the seriousness of the situation.

'At least we must presume he knows what he's about,' Gregory remarked. He was preoccupied because his full supply of anti-seasick pills had not arrived, and although they were clearly not going to have to engage any Germans immediately on arrival in France, it was still hoped to put up a good show and impress any neutral cameramen who might be around. The reason there was no immediate likelihood of encountering Germans was because the Germans were busy in Poland, gaining victory after victory. Harry found it a salutary thought, having read everything he could discover on the subject during his brief military career, that whereas the Germans were supposed to have mobilized roughly three and three-quarter million men, and the Poles had mobilized two and a half million men, the British possessed something less than nine hundred thousand men under arms, of whom only a small proportion were in the Expeditionary Force. And the Poles were being wiped out! Of course it was easy to reflect that the Poles had virtually no tanks, whereas the Germans had over three thousand, and the Poles had only four hundred planes, whereas the Germans possessed over four thousand.

But the British would be fighting alongside the French, who were mobilizing *five* million men, and were reputed to be the best soldiers in the world. They also had over two and a half thousand tanks, which, added to the British thousand-plus, gave them at least equality with the enemy, while Britain and France between them had over four and a half thousand planes, and perhaps more important than anything, nearly fourteen thousand heavy guns, more than double the amount possessed by the Germans. So, it was reasonable to wonder, why were the French not immediately invading Germany while the enemy was preoccupied in Poland? The answer was that the French and British Governments were both still hoping for a negotiated peace settlement, despite the rape of Poland. No one had a short answer to what the Poles might feel about this, or about the possibility of restoring Polish sovereignty when the shooting stopped.

As the South Midlands eventually disembarked in Boulogne, however, Harry wondered if there might not be another reason no counter-offensive had been launched in the direction of the Rhine. The battalion marched away in good order—they were going to be transported by trucks to their allotted position, but Dempster felt it would be good for everyone's morale to march through the city behind the regimental band with flags flying and bayonets fixed. This display of martial ardour certainly brought out the crowds, but children and old people apart, no one looked very pleased to see them, and Harry knew sufficient French to understand much of what was being said. 'I don't think they like this war,' he told Gregory, as they got into their truck with the huge red cross painted on each side and on the roof. 'And they blame us for starting it and dragging them in.'

'I would say they are not far wrong,' Gregory remarked. 'At least on the second count. But they're French. When they actually see a German in front of them, they'll be as keen as anyone to fight.' Harry hoped he was right.

As, just as in the Great War, the Belgians were determined to maintain their neutrality at least until actually invaded, which, putting their trust in Hitler's repeated assurances, they fervently believed would not happen, and as the concept of

134

any major offensive into Germany had been ruled out, the British and French armies occupied a line along the Belgian border. The Allied generals had no doubt at all that the Belgians were living in a dream world, and that should shooting actually start in the West, the Germans would do precisely what they had in 1914, and wheel through Belgium. In which case, the Allied plan was to meet them head on. The first sign of a German attack on Belgium would lead to a forward movement, whether or not the Belgians declared war, to the line of the Dyle River. This would involve a huge swing of four armies, the hinge of the swing being Sedan, on the Franco-Belgian border, and situated on the southern edge of the heavily-wooded hilly country known as the Ardennes, which was, so the pundits said, impassable to any large bodies of troops, and especially armour. While if the Germans attacked further east, into France proper, they would have to come face to face with the Maginot Line.

This was also regarded as impassable. Ever since the Franco-Prussian War of 1870 the French had maintained a line of fortresses along their frontier with Germany, designed to hold up any large-scale invasion. These fortresses, especially those around the city of Verdun, had played important parts in maintaining the integrity of France during the Great War, with the result that following that conflict, with the facts of life, both as regards finances and demography, indicating that while Germany had to grow stronger, France was inevitably growing weaker, the French had opted to convert the line of forts into one long, solid fortress, which had recently been completed and named after its designer. The Maginot Line, like the Forest of the Ardennes before Sedan, was regarded as impervious to any large bodies of troops, and to attacks by enemy armour. The French High Command therefore regarded their border with Germany as sealed from invasion, behind which they could make their dispositions at leisure, when it came to a fight, as now. There were those who criticized the concept as being entirely defensive, and thus in direct contradiction of the age-old traditions of the French army, which were aggressive. It certainly had created a mood where the French felt that they would fight the battle, when it came, on ground of their own choosing—Belgium—and virtually at a time of their own choosing, which was not to be in the autumn of what had in any event been a very wet year, whatever was happening in Poland.

The BEF was therefore required to take its allotted place, and await events.

There was nothing Gort and his generals could argue about in this. Not only was the British Government—with one or two notable exceptions, such as Winston Churchill—apparently entirely in agreement with the French point of view, and indeed, willing to accept French leadership in all things military, but the BEF was a very small cog in a huge wheel. There were no fewer than eight French armies arranged along the Belgian and German frontiers, from Dunkirk on the sea to Basel in Switzerland. These were arranged into three Army Groups. The BEF was merely a ninth army, slotted into Army Group One, commanded by General Billotte. They were placed on the right of the Seventh Army, commanded by General Giraud, which had its headquarters in Dunkirk, and on the left of the First Army of General Blanchard, centred around Maubeuge. The British Army was centred around Lille, and was disposed roughly between the Rivers Lys and Escaut. They were of course scattered over a considerable area, and the South Midlands found themselves encamped around the village and château of Centot, with orders to prepare to spend the winter there. Harry was intrigued by this, as he recalled that his father had mentioned Centot during his reminiscences of the last war, but he doubted anyone living here now would remember the Brigadier.

'This may seem to you to be a rather odd business,' Dempster told his assembled officers. 'The only non-British or French units in front of us are members of the Belgian Army, with whom we are not at war, nor do we anticipate being at war with them. Your men will therefore not under any circumstances advance across the border. For the rest, we stay put and make ourselves as comfortable as possible, certainly until next spring. I believe it is piously hoped in certain quarters that by next spring we will have come to an agreed peace with Hitler, whereupon we will pack up our tents and steal away, like the well-known Arabs, back to England. All I can tell you is, make friends with the natives, and keep your people out of trouble.'

'Not a happy man,' Gregory remarked. 'However, Harry old son, providing we make sure to prevent the outbreak of any unpleasant contagious disease, we should have a fairly peaceful winter. As for making friends with the natives, that is entirely a matter for the field officers.'

Gregory was no older than Harry himself, and was thus a total innocent when it came to the affairs of men; his only military experience was of the camp

138

outside Aldershot. Thus he was completely wrong on both counts. Although the male inhabitants of Centot might have regarded the South Midlands with suspicion and even positive dislike, the majority of the population—most of the men having been conscripted, anyway—were only too happy to be friendly. This led immediately to the Medical Officer being proved wrong in his first prognostication.

They had been in camp just over three weeks, and as it was the end of October the rain was teeming down and there was a general air of desolation. It had been a quiet three weeks. The campaign in Poland was now over, the Poles having been utterly destroyed as a fighting force, while what little chance they had had originally had been ended by the Russian invasion of the east of their country, apparently with the full agreement of the Germans, leaving Poland as effectively partitioned between the two major powers as it had been more than a century and a half earlier. This was depressing. Even more depressing was the fact that the offers of peace now being made by Hitler, accompanied always by his reiterated statement that he had no more territorial demands to make in Europe, were being taken seriously by a good number of people in both America and England, and more importantly, France.

'Exactly what I said would happen,' Gregory pointed out.

He was bored. Medical duties, apart from a case of ingrowing toenail and a problem with feet in general—which was normal—consisted in the main of men reporting sick and declaring they had been poisoned whereas all they were suffering from was an unaccustomed surfeit of cheap red wine in place of the beer to which their stomachs were more acclimatized.

But this morning Sergeant Cutmore was looking grave as he marched Private Davies into the office. 'Says he's not well, sir,' he announced, rolling his eyes. Gregory raised *his* eyebrows, then looked at Davies, whose face was red as a beetroot. 'It's his waterworks, sir,' Cutmore announced, and did some more eye rolling.

'Oh, Good Lord,' Gregory commented. 'All right, Davies. Drop them.' Davies obliged. He was now in such a state of embarrassment Harry feared he might have a stroke. 'And the drawers,' Gregory said. Davies obeyed, and Gregory stooped to peer at him. 'You'd better look at this, Lieutenant Brand,' he said over his shoulder. 'You'll probably see it again in the course of time.' Harry stooped beside his superior, feeling distinctly uneasy. There was no question that the testicles were swollen, and that there was an unpleasant discharge from the penis. 'I suppose you did cover VD at Edinburgh?' Gregory inquired.

'Yes,' Harry said.

'Hurts when you go, eh?' Gregory asked the private.

'Yes, sir.'

'And you want to go all the time, whether you need to or not, right?'

'Yes, sir.' Davies screwed up his face to indicate that he actually wanted to go now.

Gregory straightened. 'When did these symptoms first appear?'

'Day before yesterday, sir.'

'I see. And why have you only reported them today?'

'Well, sir ...'

'Embarrassed, sir,' Cutmore explained.

'I see.' Gregory returned behind his desk and sat down. 'Well, as you have probably surmised, you have got the clap. It's called gonorrhoea to us. I assume you have been having it off with some French bit?'

'Well, sir ...'

'I will have to have her name,' Gregory said.

Cutmore cleared his throat, loudly. 'Will I be all right, sir?' Davies asked, anxiously.

'Oh, yes, in the course of time. You will have to be excused drill for the next couple of weeks. But we will also

141

treat it. Mr Brand will mix you up a dosage of bicarbonate of soda, ten grains, to be taken every three hours. This will somewhat reduce the desire to urinate. But I will also treat the penis itself. Return here after dinner. At which time I will need the name of the woman. Dismissed.'

Davies stood to attention and was marched out. 'You mean to use permanganate of potash?' Harry asked.

Gregory nodded, 'It won't cure him, but it'll stop the discharging. And it's a sufficiently unpleasant business to make him think where he's going before he finds another hole. I am going to have to make a report to Colonel Dempster. This could be a serious business.' Cutmore coughed again, more loudly than before. 'Very well, Sergeant,' Gregory said. 'You may march the next one in.'

'There are twelve more out there, sir.'

'That's no more than normal, is it?'

'All suffering like Davies, sir.'

Gregory stared at him for several seconds. Then he remarked, 'Holy shitting cows!'

'At ease, gentlemen, and sit down.' Jimmy Dempster smiled at his two medical officers; he was always pleased to see Harry. 'Peter ...' he nodded to his adjutant,

Major Harris, 'Tells me you have an urgent problem.'

'Yes, sir.' Gregory was never one to beat about the bush.

'I have today had to excuse twelve men from drill and all duties, for a period of at least three weeks.' Dempster raised his eyebrows. 'They have VD, sir.'

Dempster sat up. 'What sort of VD?'

'Oh, these cases are all gonorrhoea,' Gregory said. 'But where there is gonorrhoea, there is always the threat of syphilis. In any event, sir, those men are in no condition to fight a battle should we have to do so, and in the circumstances, they are certainly only the tip of the iceberg.'

Dempster looked at Harry, then at Harris, and then at the fifth man present, Captain the Reverend Moore. 'This undoubtedly arises from the, ah ... house we discussed, sir,' Harris said.

'The use of which I opposed,' Moore added.

'I accept that, Padre. But as I pointed out, men away from their wives and sweethearts have to have, well ...'

'Relief, they call it, sir,' Harris said.

'Exactly. Captain Gregory, I'm afraid I will have to ask you to visit this establishment, discover the carrier, and put her out of bounds while she is treated, either by you or by her own doctor.'

143

'With respect, sir,' Gregory said. 'I must point out that if one of the village whores is contaminated, and they operate from a brothel, the existence of which I was not informed, then it is extremely likely they are *all* contaminated.'

'The place will have to be closed down,' Moore said, with some satisfaction. 'Or certainly placed out of bounds to our people.'

Dempster looked at Harris. 'The men won't like it, sir,' the adjutant said.

'You mean they would rather have the clap than be chaste?' Moore demanded.

'Very probably, yes. But there is another point: the locals won't be very pleased either. I imagine our men have proved a considerable source of income on their visits to the village since our arrival.'

'To the madame, you mean?' Moore inquired, hotly.

'I would say, through the various spin-offs their visits have involved, to the whole community.'

Dempster banged the flat of his hand on his desk to stop the argument. 'We are discussing what is at present supposition. Captain Gregory, you will visit, in the first instance, the local doctor ... do you speak French?'

'I'm afraid not, sir.'

'I speak French, sir,' Harry said.

'Of course. Very good. Lieutenant Brand will accompany you, Captain Gregory. As I say, you will visit this doctor and acquaint him with the situation, and ask for his co-operation in getting to the bottom of the matter, if you will excuse the simile, Padre. You will inform him that it is your intention, again, hopefully, with his co-operation, to visit this establishment and examine the inmates. If he will not co-operate, you will tell him that you intend to do this anyway. And if there is no co-operation from either him or the madame, or if you find that too many of her girls are contaminated, then you will close the place down, at least as regards our people. In fact, you will place the entire village out of bounds. Is that understood?'

'Yes, sir.' It was the first time Harry had ever seen Gregory looking unsure of himself.

'Do it in style,' Dempster told him. 'You may use my car, and take a couple of Redcaps with you. I wish a report on your progress by this evening. Thank you, gentlemen.'

'Know anything about brothels, Harry?' Gregory asked, as they entered the village in the Colonel's car, driven by a Military Policeman, with Sergeant Cutmore, who appeared determined to see this matter through, seated beside him in the front.

'Not about how they work.'

Gregory grinned. 'Well, just remember that *we* are working. And remember also that I am relying on you, entirely. I only have a couple of words of French, so it's up to you not to land us in any diplomatic cart.'

'I'll do my best,' Harry promised, and looked up at the bulk of the château, perched on a low hill overlooking the town. 'I wonder who lives up there?'

'Why, the Countess d'Aubert.'

'Oh, is that the old bird you lot had dinner with the other night?' You lot, in this context being all officers in the battalion of the rank of captain or above, headed by the colonel.

'That is correct, young Harry, and I wouldn't describe the countess as an old bird,' Gregory said. 'She is an absolute knockout. What you want to do, old son, is think about that gorgeous creature all alone in that huge pile.'

'You mean she's not married?'

'Oh, she's married. But her husband is with the French army somewhere; certainly nowhere near here.' He gave an artificial sigh. 'Ah, well, I imagine she wouldn't be interested in a lieutenant. She didn't give too much suggestion of being interested in captains, either. Or even colonels.'

'War is hell,' Harry agreed, slyly.

Dr Le Bouquerelle turned out to be a small, fussy man with a waxed moustache, a relic of a bygone age, Harry felt; he wondered if he had been here when Dad had last visited the place? 'Venereal disease,' he remarked disparagingly. 'I do not believe this, *monsieur le lieutenant*. There is no VD in Centot.'

'If you would care to come out to our camp, doctor, I will show you it,' Harry said.

'Ah, the English soldiers.' The doctor shrugged. 'That is to be expected.'

'They must have got it from somewhere.'

'I would say they brought it with them, lieutenant.'

'What's he gargling about?' Gregory asked.

Harry explained. 'Did we have any cases before leaving England?'

'Not one. And as we were cooped up without a woman in sight for over a fortnight before landing in this benighted country, I would say that is pretty conclusive. Put the rocks to this fellow, Harry. We haven't got all day.'

Harry cleared his throat. 'It is the opinion of my superior, Dr Gregory,' he told Dr Le Bouquerelle, 'that the contagion was contracted here in Centot. Now, sir, it is our intention to proceed to this, ah, house, and hold a medical examination.'

'But you cannot do that,' the doctor protested. 'Unless ...' he brightened. 'You pay, of course. For each examination.'

'This is a medical matter,' Harry informed him.

Le Bouquerelle puffed out his chest. 'You have no right to do this.'

'We would be very happy for you to accompany us,' Harry said winningly. 'And indeed, if you wish, carry out the examination yourself. We merely wish to be present to confirm your findings.'

But Le Bouquerelle was not to be placated. 'You have no right,' he said again. 'If you persist, I must take the matter to a higher authority.'

Harry translated. 'Tell him to bugger off,' Gregory suggested.

'You have every right to do what you think best, doctor,' Harry said. 'But you will look rather silly if you take the matter higher and we do find that these young ladies are indeed contaminated.'

Le Bouquerelle gazed at him for several seconds, then got up. 'I will come with you,' he decided.

'*Ooh, la—la,*' Madame exclaimed as the staff car drew up outside her front door, which she hastily opened. 'Officers! And

148

you, Dr Le Bouquerelle? It is not your usual day.'

Le Bouquerelle was overtaken by a fit of coughing, while Harry translated to Gregory. 'Ask her if we may come in,' Gregory said.

'But of course,' Madame declared, in English. 'You are most welcome. Helene, Eloise, Aimee, Marie, there are gentlemen to be entertained.' She showed them into a very well-furnished parlour, where they were immediately joined by four giggling but extremely attractive young women, wearing very little. 'It is early, you understand,' Madame said. 'We are just out of bed. But for officers ...'

'These gentlemen are not clients, Madame,' Le Bouquerelle said.

Madame turned to Harry and Gregory, eyebrows arched, the warmth of her greeting quite disappeared. 'We are doctors, Madame,' Harry explained, somewhat nervously. 'It is necessary that we examine your women.' Gregory cleared his throat, and Harry remembered that, as they were speaking English, his superior was capable of looking after himself.

'This is outrageous!' Madame declared, and switched back to French. 'How can you permit this, doctor?'

'It is the Army, you understand,' Le Bouquerelle said apologetically.

149

'The British Army,' Madame said contemptuously, indicating that if it had been the French Army involved, none of this would have happened.

'We haven't got all day,' Gregory remarked. 'The young ladies don't have much to take off. Tell them to get on with it.'

'This is an insult,' Madame declared. 'I shall report it.'

'Listen,' Gregory said. 'I have two of my men outside. Do you wish us to call them in to give us a hand?'

Madame gave a snort. 'You are a brute, Captain. Aimée!' Aimée came forward, apprehensively, and was made to bend over. With women, the swelling associated with the disease is often interior, but Gregory quickly ascertained by probing whether there was some. While he was doing this Aimée gave a series of little yelps, and there was clear evidence of a discharge from the vagina. Gregory called Le Bouquerelle over to have a look, and the doctor raised his eyes to heaven. The other three girls were all diseased. 'This has never happened before,' Madame declared. But she had it as well. Which presumably, if he was a regular customer, meant that the doctor was also infected. Therefore he must have known all along!

'What are you going to do?' Le

Bouquerelle asked Harry.

Harry asked Gregory. 'We are going to place this house out of bounds.'

Harry translated, but Le Bouquerelle, having seen Madame's expression, had already worked out the British intention. 'It will cause a terrible scandal,' he protested.

'In fact,' Gregory went on. 'In all the circumstances, I think we may have to put the entire village of Centot out of bounds. Either that, or we'll have to station a squad of Redcaps here all the time.'

Harry translated. 'This is an outrage,' Le Bouquerelle protested. 'Can this be called the Entente Cordiale?'

'How about the Entente Sanitaire?'

Le Bouquerelle was not amused. 'We were told that the British, when they came, would bring prosperity, not disaster.'

'Yes, but you see, old chap, we're actually here to fight a war. Fucking your women is only a secondary consideration, however enjoyable it may be. So you must understand that if fucking your women renders our people unable to fight a war, then it is the fucking which has to go.'

'I wish to see your colonel,' Le Bouquerelle announced.

Harry translated. 'I think that would be a very good idea,' Gregory agreed.

151

Dempster listened to both sides with equal concentration. 'Putting the entire village out of bounds seems a little severe,' he remarked.

'I don't see any alternative, sir,' Gregory said. 'If the men are allowed to go into the village and drink at the pub, or estaminet, or whatever, we are going to need every policeman we have to keep them out of the brothel, and even so there are going to be fights. That isn't going to present a very good image.'

'You'd better translate, Harry,' Dempster said, wearily.

'It will ruin the village,' Le Bouquerelle declared.

'Now hold on just one moment,' Dempster said. 'The village existed quite happily before we ever came here.'

'But then our men were here,' Le Bouquerelle argued, as Harry translated to and fro.

'I'm sorry.' Dempster made a decision. 'The village is out of bounds unless and until all of those women are free of disease. I leave that up to you, doctor. However, if you require some help, I will lend you my junior medical officer.'

'I beg your pardon, sir,' Harry protested. 'I'm afraid injecting women's vaginas with permanganate of potash isn't my scene.'

152

'I should have thought you would find it rather interesting,' Major Harris remarked.

'This whole episode, sir, has entirely put me off sex,' Harry said.

Le Bouquerelle had also come to a decision. 'I will have to refer the matter to the Countess.'

'What did he say?' Dempster demanded, having caught the word countess. Harry translated. 'He can't do that,' Dempster protested. 'The countess is a lady. She can't be involved in arguments about brothels and gonorrhea. I'll bet she doesn't even know what the word means.'

Harry translated. 'The countess,' Le Bouquerelle said with dignity, 'owns the brothel.' He took his departure, leaving the English officers staring at each other in consternation.

'That is of course an absurdity,' Harris declared.

'He seemed pretty sure of his ground,' Gregory argued.

'Some of these Frenchwomen are pretty broadminded,' Captain Moore remarked.

They all looked at the Colonel. 'Gentlemen,' Dempster said. 'We are going to have to grasp the bull by the horns.' A simile which Harry felt, in all the circumstances, was singularly inappropriate. 'Captain Gregory,' Dempster went on. 'You will proceed with your recommendation, and place the entire village of Centot out of bounds until further notice. I will call on the Countess and see just what she does know about this matter, and if possible enlist her assistance. Padre, you will accompany me.' He looked at his watch. 'If we leave now, we should get up there before she has her dinner.' He looked around the other officers. 'Brand, you'll accompany us.'

'Me, sir?'

'You know everything that has so far been said and done, and you speak French. The Countess's English is excellent, but I don't want any asides we may not understand.' He looked Harry up and down. 'Freshen up. You need a shave. We leave in ten minutes.'

'What am I supposed to say to this woman?' Harry asked as he dragged his razor over his chin. 'I mean, the wordage.'

'Well, obviously you can't use words like sex or VD to a countess,' Gregory agreed. 'You'll just have to generalize. I'm sure she'll get the message, especially if she's at all involved.'

'Do you really think she is? At all involved, I mean. You've met the woman.'

'Yes. And I find it hard to accept. Anyway ... enjoy the view.'

Harry thought there might have been quite a view, as he sat in the front of the staff car beside the driver, the colonel and the padre being in the back. But by now it was dark; the village was blacked out as was the château. It was also drizzling. And he was too nervous. He had absolutely no idea how to convey the situation to some aristocrat who would certainly be several times removed from the facts of life as lived by the peasantry—or the soldiery.

They drove over a drawbridge and into the courtyard, pulled up in front of a flight of broad stone steps leading up to the main doors of the castle. The three officers went up the steps, and at the top, before they could pull the bell rope, the doors swung in. Beyond was a cavern of light, but the moment they stepped inside the doors shut again behind them. The butler bowed. 'The Countess is expecting you,' he said in French.

Harry translated. 'I did telephone, to let her know we were coming,' Dempster explained, with some satisfaction.

The butler led them across the room, which, Harry realized, was a knights' hall, high-beamed and wide, with a huge table to one side and varied examples of medieval arms pinned to the walls. 'Amazing to think that we are almost certainly not the first

British officers to enter here,' Dempster remarked. Harry knew the colonel was thinking of people like Wellington or perhaps even Marlborough or the Black Prince, all of whom had campaigned across this country at some time in history. But he wondered if it might not have been more recent than that.

The butler opened the door for them, and they entered a drawing-room, a fraction the size of the hall, but still a very large room, exquisitely furnished. Having digested that, he wondered what words he could use to describe the woman standing before the roaring fire which was the centrepiece of the room. The Countess d'Aubert was a rather small woman; Harry estimated she was not much over five feet in height. She also had a rather small figure, but, as delineated by the contour-hugging black evening gown, a very well-shaped one. Her hair, which was piled on the top of her head in a vast chignon, was a deep auburn, her complexion a pale cream and flawless. Her features were crisp, and, like her body, perfectly proportioned. She was by some distance the most beautiful woman Harry had ever seen. 'Welcome,' she said in English, her voice husky and entirely in keeping with the rest of her. 'Although I do not know I should say that, in view of what I have been hearing.'

'Ah,' Dempster said, 'You have heard from the village?'

'But of course. It is my village. You will take an aperitif?'

'Well, that would be awfully kind of you, Countess.'

'Henri!' The butler went to a sideboard on the far side of the room. And Harry discovered that the countess was staring at him, with a faint frown.

'Allow me to introduce Lieutenant Brand, Countess,' Dempster said. 'Captain Moore you have already met.'

Harry wondered if he should offer to kiss her hand, but as she did not move, he merely gave a stiff military bow. 'My great pleasure, Countess.'

'Please be seated,' the countess said, and sat down herself. 'Did you say, Brand?'

'Why, yes.'

Before he, or she, could pursue the subject, Henri the butler served a tray of Pernod, and Dempster decided it was time he took over. 'You will understand that this is an intensely embarrassing situation for us, Countess.'

The countess had still been gazing at Harry. Now she turned back to the Colonel. 'For us all, Colonel. I understand that you intend to place the entire village out of bounds to your men.'

'Well ... of course, when I made

157

that decision, a very necessary decision, Countess, I had no idea you were in any way involved.'

'You mean you did not know I owned the brothel.'

'Well ...' he gazed at Moore, taken aback by the use of the word.

The countess smiled. When she did that, her beauty was redoubled. 'I do not share in the profits, Colonel. I merely own the house. I own most of the houses in the village.'

'But with respect, madame,' Moore said, 'you knew this house was being operated as, well ...'

'I believe you English call it a house of ill repute,' the countess said. 'I cannot imagine why. Yes, Reverend, I knew for what purpose the house was being used. That house has been a brothel for several hundred years. And I can assure you that for most of that time it has been a house of very good repute, rather than ill.' Moore gulped, and the countess looked at Harry. 'May I ask what part you have played in this business, Lieutenant ... Brand?'

Harry licked his lips. 'Well, you see, Countess, I am one of the battalion medical officers. It was the duty of my colleague and I to examine the ah ... ladies of the house.'

'And you found them diseased. So that

158

you have determined that the entire village must also be diseased.'

'Well, no, Countess,' Harry protested.

'If the whole village is diseased,' the countess pointed out. 'Then I am diseased. Would you care to examine me as well?'

Harry looked to his superiors for help. Moore was red in the face, but Dempster came to his rescue. 'Please try to understand, Countess,' he said. 'We are here to defend France against the Germans. My men cannot fight while they are suffering from such a debilitating disease as the ... well ...'

'I believe it is called the clap in England, Colonel.'

'Ah ...' now it was Dempster's turn to look for help, but as there was none forthcoming, he battled on. 'Yes. So you will understand, I am sure, that I cannot afford to have a large part of my command *hors de combat,* as it were ... oh, my God, what am I saying? I do apologize, Countess.'

The countess gave one of her dazzling smiles. 'Apology accepted, Colonel. And I do understand. But why the whole village?'

Dempster gave a sigh of relief. 'It is simply that, should my men go into Centot, and begin drinking at the *estaminet,* they will then wish to, ah ...'

159

'Visit the brothel,' the countess said helpfully.

'Quite so. And if they are then refused permission to do so, there will be fights, and a good deal of unpleasantness, and damage ...' he paused, hopefully.

'I see,' the countess said, and appeared to be considering the matter. 'It is quite a dilemma. So you intend to confine your men to barracks. For how long?'

'Well, until this matter can be cleared up. We really should be talking of only two or three weeks, if the proper treatment is administered. I know Lieutenant Brand and my senior MO, Captain Gregory, will take care of our people. And I have no doubt that Dr Le Bouquerelle can see to the ah ...'

'Whores,' the countess told him. 'Unfortunately, Le Bouquerelle is a doddering old fool. Who, incidentally, visits the brothel himself. As do most of the male residents of Centot. So, we will have to have a deal, you and I, Colonel.'

'Countess?' Dempster asked uneasily.

'You need to confine your men to barracks for the next three weeks. But men must have relaxation, and if they cannot obtain such relaxation from women, then they will have to obtain it from alcohol, without, hopefully, being in a position where they can wreck anything when they

160

learn that women are not also to be available. Do you understand me?'

'Ah ...' Dempster looked at his two subordinates. 'I think so.'

'Very good. Every evening, then, I will send out to your camp one of my trucks laden with barrels of wine, and your men will be able to drink to their hearts' content, at the same prices as they would have paid in the *estaminet*. Agreed?'

Dempster scratched his head. 'I assume, Countess, that you own the *estaminet* as well,' Moore remarked.

'But of course. Now, Colonel, you will readily agree that this can be nothing more than a stop-gap measure.'

'Absolutely,' Dempster agreed, fervently.

'Very good. Thus it is essential that what we shall call normal relations are restored as rapidly as possible. After all, men must have their sexual relief. Would you not agree, Reverend?' Moore gulped again. As did his colonel. 'Now,' the countess went on, having taken complete charge of the meeting. 'I have no doubt that your senior Medical Officer, as you say, will rapidly take care of your afflicted soldiers. By the way, is he that Captain Gregory you brought out the other night?'

'Yes.'

'A good man,' the Countess said sceptically. 'In his hands your people

161

will soon be ready to fight the Germans, as you say. Sadly, as I have said, we are not so well served in Centot. Therefore I must ask for your help.'

It was Harry's turn to gulp; he had a sudden intimation of what she had in mind. 'Anything, Countess,' Dempster promised.

'Very good. I am sure you will agree that it is essential the ladies in the brothel are also restored to health as rapidly as possible, and anyone else in Centot who may be afflicted. I would therefore ask you to second Lieutenant Brand to my village for a period of three weeks or until the contagion has been cleared up.'

Dempster looked at her, then at Moore, who remained absolutely po-faced. Then he looked at Harry. 'I do not think I have sufficient knowledge to handle the matter sir,' Harry said. 'Perhaps the Countess is unaware that I am not a qualified doctor, merely Captain Gregory's assistant, pending replacement ... '

'I am sure you know exactly what to do and how to do it, Lieutenant,' the countess said. 'This is an emergency. We cannot be handicapped by red tape or the lack of qualifications.'

'Then there is the matter of where I would be billeted,' Harry said desperately.

The countess smiled. 'You will be

billeted here, Lieutenant. I insist.'

'Why, that is exceedingly generous of you, Countess,' Dempster said.

'Well then, I am so very pleased that is settled. I would suggest that Lieutenant Brand takes up his new duties just as soon as possible, so that we may get this business sorted out just as soon as possible.'

'Absolutely,' Dempster agreed. 'Lieutenant Brand will report for duty, ah, first thing in the morning.'

'Why not tonight?' the countess inquired. 'Ah ...'

'If he were to move in here tonight,' the countess explained, 'then we could indeed start work first thing in the morning.'

Dempster looked at Harry, who had absolutely no idea what to say, or do. The suggestion that a woman like the countess might want to have him in her bed was just too incredible to be true. But ... 'I am sure we can organize that,' Dempster agreed. 'Shall we say, after dinner? You'll have to get your man moving, Harry.'

'No, no,' the countess said, and looked at the gold watch on her wrist. 'It is a quarter to seven. I will expect Lieutenant Brand *for* dinner. At eight. But he will not need a "man". I have enough servants to take care of him.'

'That is a very odd woman,' Captain Moore remarked, 'And, one suspects, a lonely one,' Dempster observed.

Harry, as before, seated in the front beside the driver, made no comment. He needed time to think. 'You don't suppose ...' Moore ventured.

'I really don't know.' Dempster said. 'I must say it looks like it. However, Harry, if I may speak as your father would do in these circumstances, we expect you to behave at all times as an officer and a gentleman, and under no circumstances must you allow yourself to be seduced by this woman. Do you understand me?'

'Yes, sir.' He thanked God that it was dark and thus they could not see his ears burning.

'It is of course possible that we are maligning the Countess,' Moore suggested.

'I sincerely hope we are, Padre. However, I have no doubt at all that she is pursuing *some* ulterior motive. Therefore I repeat, Harry: strict protocol at all times.'

Gregory clearly could not believe his ears. 'Of all the luck, young Brand. Why the devil did she pick you?'

'Probably because I speak French. See where scholastic neglect gets you?'

'Ha. When I think of you up at the château, drinking her wines, slipping

164

beneath her sheets ...'

'The Colonel has placed her absolutely out of bounds,' Harry pointed out.

Gregory gave him an old-fashioned look. 'In that case I suspect you are going to return to me in need of psychiatric treatment. Have fun.'

An ulterior motive, Harry thought, as he was driven back up the hill in the colonel's car, his kitbag and box of medical supplies on the seat beside him. The only ulterior motive had to be sex. So how did one resist the advances of a beautiful and obviously amoral woman who also happened to be one's landlady, however temporary, and with whom one was about to embark upon a course of curing sexual ailments? Jesus!

And the matter was complicated by the fact that he had no desire whatever *to* resist her. Indeed, the idea of slipping between the sheets of the Countess d'Aubert in order to join her there was the most attractive he had ever known. But to do that would be a direct dereliction of duty!

He had still not resolved his dilemma when the car drew up in the château courtyard. A flunky was waiting to take his gear, and another waited inside the knight's hall to relieve him of his coat and cap. Henri the butler showed him

165

into the drawing-room, where the countess was waiting; indeed, she might never have moved during the hour and a half he had been away. 'Welcome,' she said, as before. 'Henri, the Dom Perignon.'

Henri hurried to the bar. Harry swallowed. 'Ah ... do you always drink champagne before dinner, Countess?'

'As a matter of fact, no. But this is a special occasion.' She sat down on a settee and patted the space beside her. 'Come and sit down. Here,' she insisted, as he made for a straight chair. Behind him, there was a gentle pop and Henri opened the bottle. 'Harry Brand,' the countess said. 'Your name is Harry, isn't it?'

'Ah ... yes,' Harry said, more uneasily than ever. 'How did you know that?'

Henri presented his silver tray, and they each took a glass. 'Thank you, Henri,' the countess said. 'Leave the bottle, and you may serve dinner at eight-thirty.' Henri bowed, placed the bottle in an ice bucket on the coffee table, and left the room, carefully closing the doors behind him. 'Here is to us.' The countess sipped. Harry also sipped, beginning to be gripped by a consuming panic. 'My name is Nicole, by the way,' the countess said, and paused, expectantly.

'Nicole,' Harry said. 'That's a very nice name.'

'But it means nothing to you? Before I was married, I was Nicole d'Esperey.'

'There's a French general ...'

'A distant relative,' Nicole said. 'You are much closer.'

'Eh?' Harry spilled some champagne.

'My dear Harry,' Nicole said. 'Did you not know that you and I are by way of being brother and sister?'

Chapter Six

The Bridegroom

Slowly Harry put down his champagne glass. Nicole gave a little ripple of laughter, a delightful sound. 'You do not like the idea of that?'

'Frankly, Countess, I'm flabbergasted.'

'Nicole. You must call me Nicole, and I will call you Harry. You did know your father was stationed here during the Great War?'

'Yes, I did.'

'Well, he and my mother became very close friends.'

'I'm sure they did. But ...' his brain was in a spin, but there were certain obvious impossibilities in her story.

167

'I am older than you,' Nicole agreed. 'By some years, I would estimate. Yes. I was born in 1908, and you were born in ...?'

'1914. November.'

'*Ooh, la-la.* You were being born while your father was actually living in this house. I did say that we were related only in a manner of speaking, in that your father and my mother were lovers.' She frowned at him. 'You are relieved at that, I think.'

'I am. I already have a sister.'

'How splendid. I do not have a brother, alas.'

'Countess,' Harry said, not sure whether or not he was caught up in the biggest leg-pull of his life.

'Nicole, please.'

'Nicole. There are a couple of things you have to explain to me.'

'You have but to ask.'

'Well you say my father and your mother were lovers, during the Great War.'

'That is correct. I was six years old when your father first came here. I remember him well. He was very young and handsome. Is he still handsome?'

'Oh, indeed, but not quite so young. He's in France, somewhere, you know.'

'Is he? How splendid! I should love to meet him again.'

'I'm sure he'd like to meet you again,

too. But ... you say he and your mother got together, here.'

'In this very room, the first time,' Nicole said. 'As I remember.'

'But ... you are now married.'

'Ah,' she said. 'I see what is troubling you. Oh, this is the d'Esperey family home. Francois, you see, my husband, comes from a very long and famous noble family, but one, alas, that is totally impoverished. Whereas I inherited this château from my mother, along with all the land around here, and most of the houses.' She smiled. 'Including the brothel. Shall we eat?'

Harry was totally confounded. But what a delightful way to be confounded! He sat at the opposite end of the huge dining table from Nicole, so that conversation was really rather difficult. On the other hand, the food was so magnificent, and the wine such perfection, that conversation would have been an irrelevance, save on one subject. And that subject was well covered by Nicole's eyes, which glowed at him across the acres of silver and crystal.

She wants to take me to bed, he thought. Just as her mama did with Dad. And oh, how he wanted to go along with her on that. But he had been specifically forbidden to do so. And if by any chance he was mistaken, and he raised the subject, he would really be up the creek. Yet it had to be done. He waited until they had been served coffee and armagnac by Henri, in the drawing-room. The butler then retired, and they were alone. 'What exactly are your plans for tomorrow?' he asked.

She gave a delicate little shrug. 'I suppose we should start fairly early. The sooner this business is cleared up, the better. Shall we say, eight o'clock?'

'Ah ... you mean you will come with me?'

'I think I should.'

'It will not be very pleasant.'

'Disease seldom is.'

'Yes, but this is somewhat more unpleasant than most.'

'You have experience at it?'

'No, I do not.' He tried a smile. 'Frankly, I am terrified. Do you ... well ...?'

'I have never had the clap, if that is what you were going to ask. So, I am equally terrified. So, we will be terrified together, and together we will assuage each other's terror. Do not look so concerned, I manage the family farm, and thus I am fairly used to, shall we say, the more revolting aspects of animal behaviour. Besides, if I am not there, you may encounter some resistance to what you have to do. My presence will

170

give you an official stamp of approval, as it were.'

'And you are curious,' he challenged.

'Why, yes, so I am. I believe one should experience everything possible, in life, before one has to confront the ultimate experience, death.'

'It's a point of view,' Harry said, and stood up. 'Well, if we're to make an early start tomorrow, I should get to bed. I can't thank you enough for that meal. It was out of this world.'

'But you have not yet examined me.'

'Examined you? Oh, that was a joke. Not in very good taste, I'm afraid, but ...'

'Harry,' she said. 'It was I who made the joke. And it was not a joke.'

'Yes, but ...'

'Don't you *want* to examine me, Harry?'

'Yes,' he said without thinking.

'Well then ...'

'I can't, Countess. Nicole.'

'If you are concerned about Francois, do not be. He will never know of it.'

Harry licked his lips. 'I have been commanded not to touch you, by the Colonel.'

Nicole smiled. 'Was I that obvious? But Harry, you come from a military family. Do you not know that all great soldiers, and most great sailors as well, are great

171

because they disobeyed at least one order in their lifetime? And your colonel shall never know of it, either.'

A cock crowed, and Harry was awake. For a moment he did not know where he was; it was some weeks since he had slept in a comfortable bed. And never in his life had he slept between scented satin sheets. He turned his head, sharply. It had all, surely, to be a dream. But there she was, her hair now loose and scattered in auburn delight across the pillow, her arms extended in front of her so that they almost touched him, even in a bed that size. The sheet was folded across her waist, and between her arms was the pink-nippled perfection in which he had buried his face last night.

Would he ever tell Dad of this? Dare he? I am the luckiest man alive, he thought. When he recalled his almost febrile, immature desire for Marion Shafter, just because she had offered herself, or his aggressive, destructive desire for Constance Lloyd, simply because when he had met her he had hated all women ... of course he could not allow himself to fall in love with Nicole. She was married, she was a social strata above him, and she was several years older than him. But ... He kissed her on the nose. 'I love you,' he said.

She opened her eyes. 'It was fun, wasn't

it.' He rolled on his back in a paroxysm of frustration, and she rose on her elbow and in turn kissed his nose. 'You are serious.'

He caught her shoulders and brought her down on to himself. 'I'm a serious person.'

She wriggled her body on top of his, straddled him with her legs. She had such perfect legs. 'There would be problems.'

'I have just been considering them, and decided they aren't worth the trouble.'

She kissed him several times. 'It is something we both need to consider, very seriously.'

'You mean you *would* consider it?' He could not believe his ears.

'I am a very serious person too. So we have slept one night together. And had sex three times. Every time better than the last. That is a very serious consideration.'

'Isn't it good with Francois? I thought Frenchmen ...'

'Frenchmen,' Nicole said, 'are the greatest lovers in the world. But that does not necessarily mean that they are the greatest love-*makers* in the world.'

'Then what would you say of Englishmen?'

She gave one of her delicious little gurgles of laughter. 'Englishmen are without doubt the very worst lovers in the world. But when you do manage to get one into bed and strip away his inhibitions ...'

He was instantly jealous. 'That sounds as if you have had quite a few.'

'You are the first. But Mama told me about your papa. She loved him. But of course she could not marry him. She was already married to my papa, and he was already married to your mama.'

'We're one stage better off than that.'

'It is still something to be seriously considered. And we have a lot of time to consider it. Not less than three weeks, *n'est-ce pas?* And now ... down in the forest something is stirring. We do not have to get up for another half hour.'

Definitely the luckiest man in the world, Harry thought. To have known, in the most Biblical of senses, three such magnificent women, and to have wound up with the most magnificent of them all ... he sometimes wondered if he was indeed dreaming. Not even the realities of syringing the prostitutes, an utterly distasteful task, remained a chore with Nicole at his side, observing, recommending, and soothing, where necessary. And as she had promised, her presence removed any hint of resentment or animosity towards the English doctor, even when she extended the search for the disease, and the treatment, to almost the entire remaining population of

Centot. 'You do realize,' he pointed out, 'that if this ever becomes widely known, I shall be struck off?'

Nicole laughed. 'How can you be struck off, my darling; you have not yet been struck on? And you are acting on orders from your commanding officer.' Certainly Gregory and Dempster seemed well content with the work he was doing. The only problem, from Harry's point of view, was that with such a strict control of the sexual habits of both villagers and soldiers, the disease was being cleared up in rapid time. Once it was completely eradicated, there would be no more reason for him to stay at the château; his only hope was that both villagers and soldiers were so obviously counting the days until they could get at each other again, he didn't doubt that there would very rapidly be another outbreak.

The war seemed very remote. It continued at sea, of course, and there was news from time to time of a ship being sunk by a submarine, or a submarine being sunk by a warship. There were rumours that there had been patrol clashes between the French and the Germans further to the east, but there was absolutely no activity in front of the British lines, while such planes as flew overhead were carrying leaflets. In all the circumstances it was determined by the high command that Armistice Day, 11 November, should be fully celebrated, and the entire battalion, now almost wholly fit again, was paraded before the Centot war memorial while the Reverend Moore and l'Abbé Dudevant conducted services. Harry naturally took his place beside Gregory and the medical orderlies, while Nicole stood between Colonel Dempster and the mayor. She wore black and was black-veiled as well as black-hatted, but some of her auburn hair escaped to float in the breeze. 'A great occasion,' Gregory commented, when he and Harry returned to the field hospital for a glass of bottled beer after the ceremony. 'Things are really going very well. Do you know there are only a couple left on our sick list? What's the score in town?'

'Ah ... more than a couple, I'm afraid.'

'But still, another week at the outside will see us clear. And then, Harry my lad, do you know what I am going to do?'

'No,' Harry said, uneasily, because he had a distinct suspicion that he did know.

'I am going to recommend that you be sent home to go back to medical school, and qualify. I don't know why you dropped out before, and I don't want to know. But I do know that no man could have had a better assistant than you. You're a born MO, Harry.'

'It's very kind of you to say so,' Harry said. 'but I couldn't possibly leave you here with no help. I thought we weren't going to discuss my going home until after my replacement arrived.' And there was absolutely no sign of that happening.

'Not necessary,' Gregory said. 'I have lacked your assistance for the past three weeks, and I've managed perfectly well. It isn't as if we were engaged in a shooting war, and having to attend to casualties. No, no, I am perfectly capable of holding the fort here and you deserve a bump up. Besides, I know how frustrating it must be for you, living up at the chateau and being unable to do anything about the Countess.'

Harry gulped.

Nicole was not concerned. 'The one thing we must not do is let them suspect anything about us,' she said that night. 'Indeed, I think it is all going to work out very well. Once the disease is entirely eradicated, you are going to have to move back to the regiment, and then we are only going to be able to meet clandestinely, like two schoolchildren. But if you are sent back to England ...'

'We won't be able to meet at all,' Harry said disconsolately.

She laughed, and kissed him. 'But of

course we will. I have business interests in England. You will go, and after a suitable, but not too long, period I will follow. I should think we will be able to spend at least every weekend together.'

'That sounds tremendous. And perhaps ...'

'We still have to consider every angle,' she told him. 'By the way, this came for you today. It was delivered up here by your postman.' Harry frowned at the envelope. It was in a hand he had never seen before. But it gave off a faint whiff of perfume. 'Should I be jealous?' Nicole asked.

'Definitely not. It's from one of two people, and neither of them means anything to me now.' Actually, he reflected as he slit the envelope, it could only be from one person: there was no reason for Marion to write to him after this long. And as he surmised, it was from the Lloyds' London address.

My dearest Harry, Constance had written. *I am sending this to you care of the BEF, somewhere in France. I am assured that it will reach you, fairly quickly. Your mother has told me this.*

Why your mother, you will ask yourself, when it was our mutual desire to keep our liaison a secret? Sadly, as Thomas à Kempis would have it, Man proposes but

God disposes. *This would appear to apply even more forcefully to woman.*

Harry, I wish you to know that I do love you, most deeply and sincerely. Had I not done so I would never have yielded myself to you. Any hesitation on my part in accepting your proposal of marriage may be put down to a desire to be absolutely certain that we were right for each other. Please believe me when I say I had already reached that certainty before I became aware that there was another factor binding us together. But for that other factor I would not have pressed the matter until this business with Hitler was concluded, which cannot now be long delayed, everyone says. Unfortunately, waiting is no longer possible. I do not wish to be indelicate, but as nearly three months have elapsed since last we met there would not appear to be any doubt about my situation.

I have told no one, to this moment, and I will tell no one, pending your reply. Sadly, in a few months' time there will be no necessity to tell anyone, as they will be able to see for themselves. I am therefore placing my future in your hands, confident that as you love me and are an officer and a gentleman you will not fail me.

With my most dear love. Constance.

Nicole had been watching his expression as he read. Now she commented, 'That looks like bad news.' Harry held out the letter. She frowned. 'You wish me to read it?'

'I will need your advice.' His mind was in a turmoil. Of all the women with whom he had been intimate, Constance was the one he had loved least. Indeed, he had not loved her at all. Nicole was the only woman he had ever truly loved; he was certain of that. But now ...

Nicole raised her head: 'You are a masterful fellow, Harry,' she said softly.

'You mean I am the most wretched man on earth.'

'Becoming a father is more often regarded as an occasion for great personal satisfaction.'

'In these circumstances?'

She made a moue. 'Tell me of this woman.'

Harry did so, while she lay on her back with her hands beneath her head. 'Now I suppose you wish me to pack my bag and return to camp,' he said when he had finished.

'You are so vehement, so determined to be terribly right or terribly wrong,' she remarked. 'Do you imagine I was unaware that you had had women before me? One must always look on the positive side. From what you say, this Constance would appear to be a well-bred young lady of some social standing. And also, a friend of your family.

Now, consider the consequences had she been some barmaid?'

'What are the consequences?'

'You have to marry her.' Harry sat up. 'You *are* an officer and a gentleman, Harry,' Nicole pointed out. 'She has appealed to you in that guise. And you carry on your shoulders the burden of the honour of generations of officers and gentlemen. You cannot let them down any more than you can let her down.'

He threw himself down again. 'You talk of honour. Do you know what is involved? I will have to go to Dempster and tell him the facts, and ask for leave. He will give it to me, I am sure, and he may even hush it up as far as possible, but it will have to go in an official report. I will have to tell my mother and father the truth, and Constance will have to tell her parents the truth. They too may do all they can to keep it quiet, but the fact is that she will be at least four months gone before we can get married, and there will be no disguising the fact that she will give birth after five months of marriage.'

'All of which will prove a grave embarrassment to you,' Nicole said gently. 'But whether you ride such an embarrassment or not will determine, and not only to yourself, whether you are a callow youth or, an officer and a gentleman.'

181

He raised his head. 'You think I have behaved despicably.'

'In taking a woman to bed? I think you have behaved most naturally. I am sure she is at least physically attractive.'

'But I do not *love* her. I love you.'

She kissed him. 'I think we both understand that our love can never come to fruition, Harry.'

He held her close. 'And suppose you are pregnant?'

She smiled into his mouth. 'I assure you that I am not.'

'Well, of course, you will have to have leave,' Dempster said, and peered at Harry. 'You do love this girl, I hope?'

'Oh, yes, sir,' Harry said. 'Absolutely.'

'Well that's a relief. Lloyd. Something in the City, isn't he?'

'Yes, sir.'

'That's a relief as well, I'm sure. Would you like me to inform the Brigadier, or will you do that?'

'I will, sir. But if you would like to as well ...'

'Give my blessing, you mean? I'm not sure I can do that, in the circumstances. But ... ' he grinned. 'I'll give you a character reference.'

'Thank you, sir.'

'You'll have three days,' Dempster said.

'You have my permission to use the battalion phone to get in touch with your, ah ... fiancée, and with your mother. They will have to arrange things.'

'I understand, sir.'

'Good. Well ... today's Monday. We'll have to give them some time. Your leave will begin on Friday the Seventeenth, and we will expect you back here on Monday the Twentieth. I'd like to let you stay over Christmas, but it simply can't be done.'

'Thank you, sir. But what about my duties?'

'Gregory can cope until you return. From what he tells me, the crisis is just about over anyway.'

'You really are quite a lad, Harry,' Gregory remarked. 'Although now I can understand why you haven't been turned on by the countess, eh?'

'Yes,' Harry said. 'I'd better go up there and say goodbye.'

'Oh, Harry: you look so *miserable*.' Nicole held him close.

'I am so miserable,' he said.

'Don't you love her at all? You must have found her attractive.'

'She's an attractive woman. But I hit her on the rebound, when I was on a high at being commissioned. I really am a cad, Nicole.'

'You are a very average human being,' she corrected. 'But I suppose you would regard that as an insult. All right, you are an above-average human being, who went over the top. But I am sure she will make you a good wife, and that you will be very proud of your son.'

'And you and I are through, is that it?'

She kissed him. 'Not at all. It is not as good as we had both hoped and planned. But then life seldom is. One must cope with changed circumstances. You are coming back here?'

'You bet.'

'Then we will meet whenever we can. We will still love, my darling.'

Harry was in a thoroughly confused and somewhat distraught frame of mind when he stepped off the boat at Dover. For one thing, it was very difficult to grasp that he was part of an army that was at war. Or a country! From Britain's point of view, hardly a shot had been fired by any of her soldiers, and there had not been a single casualty, cases of VD excepted. According to what his father had told him, by the second half of November 1914 the BEF had already lost more than a hundred thousand men! He knew

184

he was not the only frustrated soldier. There were those who regarded it as a gigantic holiday, who had very little idea of where Poland was much less of what the Polish people might be like, and who reckoned the whole business would soon be called off and they'd all be home for Christmas.

He was not one of them. He could not have been named Brand if he was. But apart from that, he knew sufficient history to be certain that Great Britain had only ever become involved in one war they had not fought to a victorious finish, and that had been against their own kith and kin in North America in 1776. But sometimes their neglect of militarism, when not actually fighting, had led them into some very lengthy businesses. The Government had already announced a blockade of Germany. Most analysts recognized that it had been the blockade far more than any Allied military successes that had forced the Kaiser's Germany to its knees, just as a hundred years previously it had been the blockade of Napoleonic Europe that had forced the Little Corporal to expand his conquests until they had collapsed of their own weight.

But the war against Revolutionary France had lasted twenty years. Even that against the Kaiser's Germany had lasted four, and that Germany had been entirely surrounded by enemies. Hitler's Germany could draw on its strange bedfellow, Stalin's Russia, for the sinews of war. Twenty years, he thought! Supposing we just sit in France for twenty years, because neither side can afford to risk the cataclysm of a battle fought with modern weapons? My son will be twenty years old!

Which brought him back to the real problem. His son! Which was an absurdity in itself: his child could easily be a daughter. But it would be his child. With a woman with whom he had done nothing more than amuse himself. He had to be the most wretched bastard on the face of the earth. What was as galling as any other aspect of his situation was that from the moment Constance's letter had arrived, the event had been taken right out of his hands, with everyone, from Nicole down, telling him exactly what needed to be done. As if he had not known what had to be done.

Perhaps they all felt that, without direction, he might shirk his duty. Would he have done that? He knew he would, if Nicole had said, stuff her and marry me instead. But Nicole had not said that. Nicole was no doubt glad to be rid of such a callow youth, for all her promises. He wondered who would be the next young officer to be invited to Centot Château?

186

Landing in Dover was equally unreal, when he remembered their departure, six weeks before. The ferry had crossed the Channel at high speed, accompanied by a destroyer, but no submarines had been seen and the sky had been clear. Now Dover, while the actual getting ashore was submerged beneath a mass of red tape, was utterly peaceful, sheltering beneath a steady drizzle. There were sandbags everywhere, however, and the officialdom of the docks were intensified at the railway station, where the ticket collector seemed offended that Harry was travelling on his train at all. He had expected Constance to be on the platform at Waterloo to greet him, but instead it was James Lloyd himself. He braced himself as he stepped off the train. 'You're looking well,' Lloyd remarked.

'Thank you, sir.'

'So is Constance,' Lloyd added, by way of answering Harry's question before it was asked. 'I've a taxi waiting.'

Harry was carrying only an overnight bag, so they did not need a porter. They sat together in the back of the taxi. 'I would like you to know, sir,' Harry began. He had prepared a statement, although he had not expected to have to deliver it so soon.

'Later,' Lloyd said, nodding his head at the half-open glass partition. 'How long have you got?'

'I'm due back on Monday.'

'And we can't have you posted AWOL, eh?' Lloyd did not smile as he made the joke. 'Here will do, cabbie.' The taxi drew up outside a very smart building, although its front was obscured by a mountain of sandbags. 'My club.' Lloyd paid off the taxi.

'Is Constance here?' Harry asked.

'This is a man's club. A *gentlemen's* club,' Lloyd added, with some emphasis. 'I thought you and I should have a chat.'

Harry gulped, but followed his prospective father-in-law into the sumptuous interior. He was signed in at the desk, and then escorted into an even more sumptuous smoking-room. Lloyd nodded to one or two people, and led his guest to a couple of leather armchairs in the far corner. Whiskies and soda appeared and were placed at their elbows. By this time Harry had got over his initial attack of nerves and was becoming just a little bit irritated. 'You do realize, sir, that I have only two days after this one. And it is already nearly noon.'

'Impatient, are you? That surprises me, seeing that ... well ...'

Now Harry was definitely angry. 'That,

188

Mr Lloyd, was a totally unnecessary piece of vulgarity.' Lloyd sat straight, staring at him. 'Constance and I happen to be in love with each other,' Harry went on, speaking in a quiet, even tone which went with the room, and wishing that he was not lying, which did *not* go with the room, 'You may put down what happened to the exigencies of the time, but we fully intended to get married anyway, as soon as possible. You were the only obstacle. Well, sir, are you going to refuse us permission now?'

Chapter Seven

A Botched Affair

'You certainly shook Daddy up,' Constance said. 'But I think he respects you for it.'

'Do you respect me, Connie?'

'I love you, Harry.' She kissed him. He was alone with his bride, after a very hectic twenty-four hours.

First of all there had been the Lloyd family luncheon, at which he had been introduced to all of Constance's large circle of relatives, which had varied from elderly aunts with condemnatory sniffs to

189

small boys and girls who all seemed aware of what he had done to their Connie. But all wanted to ply him with questions about the situation in France, whereupon he had got his own back by simply refusing to discuss it.

Then there had been the Brand family dinner, a much more muted affair, because there were so few Brands available. Both Father and Hector were serving in France and could not get away, while Jocelyn, who had begun the whole thing, was with her mother in Scotland and was too heavily pregnant to make the journey south. She had, however, written them a joint note: *You darling devils. But I know you will never regret a moment of it.* Jocelyn, Harry reflected, was still living in cloud-cuckoo-land.

He was actually relieved not to have to confront Father at this moment. Confronting Mother was bad enough. He gathered that she and Constance had become good friends, and that she regarded her son as entirely responsible for the while thing. Well, he supposed she was right about that. Louise, on the other hand, was entirely on his side. 'She's very pretty,' she whispered, smiling at Constance across the table. 'But do you love her?' Harry had stirred his tea vigorously. 'I don't think you should marry someone if you don't love them,' Louise said. 'Not even if she is in the family way.' Louise was clearly emancipated.

'Of course I love her,' Harry whispered back. 'I love her very much.'

Louise looked sceptical. 'And what about that woman in Africa?'

'She was a nothing,' he snapped. The first truth he had uttered in some time. And now, nearly twenty-four hours later, the list of lies had grown beyond belief. Honour and cherish. Till death do us part.

'You're terribly serious,' Constance said.

'Marriage is a serious business.'

She had been looking out of the window at the Thames; they had decided to spend their two-night honeymoon at the Savoy rather than the Ritz, where they might be remembered. Now she turned back to him. 'You didn't really want to, did you?'

'Now, Connie!' He got up to offer her a glass of champagne. 'What on earth makes you say that?'

'Your expression, from time to time, during the service. Last night, as well.'

'Well, the whole thing is a bit traumatic. I mean, I had looked forward to one of those romantic courtships, and then an announced engagement, and then ...'

'Those things would not have been

possible anyway, with a war on.'

'I suppose not.'

'And I'm glad it happened the way it did. Now we've told the world, we have loved, we love, we will love.' She paused, just a little anxiously, waiting for his reply.

He took her in his arms, still holding the two glasses of champagne, kissed her on the mouth. 'There's an orchestra downstairs. Would you like to go down and dance?'

'With only tonight and tomorrow? I want to stay up here, and make love.'

'Oh. Can we?' She raised her eyebrows. 'I mean, well ...'

She laughed. 'You're not going to hurt the baby, silly. He's just dying to have some more of you.'

How peaceful Centot looked, nestling in its valley as the trees bared themselves and waited the first snow. 'All well?' Dempster asked.

'Yes, sir.'

Dempster looked at his subordinate; the boy was not exactly exuding happiness. 'I've heard from the Brigadier.'

'So have I, sir.'

'Oh, quite.' Which obviously explained much of his demeanour, the Colonel concluded. 'I'm sure he'll soon get over it.'

'I would imagine so, sir. His attitude is rather like the pot calling the kettle black.'

Dempster digested that. But he wasn't sure just how much this lad knew of his father's reputation as a philanderer. 'Yes. Meanwhile, there have been some developments.'

'The Germans aren't making a move, are they?' Harry was eager.

'Good Lord, no. They're too busy talking peace. I believe there has been some patrol activity in the Ardennes, but that can't mean anything much. No, this is personal, as regards yourself. Did you know that Gregory had recommended you for training as a doctor?'

'Yes, sir.' Harry's heart sank.

'Well, it's been accepted by GHQ.'

'Oh, good lord, sir. I'd far rather stay here.'

'That's very loyal of you, Harry. However, you have your way to make, and I am certainly not going to stand in your way. I endorsed Gregory's recommendation, and GHQ have accepted it, as I say. However, it can't be until next year. I know Gregory claims he can manage without an assistant, but they are adamant that he shall have one. They're still all in a muddle, sorting out who goes where and replaces whom, and when, and they can't let us have our new man right away, so it'll certainly be next year before they'll be ready for you. Still, something to look forward to, eh?'

'Yes, sir,' Harry said.

'Don't looked so buggered, Harry. You'll almost certainly be sent to a London training hospital, and that means you'll be able to spend the weekends with your wife. Won't that be splendid?'

'Yes, sir.'

'When is your baby due, by the way?'

'End of May, sir.'

'Well, we shall certainly hope to have you home by then. How are things in England?'

'Except for the black-out, you wouldn't know there was a war on, sir. And what the black-out is for, no one seems quite sure; there certainly aren't any German planes about. Oh, and there is talk that one or two things are going to be rationed.'

'It certainly is a rum old war,' Dempster said. 'But as long as it continues like this, who's complaining?'

'Hello,' Harry said. 'Hello!' He looked over his shoulder, but Gregory had not yet returned to the office. 'Hello?' At last. 'Is that you, Henri? May I speak with the Countess, please.'

'The Countess is in Paris, monsieur.'

194

'Oh, sh ... heck. When will she be returning?'

'I do not know, monsieur. She went there to be with the Count, you understand.'

This time Harry did not bother to choose his words. 'Shit!' he commented.

It was a thoroughly miserable December, but then, it might have been anyway, for Harry. Constance had been so eager, so loving, so anxious to *be* loved. He could only hope he had fooled her into believing he was no less in love, while hating himself every time his thoughts drifted away to Nicole, which happened every few minutes. And she was in Paris with her husband!

But apart from his personal problems, the War continued to be a non-event, on the Western front. At the beginning of the month the Russians attempted to invade Finland, and promptly received a bloody nose. That the Russians would eventually be able to beat Finland, however, was obvious, which opened a whole can of diplomatic worms. The Allies were not at war with Russia, and did not wish to be; there was always the chance that Stalin might change his mind about being Hitler's pal, and in any event, it was an alarming thought to consider Britain and France being opposed to the two totalitarian superpowers. Additionally, Finland was a traditional ally of Germany, and therefore a natural enemy of the West. But public opinion in the West, already aroused by the Russian rape of what the Germans had left them of defenceless Poland, clamoured for something to be done to help poor little Finland. The pressure grew to the stage where Britain and France determined to take action, but then were stymied by the refusal of the Norwegian and Swedish governments, both presumably afraid of antagonizing Hitler, to permit the passage of any aid, much less troops, through their territory. So that was that.

Along the Belgian front rumours abounded, of German troop movements and plans, but nothing was very visible, and it came as a shock to the entire Field Force when on 10 December it was reported that the previous day the British Army had suffered its first fatality of the War, Corporal Thomas Priday of the King's Shropshire Light Infantry being shot leading a patrol. The shock was less the sad loss of Priday than the realization that they had been at war more than three months before such a thing had happened, or that it had happened in the middle of an official visit to the troops of King George VI. 'Must have known he was coming. But at that rate,' Gregory commented, 'we could be here for five years before losing a platoon.'

He was itching to have some real wounds to deal with, and was stirred by the visit of the Prime Minister a few days later. 'We are going to drive Hitler out of business,' Mr Chamberlain told the battalion. 'You may rely upon that.'

Harry was less convinced, and was in any event irritated that the Prime Minister had been given the run of the château during his brief visit, but Nicole had not hurried back to entertain him. In fact she did not return until well into January, by which time the battalion was snowed in. Now at last Harry received an invitation, to tea. 'You alone?' Gregory asked, somewhat peeved.

'I imagine she wants to ask me about the wedding,' Harry said.

The Countess sent her car for him, and she was waiting in the doorway of the knights' hall when he arrived. 'You must be frozen.' She led him into the drawing-room, where there was a roaring fire and Henri was serving mulled wine. 'At least you can be sure there will be no fighting in this weather.'

'I do not think there is ever going to be any fighting, in any weather,' he remarked.

Nicole raised her eyebrows, and nodded to Henri. 'Thank you, Henri, we will help ourselves. I assume you do not really want tea, Harry?'

Harry waited until Henri had closed the door. 'I want you.' She took him into her arms for a kiss. 'How was Paris?' he asked, hating himself for his gaucheness.

'Paris was Paris. How was London?'

'London, I suppose.'

'And as we were both with our respective spouses, there is no necessity for jealousy, *n'est-ce pas?*'

'God, I am just jealous of the air you breathe, when I am not breathing it with you.'

'That is a very romantic thing to say. How long can you stay?'

'Until six.'

'But that is less than two hours. We must make haste.' She unbuttoned her blouse.

'Here?' He looked at the door.

'Henri will not come in now unless I call him, and for us to go upstairs in the middle of the afternoon would be too obvious.'

'You think us being here alone isn't obvious?'

'It may well be, but no one can prove anything. Don't you want to make love to me, Harry? Anywhere, any time?' He

198

lowered his head to kiss her breasts as she uncovered them.

She was as passionate as ever he remembered. 'Because I have missed you so,' she explained. 'And because ...'

'Tell me.' They lay together on the settee, naked, their limbs entwined as there was not much space. But it had been the best one Harry had ever had, as she had wanted him to enter her from behind, something he had never suspected a civilized white woman could ever desire ... and it had been heavenly. He wondered if Constance would ever let him do that?

But he could also tell that Nicole had things on her mind. He could only pray that Francois had not for some reason been demobbed, and would be coming home. She sighed. 'There is a rumour in Paris that a German reconnaissance plane crash-landed in Belgium a couple of weeks ago. The pilot was captured. He was a Major Reinberger of the Parachute Corps, and he had on him secret documents outlining Germans plans to seize certain key Belgian and Dutch areas by parachute drop, as part of a general offensive in the west.' She raised her head as Harry did not immediately reply. 'You do not believe this?'

'Are you saying a major in the German

army did not have the nous to destroy any papers he might have been carrying when he realized he was down in foreign territory?'

'Apparently he tried, but made a mess of it. The Belgians were able to piece everything together.'

'And what have they done about it?'

She shrugged. 'Nobody knows. They are so determined to maintain their neutrality it is possible that they are deliberately doing nothing about it for fear of provoking Hitler. But it surely means that he intends to attack France as soon as the weather improves.'

'Unless it was a plant. I still find it difficult to accept that a German officer would not have destroyed his papers. He could have been ordered not to do so. Thus, as you suggest, all our top brass are now anticipating an attack, while Hitler might be meaning to move somewhere quite different.'

'Where?'

'I have no idea.' He kissed her. 'Let's talk about something more certain, and important. Dempster is determined that I should go back to medical school and qualify, just as soon as he can find me a replacement.' This time it was her turn not to speak. 'Will you still be able to come over?'

'When are you going?'

'I have no idea. Neither does anyone else, it seems. But he's going to try to wangle it for early May. My baby is due at the end of that month.'

'You mean, your wife's baby.'

'Well ... yes.'

'And you seriously want me to be about? I thought this whole business had made a man out of you.'

'For God's sake. I love *you*, Nicole. Nobody else.'

'Then let us make the most of what we have. But I am not going to muscle in on your wife.'

Crumbs from the table, he thought. But he took her advice and made the most of them.

Nicole had him up to tea at least once a fortnight; to do so more often, she felt, might arouse suspicions. And certainly Gregory found it cause for comment. 'You're not having it off with her, I hope?' he asked.

'If you must know,' Harry said, skirting around the truth, 'the Countess regards me as her brother.'

'What?'

Harry told him about the Brigadier and the previous countess.

'Holy smoke! The old devil,' Gregory

201

commented. But he seemed entirely satisfied with the explanation.

On 9 April, the Germans invaded both Denmark and Norway. As this was a Tuesday, and Harry was not due at the château again until Saturday afternoon, he could make no comment to Nicole for several days, and by Saturday it was clear that both the British and French governments intended to support Norway as fully as they could—by then it was already too late for Denmark, which had been overrun in twenty-four hours. 'Nevertheless,' Harry pontificated. 'It just goes to show that your Major Hamberger or whatever his name was, was indeed a plant.'

'Would it be awful of me to say that I am so glad he was a plant?' Nicole asked. And then added, anxiously, 'You won't have to go to Norway, will you?'

'I doubt it.' But amongst the British troops which were pulled out of France to sail north was the Brigadier. 'All because he knows how to ski,' Harry suggested. But he was actually worried for his father. They had not seen each other since the War had begun, but of late his letters had been more forgiving than immediately after Constance's news had broken, and he hated to think of the old boy going into action before himself.

He became even more worried when the Norwegian business became more and more botched. The Royal Navy seemed to be doing everything that could be required of it, but the Army appeared to be always on the run. This was galling, and not only to the Army itself. 'There's to be a general debate as to the conduct of the War in Parliament,' Dempster told Harry. 'Might be worth dropping in on.'

'If one happened to be in London, sir,' Harry agreed, wondering why he had been summoned to battalion headquarters to discuss the situation with his commanding officer.

'Oh, quite.' Dempster agreed. 'You will, unfortunately, probably miss it, as I believe it is going to be next week. However, you will be in London the week after. Your transfer has finally come through.'

Harry gulped; he had almost forgotten all about his transfer. 'With respect, sir ...'

'Don't you want home leave, Harry? I cannot think of another man in the regiment who would not give his eye-teeth to be in England this spring. Look at the weather! It's simply magnificent.'

'It's just that I feel I should be here when the balloon goes up, sir.'

'Harry, there is simply no prospect of any

balloon going up here until this Norwegian business is completed. We may not be doing very well, but Hitler is fully committed.' He pointed. 'You've been listening to the Countess, haven't you?'

'Well, sir ...'

'I know all the rumours. So and so whispers to the Papal Nuncio, who whispers to the Pope, who whispers to some Italian countess who just happens to be the sister of the King of the Belgians, who whispers to her brother ... and somehow it immediately becomes known to all of Parisian high society, just what Hitler is going to do next. Just answer me one question: did the Countess, with her claims to know exactly what is going on in Berlin, give the slightest suggestion that she knew Hitler was going to invade Norway?'

'Well ... no, sir.'

'There you have the truth of the matter. People like the Countess, God bless her, exist on rumour. And long may it be so. But one thing I can promise you, when you come back, a fully qualified doctor, Harry, we shall still be right here, waiting for you. And do you know something else? Gregory has done a great job, this winter, in difficult circumstances. I'm recommending him for a Brigade post and ...' he smiled. 'I am requesting that you be returned to us, as our MO, with, of course, the rank of captain.'

'That is exceedingly kind of you, sir.'

'It's only what you deserve, and what this battalion deserves. Now, I know you'll want to write to your wife and give her the good news; it means you'll be home for the birth.'

'Yes, sir. Am I allowed to write, sir? I mean, troop movements ...'

'I think, in the circumstances, that we can condone the information that one second lieutenant is coming to London for medical training to be disseminated,' Dempster said with a grin. 'If Hitler gets hold of such a priceless piece of information, he may well sue for peace more vigorously than he is doing at the moment. You leave on Saturday morning.'

This was Thursday. Again it was a matter of waiting for Gregory to leave the office for a few minutes and then desperately telephoning. 'I'm off on Saturday,' he said.

'That's rather sudden,' Nicole said.

'I'm afraid that is how the Army operates. Are you free this afternoon? I'm sure I can get away.'

'No,' she replied. 'I am expecting the nuns from the convent for tea. I do not think it would go down very well with them if you were to turn up. Tomorrow. Can you make it tomorrow?'

'I'll make it. Oh, Nicole ...'

'Tomorrow,' she said. 'I am counting the hours.'

'Pity you can't let your wife know you're coming home,' Gregory remarked. 'When you walk in the door, she'll probably get so excited she'll deliver there and then.'

'You are a terribly vulgar bastard,' Harry said, and went to bed. But not to sleep, immediately. There were so many thoughts roaming through his mind. He was unlikely to return to Centot for several months, perhaps even longer. He adored Nicole, but he knew she was as randy as hell, and the thought of her getting aereated over some other young officer ... or Gregory! He'd go stark raving mad. He didn't even know if she'd be interested in him at all, once he was a father as well as a husband.

He dosed off just before dawn, awoke with a start to the sound of the camp siren. He fell out of bed and landed on his hands and knees, and for several seconds was unsure where he was. Gregory came in, dragging on his clothes. 'It's happening. The Germans have invaded Holland and Belgium. And France. Through the Ardennes, would you believe it.'

'Holy Jesus Christ! When?'

'Only a couple of hours ago. First light. Make haste, boy. We're moving out.'

'Where?'

'Into Belgium. We're going to have a crack at the buggers.'

Harry got dressed, and ran into the office, where Croom and Gibbons were busily packing medical supplies and files. He gazed at the telephone, biting his lip. But not only was it impossible to have an intimate conversation in front of the two orderlies, it would be a grave dereliction of duty to tell anyone, even Nicole, where they were off to.

'Officers call!' He hurried to the command hut, before which Dempster waited, together with Harris and the Reverend Moore. The Colonel smiled at his hastily assembled officers.

'The moment we have all been waiting for, eh? Now, in accordance with the decisions of our commanders, we are going to advance across the border, and across Belgium, to the line of the River Dyle. We should get there just about the same time as the Germans. Then we are going to show those bastards what war is all about. You with me?'

'Hip, hip, hoorah!' shouted Nelson, and the cry was taken up.

'Then let's go! A word, Lieutenant Brand.' Harry hurried forward. 'I'm afraid all plans are on hold, Harry,' Dempster said. 'I'm sorry.'

'I wouldn't have it any other way, sir.'

'Good man. But I'm afraid there isn't any way that you can let your wife know.'

'She didn't even know I was coming home at all, sir.'

Dempster raised his eyebrows. 'Oh! Right. Well, let's get at it, The sooner we do that, the sooner you'll be able to get to her.'

The trucks were loaded, and the battalion moved out. It had all happened so quickly the people of Centot didn't really know what was going on; they had not yet heard the news from Belgium. Thus only a few emerged from their houses to wave their friends off, the brothel, needless to say, was firmly closed at eight in the morning. Nor was there any sign of life at the château, although they must have heard the growl of engines up there. The border barriers were up, the douanes on both sides standing to attention with hats doffed as the Field Force drove through. Immediately on the Belgian side of the frontier there were cheering crowds, and these continued for some time. It was some sixty miles from Centot to the River Dyle, which itself was some ten miles east of Brussels. The British Army in general was to take up a position south of the city, and a glance at the map had Harry's excitement and sense of history overcoming his disappointment at not being able to say goodbye to Nicole, for their route lay directly through country steeped in British military history, including the battlefield of Waterloo, while Wavre lay on the river itself.

The journey should have taken about four hours; instead it was nightfall before the battalion reached its appointed bivouac position, within a mile of the river. This was partly because of the crowds on the roads certainly, refusing to be intimidated by the bellowing, red-faced military police, but also partly because there was simply too much movement for the roads to handle. In addition to the entire British Army hurrying north-east there was a French corps hurrying north to help defend Holland, crossing the British path; the medical corps found itself mainly treating cases of nervous exhaustion, usually from other units. Not an enemy was to be seen, and although there were planes overhead, they were very high and might have been British or French as much as German.

Bivouacing was the usual scene of ordered chaos, as the tents were thrown up, and as the men were ordered to dig slit trenches on their eastern perimeter. No one slept that night, although many fell asleep with first light, and still no sign of any enemy. Dempster called an officers' conference. 'I have to tell you,' he said, 'that Prime Minister Chamberlain has resigned. Churchill is the new Prime Minister.' He paused, and the reaction was predictable. 'Hoorah!' shouted Nelson. And the rest joined in.

'Do you think they are out there?' Gregory asked. He and Harry stood on the banks of the river, and peered across in the morning mist. The river itself was not very wide or very fast, and would not, Harry felt, present much of an obstacle to determined men. But they would certainly be opposed; to either side the Field Force were dug in, with their tanks and their artillery as well as their rifles, glaring grimly to the east. On the other hand ...

'If they are, they're keeping bloody quiet about it,' he commented.

But the Germans were there. That morning the first refugees arrived, pitiful columns of people of both sexes and all ages, from babes in arms to old men walking with sticks, and accompanied by their dogs and their cats and their caged birds. Some were driving cars, others pushing cars which had run out of petrol—and which were moving just as fast owing to the congestion—others pushing handcarts or guiding horse-drawn carts, some on bicycles, the main part on foot; everyone carried a bundle of belongings, those who had some sort of transport equipped with heavier stuff, from paintings to cutlery and crockery to, in more than one case, a piano, not to mention the odd bedstead.

There had been no orders to blow the bridges as yet, and the British soldiers gazed at the terrified people as they filed across, being carefully watched by the MP's who had been warned that there might be fifth-columnists inserted in the throng. 'Miserable blighters,' Gregory commented. 'Can you imagine that happening at home?'

'Not really,' Harry said. 'At home there wouldn't be any place to go.'

That afternoon they heard the sound of the guns, and then the first Belgian soldiers reached the river. They gave an appearance of conducting an orderly retreat; certainly there was no panic. But so many of them walked with bowed heads, and trembled, as they contemplated the past twenty-four hours. Too many also had lost their weapons in their haste to be away, while too much of what transport they

211

had saved was horse-drawn. The British soldiers offered them cigarettes and rum. 'You will see them soon enough,' said one of their officers who spoke English. 'and you will have seen nothing like it. The dive-bombers, the artillery, the tanks ...'

'We have a few of our own, old son,' Gregory said, and pointed to where several of the huge armoured vehicles were waiting in the concealment of a wood.

'You will see,' the Belgian said again, and rejoined his men.

The Belgians had been withdrawing to rest and recuperate after their shattering experiences on the border, a further sixty miles to the east. They were indeed being followed by German troops, but these were only skirmishers. They took pot-shots at the British, and the British took pot-shots back at them, but there were no casualties, at least on the British side. 'Beats me why, as they're so thin on the ground, we don't cross the river and smash the buggers,' Gregory said, as belligerent as ever.

On Sunday, following a brief church parade, Dempster gave them one of the answers. 'The French have pulled back across the Meuse,' he told his officers. 'It appears that the Germans are advancing in considerable strength, and using their dive-bombers to devastating effect. They have actually penetrated the Ardennes with their armour. But it is not supposed they will be able to cross the river, although it is certainly anticipated they'll try.'

'When are we going to have a crack at them, sir?' Price asked.

'All in good time. If they do get bogged down on the Meuse, then it may be possible for us to swing in against their flanks. But the people at the top know more than we do.'

That afternoon they thought they could hear the sound of the guns, but no one was sure. What was sure was that next day they learned that the Germans *had* forced the Meuse in strength, and that the French Ninth Army had virtually been destroyed. 'Jesus,' Nelson remarked. 'I thought the French were the best soldiers in the world?'

'Well, they're not doing very well at the moment,' Dempster said, unwilling publicly to condemn Britain's allies for lack of fight. 'One thing is certain: they'll be after us next.'

They actually came on the Wednesday.

The battalion was stood to at dawn with the warning of approaching aircraft. Harry and Gregory stood outside the field hospital and watched the single-engined monoplanes, flying surprisingly low, and not very fast. 'Those aren't Messerschmitts,' Harry said.

'No, they're Stukas,' Gregory said. 'Junkers 87s. They're dive-bombers. They're the chaps who destroyed the Polish army, and caused the French problems at the Meuse.'

There was no shelter worth taking; they had to rely on the huge red cross painted on their truck. And in fact the Germans did leave them alone, but they attacked the positions along the banks of the river, their engines making a high screaming sound as they hurtled downwards. A nearby anti-aircraft battery, opened up, while the troops fired their rifles and the machine-gunners endeavoured to elevate their weapons sufficiently. The noise was tremendous, but the actual results of the attack, Harry estimated, were limited. A good many of the bombs, released when the Stukas were perilously near the ground, went into the river itself. But enough struck the banks to bring the medical team their first casualties of the war. Harry gulped as he saw the shrapnel-torn body stretched out on the rudimentary operating table. 'Morphine,' Gregory commanded, in total command of the situation. 'Swabs. Sutures. This one for evacuation, Corporal. Next!'

And the routine commenced again. Harry's role was that of head nurse, while Croom and Gibbons did the dirty work, quite literally: a man struck by flying shell fragments invariably loses all control of his body functions. But all four of them were soon covered in blood. There was no time to feel sick. In the noisome heat and tension of the medical tent it was impossible to have any idea of what was happening outside. The Stuka attack only lasted a few minutes, although there were at least a dozen casualties, and these did not include the five men killed outright. Before Gregory had dealt with the last one, however, there was another series of explosions, these much heavier and more dramatic, in that the entire tent seemed to shake. 'Guns,' Gregory commented, without lifting his head from the wound he was probing.

The British guns were already firing, and the artillery duel joined with even more earth-shaking effects. Surprisingly, there were less casualties as a result of the bombardment. 'Right,' Gregory said, when there was a temporary break in the number of men being brought in. 'Now we can look at the walking wounded. And you, Harry, get that truck moving back to Brigade with those serious cases.'

'Yes, sir,' Harry said. In an hour his estimation of Gregory, both as a man and as a doctor, had quadrupled. He went outside, where the May sunshine was startlingly bright. Lying or sitting on the grass were another dozen soldiers, smoking cigarettes and muttering at each other; these were the men with superficial wounds. Some of them struggled to their feet to salute, most ignored the young officer. Harry ran to where the truck was waiting, in the shelter of some trees, its back filled with stretcher cases. 'Off you go,' he told the driver.

'Yes, *sir*,' the corporal agreed, happy to be away; a shell had burst not a hundred yards away, creating a deep crater and bringing down several trees. Harry turned to look at the river, and gulped. Clearly visible from where he stood was a brigade of German tanks, advancing across the open country to the east, guns belching red. The British guns and tanks were returning fire, and as he watched one of the German machines swung hard to its right and burst into flames. The rest then came to a halt, still firing. They were aiming mainly at the west bank of the river, and only the stray ricochet came his way, but they were having an effect, as he saw the stretcher bearers making their way back from where the infantry were dug in. He hurried back to the tent to resume work.

The battle raged all day, but died down at nightfall. By then both Gregory and Harry were exhausted, as were Croom and Gibbons. The truck had been back and forth to Brigade three times, but there were still several more men waiting to be evacuated. It was Gregory who raised his head. 'Listen!'

Harry listened. 'The shooting's stopped.'

The night was by no means quiet. Apart from the cries and groans of the men they were tending, there were words of command and the grinding of engines as the tanks changed their positions ... but they were still here, he thought with a sense of wonder.

Dempster arrived as they were rigging the oil lamps. 'Not too many of those,' he recommended. 'You're creating a target.'

Gregory merely snorted. Harry looked at the colonel, whose uniform was mud and dust-stained and who looked as exhausted as himself. 'How did it go, sir?'

'Pretty well, I would say. We certainly saw them off. But I imagine they have plans for tomorrow.'

'Can we hold them?'

'I would say we can, with a little bit of help from our friends. Unfortunately, we've just been informed that the Dutch Army has asked for a ceasefire.'

'Heck. But we didn't expect too much

of them, did we? As long as the Belgians hold firm ...'

'There's no problem,' Dempster agreed. 'I'll leave you to it. But get some rest whenever you can.'

'Lucky for some,' Gregory muttered.

They did get their heads down about midnight, all four of them exhausted and sleeping in the midst of all the blood and guts that were still lying about, in and out of the tent. But they had been sleeping only a couple of hours when they were awakened by Sergeant Cutmore, shaking their shoulders to get them up. 'Time to go, sir,' he told Gregory.

Gregory sat up. 'Go? Go where?'

'I don't know, sir. But we're pulling out. Retreating, sir.'

Chapter Eight

Ever Backwards

The troops were bewildered by the command to retreat. But they were more angry. They had taken everything the Germans could throw against them, and driven it off. 'I know how the poor devils feel,' Dempster said, as he watched Gregory and

Harry loading their gear into the medical truck. 'Unfortunately, while we may have held them here, it's all hell further south. The Panzers have broken through at Sedan and are out in open country. If we don't fall back, now, they'll be round behind us, and that will be that. Now ...' he indicated the map. 'You will retire behind the line of the Scheldt, and set up your station here. The battalion will fall back on you. Brigade is taking up a position a little to your rear.'

Harry peered at the position marked. 'The Scheldt is west of Brussels, sir.'

'Yes. It's been decided the capital cannot be defended without unacceptable loss of civilian life. The Belgian Government is declaring Brussels an open city and moving to Ostend.'

Harry continued to look at the map. 'And where do we go if we have to retreat from this new position, sir?'

Dempster gave a twisted grin. 'Looks like the beach, doesn't it, Harry? What we have to do is make sure we don't have to fall back, from there.'

The retreat was even more chaotic than the advance, because now the troops were in the midst of hordes of refugees, also moving back. The next twenty-four hours were the most traumatic of Harry's life, to

219

that moment, far outweighing the horror of watching the two Italian soldiers castrated. In Belgium he was surrounded by fear and bewilderment, that such a thing should be happening—and the fear had spread to a good number of the soldiers they encountered, stragglers who didn't seem sure where they were going, or why. Occasionally they encountered a motorized column, and sometimes drove with them for a while, before diverging towards their directed objective. These men attempted to maintain the traditional British attitude of good-humoured banter, but in too many of their eyes was the dead look Harry had first noticed with the Belgians. And everyone watched the skies, because on this beautiful May morning there were few clouds, and it was from the skies that there came the enemy that turned fear and bewilderment into terrifying horror.

The first attack came quite soon after they had commenced their journey. They were concentrating on the road ahead, driving at a snail's pace as they attempted to thread their way through the people thronging the road, careless of what might be behind them, when they were overtaken by what seemed to be a wave of living humanity, running, screaming, jostling against the truck, trying to climb into it, to the consternation of Croom and

Gibbons, in the back. Then they heard the screaming of the engines. 'Stukas!' Gregory shouted.

Harry was peering out of the window. 'Messerschmitts,' he corrected. 'Get off the road,' he told Corporal Henley the driver. This was easier said than done; there was a steep parapet down one side. But on the other the ground was reasonably flat, and there were trees. The driver swung the wheel hard right, and the people on that side screamed anew as the truck threatened them. They threw themselves right and left as the huge vehicle surged beneath the trees, ripping off branches before coming to a stop. Harry jumped down to look at a sight he would never forget to his dying day. Behind them, the road had been packed with people, shoulder to shoulder, some twelve abreast. Also back there were several more military vehicles, trying to find a way through the throng. Now, as the fighters swooped lower, it was as if some invisible force was driving a bow wave through the crowd, which split and ran to either side, abandoning carts and automobiles.

Not all of them made it. Wings spitting red, the Messerschmitts came in lower even than the Italian planes in Ethiopia. Their bullets carved along the road, and carved into anyone or anything on it.

Harry watched people throw up their arms and collapse into the dust, watched too several vehicles burst into flames, saw a horse seem to explode as it was hit by several bullets at once. Then the planes were gone, droning into the blue. Harry dashed onto the road, knelt beside the nearest casualty, a woman who had been carrying a child. But both were dead, split open with almost surgical precision by the bullet stream, their internal organs mingling with the blood soaking the dust. He vomited. 'Come back, you silly clot!' Gregory was shouting. Because the aircraft were also back.

Harry hurled himself to one side, rolling over several more bodies as he sought the shelter of the ditch. Here he found himself in the midst of several people, bodies pressed flat to the earth. But now they too were under attack as the Messerschmitts swung to either side, spraying the trees with bullets. Another vehicle exploded, close at hand, and there were more shrieks. A little girl stretched out her hand against his, and Harry squeezed her fingers and grinned. She was weeping, but she managed a grin in return.

Now the planes had disappeared, back to their base to refuel and reload. For several seconds an uncanny silence reigned, then the moans and the shrieks began again. 'Harry!' Gregory was standing on the road above him. 'Come on! We have to get on!'

Harry pushed himself up, having to release the girl's fingers to do so. 'We can't leave these people.'

'We can and we must.'

'But ...' Harry looked up and down the road, at the heaps of bloodstained clothing which had once been human beings. But there were an equal number of bloodstained heaps who were moving, and beginning to scream as the shock wore off and the pain set in.

'We can't help all of them, Harry,' Gregory said urgently. 'That means we can't help any of them. Our business is to be in position when the battalion gets back to us.' Harry looked down, at the little girl, who was attempting another shy smile. 'And the answer to your next question is no,' Gregory said.

Harry sighed. 'Take care,' he said in French, and returned to the truck.

They reached their destination just before dusk, having been strafed three more times. Miraculously, while all around them was death and destruction, their vehicle escaped with nothing more than a flat tyre, changed with great expertise and speed by Croom and Gibbons. They had more trouble with the MPs, who were directing traffic at the various crossroads and did not appear to have the same map references. Gregory soon saw them off, however, and although they were held up for two hours at their designated bridge, where the chaos was greater than ever as there were too many people trying to cross the river, they established themselves on the outskirts of the village to which they had been nominated shortly before dusk. Croom immediately went to investigate, and returned to inform them that the place was deserted. 'Just walked away from it, sir,' he told the officers, doing a great deal of eyebrow waggling.

'There can be no looting, Corporal,' Gregory said severely. 'But we'll all have a drink.'

The battalion came in during the night. They too had been strafed, and had suffered casualties, which meant that the medical unit worked until dawn. Dempster visited them, and Harry asked what was happening. 'God alone knows. There's talk of a counter-attack with our armour. We'll keep our fingers crossed. How was your journey?'

'Horrendous,' Gregory told him, busy with a shrapnel wound. 'But you didn't have much fun yourself, sir.'

'Not a lot,' Dempster agreed. 'However, we're here for a few days, for rest and recuperation. Things have got to improve.'

In fact, they didn't. The battalion had a fairly restful time of it for a day or two, as the colonel had promised, but all around them was catastrophe. The French armour duly launched a counter-attack on the Panzers, led by an unknown young colonel named De Gaulle, but was beaten off, and on Friday 17 May the Germans entered Brussels. Just a week ago, Harry thought, I was looking forward to spending a glorious afternoon with Nicole. He wondered if he would ever see her again, or if by now she was being raped by the Germans? Although knowing her, it was far more likely that she would be entertaining them to tea, before being raped. Or even after!

The following day the Germans took Antwerp, and the day after that the French decided they had had enough of General Gamelin, fired him, and appointed General Weygand in his place. Weygand, who had had a most distinguished career, thus became the British Commander-in-Chief as well. 'Now things will look better,' Captain Moore said. They certainly didn't *get* better; the very next day the Panzers entered Abbeville, at the mouth of the

Somme; the Allied front had been split in two.

That evening, it was Monday 20 May, and the war was ten days old on the Western Front, Dempster returned from a visit to headquarters and assembled his officers. 'I have no need to tell you that the situation is serious,' he said. 'However, it is not irretrievable. There is evidence that the Germans are outrunning their logistical support, and General Weygand is confident that we will soon be able to launch our counter-attack. For the time being we have to fight as two groups. Our Northern Group is to be under the command of General Billotte, and consists of General Blanchard's First French Army, which is situated on our right, and the Belgian Army, commanded by King Leopold himself, on our left. We hold the centre. Now obviously we have Germans to the south of us, to the east of us, and to the north of us. To the west of us is the sea. However, as you will no doubt have noticed, the enemy have been somewhat reluctant to attack us, after the bloody nose we gave them on the Dyle. Our business is to hold our positions while the French armies to the south of us regroup and prepare their counter-attack, and while we ourselves are reinforced by sea from England; in this regard I can tell you that the main part of our forces committed to the Norwegian campaign are being recalled and will be joining us here.'

'Does that mean that the Norwegian campaign is lost, sir?' asked the irrepressible Nelson.

'I have no knowledge of that,' the Colonel riposted. 'I am putting you in the picture as regards our situation. So, we stand firm.'

'Maybe your old man will be joining us,' Gregory remarked. 'We could do with some proper soldiers. What the hell is that racket?' They went outside.

'More refugees, sir,' Croom explained. 'Just let across the bridge by the MPs. They've even got some Frogs with them. Caught on the wrong side of the divide by the Jerries.'

'Poor buggers. I suppose we can't blame them for shouting and screaming,' Gregory said. 'Well, I'm for bed.'

He went inside the tent. Harry remained watching the flow of people past the encampment. It was exactly as it had been at the Dyle, as again the order had not yet come to blow the bridges. Then he watched an MP sergeant marching towards him, accompanied by a civilian. 'I'm looking for Lieutenant Brand,' he told Croom.

'I'm Brand,' Harry said, stepping forward, and peering at the civilian, who, although wearing man's clothing, was obviously a woman, he realized. His heart started to pound.

'Says she has urgent information, sir.'

'Hello, Harry,' Nicole said. 'Thank God I found you.'

The sergeant cleared his throat. 'Yes, Sergeant,' Harry said. 'You did the right thing to bring her to me. You may leave her, now.'

Another loud throat clearance. 'It must go on my report, sir.'

'Of course,' Harry said. The sergeant saluted, and marched off into the darkness. 'When last did you eat?' Harry asked.

Nicole made a moue. 'Yesterday. I think.'

'Croom ...'

'Right away, sir.' Croom hurried off.

Harry took her in his arms. 'Oh, my darling! What happened?'

'The Germans were coming, so we had to flee. We knew they were already south of us, so I decided to come up here and look for you. It was simply a matter of homing on your regiment. I told the servants to go wherever they felt would be safest.' She nuzzled against him. 'And I have found you.'

228

'And I'm so glad you did. But ... are you all right?'

She shrugged. 'It has not been easy, and especially for a woman travelling alone, even if she is dressed as a man.' She smiled. 'Perhaps more so, if she is dressed as a man and has a pretty face. But I am not a child, and now I am here. Can I stay with you?'

Harry did some rapid thinking. 'Of course,' he said. 'Were you not our landlady for six months? It'll mean handing you over to the Colonel ...'

'But not right away,' she said.

He kissed her. 'No, not right away.'

Croom gave a warning clear of his throat. 'Grub up, sir.' He had even found a bottle of wine, undoubtedly pinched from the village, despite Gregory's stricture about looting.

'Corporal, you are a man amongst men,' Harry told him.

'Thank you, sir. May I say, Countess, what a privilege it is to have you back with us.'

'Why, thank you, Croom. I shall volunteer to be a medical orderly.'

He left them again, and they sat together beneath the trees, Nicole leaning against Harry while she ate. 'It's just Army rations, I'm afraid,' he said.

'It tastes like nectar to me,' she said.

'Oh, my darling ...' he took her into his arms.

'Harry! I haven't had a bath in four days.'

'Do you think that bothers me? I'm not all that clean either. Anyway, there isn't one available, and if we dip in the river we'll have every sentry in the battalion shooting at us. And I can't even offer you a bed.'

'It is a beautiful night,' she said. 'And there are trees over there.'

How incredible, he thought, that it should be possible to be happy, in the midst of so much horror. He thought of that little girl. Had she survived thus far? Would she survive much longer? And if she survived, would she be happy? Then what of the hundreds, thousands, who lay scattered along the roads from the Dyle? He was not thinking of his comrades. If few soldiers actually expected to die, every soldier knew death was an occupational hazard. But the Belgian civilians had expected nothing so catastrophic. Their leaders had assured them that whatever the quarrel between Britain and France and Germany, they would be kept out of it, to remain secure in their homes and their businesses, and to die in their beds. Now in the space of ten days that secure world had been ripped apart—for those who could remember it happening before, a quarter of a century ago, the trauma had to be even greater.

But he was happy, lying here with the woman he loved in his arms. Despite the fact that he was part of a defeated army, which was likely to be defeated again in the not too distant future, and despite the fact that he was behaving in the most criminal fashion. He was a married man, with a son about to be born—his child might already have been born, for all he knew. And he was lying with another man's wife in his arms. And he was happier than he had ever been in his life before. He slept, and awoke to find Gregory peering at them. 'Good God,' the doctor remarked.

'Well,' Colonel Dempster said. 'Of course we'll look after you, Countess. But ... ah ...' he looked at Harry, standing rigidly to attention. A chair had been found for Nicole.

'You must not punish Harry, Colonel,' Nicole said. 'I came to be with him.'

'I see.' Again he looked at Harry. 'Are you aware that, well ...'

'I also have a husband,' Nicole said, and gave one of her devastating shrugs. 'I am sorry, but these things happen.'

'Oh, quite. However, ah ...' this time

he looked at Captain Moore, then decided he had to grasp the nettle himself. 'Your domestic matters you will have to sort out for yourself, Lieutenant Brand,' he said. 'Although I have no doubt the Padre will be happy to assist you in any way he can. However, you must understand that there can be no ... well ...'

'Liaison?' Nicole suggested, helpfully.

'Quite, Countess. No liaison between yourself and the Countess while we are on active service. The Countess is welcome to remain with us until we can make arrangements for her to rejoin her husband ...'

'Suppose I do not wish to rejoin my husband?' Nicole inquired.

'Well, ah ... that has to be your decision, Countess. But obviously you cannot stay here. Indefinitely.'

'Can you not employ me?'

'Eh?'

'As a nurse,' Nicole said. 'I have actually had nursing training. And I assisted Harry ... Lieutenant Brand ... when he was coping with that little trouble we had in Centot. I am sure you could do with some additional help here.'

'My dear lady, we are liable to find ourselves in the middle of a battle, any moment now.'

'And where do you suppose I can go?'

Nicole asked, 'in France, or Belgium, at this time, and not find myself in the middle of a battle?'

Dempster gave up, and turned to Moore for support. 'Perhaps the Countess *could* be helpful, sir,' the padre said. 'Until things sort themselves out. I do not feel, in view of her great help to us in Centot, that we can turn her out.'

'Absolutely,' Harris said, apparently without thinking, for he immediately flushed.

'However,' Moore went on. 'I think we must again make it absolutely clear that there can be no, ah ...'

'Liaison,' Nicole said again.

'Quite. Between yourself, and any officer in this battalion.'

'Or man,' Nicole suggested, obviously enjoying herself.

'Well, really, Countess ...'

'Will you give us your word on that, Countess?' Dempster asked.

'I do not think I can do that, Colonel. Who knows what the future may bring?'

Dempster gulped, and looked at Moore again. 'One possible answer would be to put Lieutenant Brand under arrest,' Moore suggested.

'You cannot *do* that,' Nicole protested. 'It would be unjust and unfair. I will take the matter up with Lord Gort.'

'However,' Moore went on, not apparently concerned at her threat, 'as Lieutenant Brand's services may well be very necessary when next we are attacked, I would suggest, sir, that it is the Countess who is placed under restraint.'

'You would not dare!'

Moore continued to ignore her. 'I would suggest, sir, that while the Countess can assist at the medical unit during the day, and take her meals with them, that she be assigned a tent, situated well away from the main camp, for sleeping, and that this tent be under Military Police guard whenever occupied by the Countess.'

'Well, really,' Nicole remarked.

'I think that is a very sensible arrangement,' Dempster agreed, and smiled at both Nicole and Harry.

'Officious old men,' Nicole grumbled.

Which Harry thought was a bit hard on both the colonel and the padre, who were both well short of forty. 'They have to think of the effect your presence will have on the men,' he explained.

'Ha!' she commented. 'We will find a way round them, Harry.'

He reckoned they'd have to play it very carefully. He was just glad to have her near him. So was Gregory. 'You're to work with us?' he cried. 'Why, Countess, that's the best news since electric light. But we'll have to find you some proper clothing.'

Gregory could be both efficient and pushing, when roused. He sent off messages to Brigade, where the main medical unit was staffed with nurses, and back came a uniform. The most enjoyable part of the operation, from his point of view, was taking Nicole's measurements, which left Harry seething, although as usual she seemed to enjoy it thoroughly. When she was dressed in her new outfit she paraded before the assembled medical staff. 'You look tremendous, ma'am,' Croom ventured.

'Why thank you, Corporal. Gentlemen?' She faced the officers.

'What can I say?' Gregory commented.

'They even sent underclothes,' Nicole said. 'Would you like to see?'

'Ah ... perhaps later.'

Nicole smiled at Harry. 'You are like a bear with a sore head,' she whispered.

Meanwhile things were going from bad to worse, assisted by bad luck. On the very day that Nicole had reached the battalion, there had been a high level conference at Ypres, between Generals Gort, Blanchard, Weygand and the overall commander of the Belgian front, General Billotte. Returning from the conference, Billotte was involved

235

in a car accident and left in a coma—he never did regain consciousness. This made Blanchard the senior officer in the North, but for more than twenty-four hours this front was left without a commander-in-chief. The Germans put this opportunity to good use, and with Nicole's uniform, which arrived on Thursday 23 May, there came the news that the Panzers were across the Scheldt, at Oudenarde, which was only a few miles north of the battalion's position, although they had as yet not been attacked ... and that because most of its supply dumps had been captured, the BEF in Belgium was to go on half rations. 'Bloody hell,' Gregory said. 'With respect, Countess.' He liked his food.

'What does it mean, Harry?' Nicole asked, as he walked her home that night. The MP assigned to stand guard remained at a benevolent distance; his job was only to make sure no one actually entered Nicole's tent.

'It doesn't look very good,' he said.

'Whatever happens, you and I will stick together,' she told him. 'You must not mind my flirting with those others. It is my nature. But it is only you I truly wish to be near.'

He ignored the sentry and took her in his arms to kiss her several times. 'We'll stick together,' he promised. As long as we can, he told himself. But if they were forced to surrender there would be no hope.

Dempster called his officers together at dawn the next day. 'I have to tell you that we're pulling out again today. Captain Gregory, you and the medical unit will leave first. Your destination is Dunkirk. Set yourselves up there and await our arrival.'

'Dunkirk, sir? Are we being evacuated?'

'I understand that we still mean to hold a bridgehead. This army has nearly half a million men in it, and we are not going to be lightly knocked over by the Germans. However, there *is* a supply problem, as you know, and it appears the Germans are already pushing up the coast behind us. Boulogne is being evacuated by sea at this moment. The idea up here is, very sensibly, that we should shorten our lines of communication and generally prepare for what might well be the climactic battle of the war. Thank you, gentlemen. Captain Gregory, Lieutenant Brand, a word.' Harry and Gregory waited until the other officers had dispersed. 'The moment you reach Dunkirk,' Dempster told them. 'I wish you to arrange passage for the Countess to England. There are destroyers nipping in and out of there all the time, so it should not be difficult. I will give you written orders to be conveyed to any naval officer. The fact is that there is about to be the most enormous last-ditch battle, and we cannot have her in the middle of it. Understood?'

'Yes, sir,' both Gregory and Harry said together. Of course getting Nicole to safety was of paramount importance.

'However,' Dempster went on, 'I think it would be best *not* to tell the Countess our plans for her. As I am sure you are both well aware ...' he looked at Harry. 'She is a young woman with a most pronounced character, and we cannot risk her refusing to go and causing trouble. So you will say nothing until a berth has been arranged for her, and then you will have her conveyed on board the ship, if necessary under guard. Understood?'

'So off we go together,' Nicole said enthusiastically. 'Will we be accompanied by the MPs?'

'I shouldn't think so,' Gregory said.

'Ah,' Nicole commented.

'Shit! Begging your pardon, ma'am. But you two are going to get me in all kinds of trouble.'

'Only if you persist in making an issue of it,' Nicole pointed out, severely. 'Now, what time are we leaving?'

'First light.'

'Well, then, I think, in all the circumstances, I will sleep in the truck tonight, in preference to my tent. I do not wish to oversleep. I am sure a guard other than that MP can be found for me.' Gregory looked at Harry, who waggled his eyebrows.

'You're probably going to get *me* courtmartialled,' he told her, as he inserted himself into their sleeping bag.

'I will take the blame. Do you know, I have never made love in a sleeping bag?'

'There's not a lot of room to manoeuvre,' he agreed.

'So aren't you glad I'm wearing a nurse's uniform, instead of pants? Now, we must do this by rote, army fashion. You go first. Take off your pants and drawers.'

'And do what with them?' They had both already discarded their shoes.

'Oh, kick them down into the bottom of the bag.' He eased his pants down his legs, and kicked them off. 'Now I will do the same with my knickers, and ... *voilà.*' She hugged him against her.

'I want your breasts as well,' he said.

'You are a greedy fellow. However ...' she reached behind her to unfasten buttons. 'You are going to have to insert, and grope.' She smiled into his mouth as he kissed her. 'But you're good at that.'

Gregory had the good sense not to comment on Nicole's crumpled uniform the next morning, accepting that she had slept in her clothes, no matter what might have gone on under them or above them. The medical truck was duly ready to roll at first light, and as usual Dempster came to see them off. 'There is really no need to look quite so happy, Countess,' he remarked. 'This is a most unhappy business.'

'I am looking forward to seeing Dunkirk, Colonel.'

'Well, we'll be with you as soon as we can. *Bon voyage.*'

He saluted, and the truck rolled out of the encampment and onto the road. And into immediate chaos.

It was another beautiful spring day, with hardly a cloud in the sky. Over the couple of days the battalion had been encamped on the banks of the Scheldt they had seen very little of the enemy; even the ubiquitous aircraft had only dropped in from time to time, in passing, as it were. While of the enemy infantry and tanks nothing at all had been seen however close they had been to the north, so close, indeed, that they had heard the sound of firing. It was almost as if Hitler were deliberately holding back from attacking the British,

240

because he was certainly attacking the Belgians to the north and the French to the south, by all accounts. But now they had to expect the crowded roads to be attacked. For these were not the refugees to which they had become accustomed since entering Belgium; everywhere there were no civilians to be seen—they had long made themselves scarce—but soldiers and the implements of war, trucks and lorries, and columns of marching men. At least there were no tanks; these were all presumably covering the retreat.

But with every road clogged with military men and material, progress was even slower than through the refugees; other soldiers were simply not to be shunted off the road by blaring horns or shouted curses. By noon they had covered a bare four miles, and Dunkirk was still some thirty miles away. The very slow progress was caused partly by the delays involved in crossing the Lys, whose bridges, like all the bridges in Belgium, had not been designed to accommodate modern armies. The other reason was far more alarming, for the Germans, having secured their bridgehead at Oudenarde, were now probing to the south-west, and the sound of the guns was very close. Now they saw a great number of enemy aircraft, but these were mostly strafing those troops in immediate

241

contact with their own forces. There were also planes to be seen in the distance, however, wheeling over what had to be Dunkirk itself. To the great morale of the retreating troops there were also RAF planes up there; they hadn't seen too much of their own side.

The crawling along in low gear in the increasing heat had its inevitable result, and at two that afternoon, when they could actually see the bridge they were aiming for, and beyond it the rooftops and spires of Menin, there was a loud bang and a cloud of steam shot into the air from the truck's radiator. Henley promptly braked, hard, and there was a thump from behind as the following vehicle drove into them. 'Get that fucking truck off the road!' someone shouted.

Gregory, always bristly, looked at Henley. 'We will have to make some kind of repair, sir,' the driver said.

'Right. Pull off.' There was another bump from behind as the officer in charge there lost patience. Gregory jumped down to bellow curses at him while Henley turned the truck off the road, and lurched down a shallow parapet into a field. Then he also got down, and Nicole and Harry followed him.

When Henley raised the bonnet there was an even greater cloud of smoke: the bang had been the radiator cap blowing off. By now Gregory had returned, fuming and still muttering curses, and Croom and Gibbons had also joined them. 'Dry as a bone, sir,' Henley said.

'Shit!' Gregory commented. 'Begging your pardon, Countess. Where the hell are we going to find any water around here.'

They had very little left even in their canteens, and they were still a couple of miles from the river. 'One of us will have to walk it,' Harry said.

They looked at each other. It would mean a delay of at least an hour, if not longer, before they could move again, and the road was becoming more thickly packed with every minute. 'Five men and a woman?' Nicole inquired. 'Do we not have sufficient liquid between us to get us going?'

The enlisted men looked scandalized, but Gregory was a pragmatist. 'You'll burn your bum, Countess,' he pointed out.

'Have you not a funnel in your gear?' she asked. 'And you and Harry can hold me in place.'

'Countess,' Gregory remarked, when the engine again roared into life, 'you are one hell of a woman. With respect.'

'So how long do you think we've got?' Nicole asked.

'A couple of hours, anyway. We'll get across the bridge, and we shouldn't have any trouble with water once we're there.'

They eased their way up the slope and into the line of traffic, and inched towards the bridge. They were actually on it when they heard the drone of planes, and saw a squadron of Stukas dropping down on them. 'Shit!' Gregory commented.

But there was nothing they could do, as the vehicles were bumper to bumper. 'Where the hell is the RAF?' Henley grumbled.

They listened to a whining sound, and Nicole threw both arms round Harry, hugging him close. The bomb struck about four vehicles along, however. Two trucks went up with huge plumed explosions, and the rest clattered to a standstill, windshields shattering in the blast. 'Out,' Gregory commanded. 'Everybody out!'

Harry pushed open the door and jumped down onto the bridge, turning to take Nicole as she followed him. Now the whining sound was back. Harry looked up and saw the Junkers hurtling, it seemed, straight at him. Still holding Nicole, he threw himself backwards, against the low railing, and went right over, falling some ten feet into the river itself, the woman in his arms. They entered the river with a tremendous splash, struck the bottom—it was only a few feet deep—and came back up, to go under again immediately as there was an enormous explosion from above them. When they came up again they were surrounded by flotsam, and still being bombarded by bits of debris. The bridge itself had collapsed, and several trucks were in the water, mostly upside down. From the point of view of Harry and Nicole they had been very lucky, as the second bomb strike and the consequent collapse had happened on the right side of the bridge, while they had jumped to the left, or they would almost certainly have been killed by the trucks plunging into the water. But the bomb had equally certainly struck the battalion medical truck. 'Can you reach the bank?' Harry asked Nicole.

She nodded, gasping; her starched cap had come off and red hair was plastered across her face. 'I'll be with you in a second,' he promised, and made his way under the bridge, moving from collapsed span to collapsed concrete pillar, and then into the midst of the shattered trucks, around which there floated shattered men.

The noise was tremendous; he only became aware of it as the singing in his ears diminished. There were men all around him, like him searching for their comrades, cursing and spitting water as they stumbled through the various mud and weed patches. Officers stood on the bank and bellowed orders, men shouted their responses, but it was clearly going to take several hours to repair the bridge, if it could ever be done. Harry reached the medical truck, which had fallen upside down. He ducked his head beneath the water to peer at the driver's cabin, gulped and nearly choked as he gazed at Henley and Gregory, crumpled against the floor and the gears, hair drifting in time to the water flowing past them, bodies inert. He came back to the surface, took a huge swallow of air, and moved to the back of the truck. But this was where the bomb had struck, and there was nothing but blood and the shattered remains of Croom and Gibbons.

Harry surfaced again, taking great gasps. 'You, there! Lieutenant!' Harry looked up, saw a man with a major's tabs standing above him on the bank. 'Regiment?'

'Medical officer, First Battalion, South Midlands, sir.'

'Are those men all dead?'

'Yes, sir.'

'Where is your battalion?'

'Following, sir.'

'Someone says you had a nurse with you. Is she all right?'

'I believe so, sir.'

'Well, there's no point in waiting for

your people here. Take the woman and make Dunkirk.'

'Those poor men,' Nicole said, as Harry helped her up the slope. Her hair was still plastered to her head and water squelched out of her shoes with every step. He was in no better condition, and like her he had lost his hat.

'Don't think about them,' he told her.

'I suppose you have seen so many dead men a few more don't matter.'

'Those were my comrades,' he reminded her.

'I'm sorry. Harry, what are we going to do?'

Harry surveyed the road, There was still a lot of activity on this, the west bank, for some of the bombs had fallen here, and shattered and burned out trucks littered the road. But most of the survivors had got away, although they were still in sight as they crawled on their way. The east bank was a milling mass of men and machines, with MPs and officers vainly trying to get them into some order. 'Makes one think of the *Grand Armée* crossing the Beresina,' he remarked. 'If we hurry, we can catch those chaps up and bag a lift.'

Nicole made a moue. 'How far is it to Dunkirk?'

Harry tried to think. 'This town is

Menin. So it would be about thirty miles.'

'Menin?' Nicole scratched her head. 'Good heavens! I did not recognize it. If this is Menin, then we are only about twenty miles from Centot. Down there!' She pointed to the south.

'Which is full of Germans, you say.'

'Well, it was, but perhaps they have passed on. I should so love a change of clothing and a proper bath.'

'Rivers not good enough for you?' He grinned. 'I don't think we can chance it, darling. Dunkirk is the only place we know is clear.'

'All right. But let's walk it.'

'Thirty miles? With no food, or water?'

'We can fill our canteens here ... or will we poison ourselves?'

'They'll have anti-cholera pills in Dunkirk. And we may be able to get some food in Menin. Then we'll see about picking up a ride.'

'If we can find food, I'd rather walk to Ypres,' she pointed out. 'I don't want to be in a truck again, Harry. Please.'

Actually, he agreed with her.

Menin was mostly in flames, which made doing a bit of discreet pilfering easier; they found an abandoned grocery and secured some smoked ham as well as a loaf of bread. 'Do you realize I could be the first British officer ever shot by an MP for looting?' Harry asked.

'Then let's get out of here,' Nicole recommended. They did so, moving away from the road west of the town, and found themselves in a wood. It was still only just noon, and the day was warm. Above them they could hear planes wheeling and bombs exploding. But in the wood they felt secure. 'I think we should stop here, and eat, and rest, and make love,' Nicole said. 'We can dry our clothes at the same time.'

Harry wasn't going to argue with that, especially as they were still squelching. It was like Ethiopia all over again, save that Gregory and Henley, and Croom and Gibbons, had died quickly and cleanly. But the adrenalin was still flowing in his veins. They found a copse which really seemed secluded from the world, and draped their clothes over various bushes, then lay together on the grass. They ate first, then made love. 'We could be the only two people left in the world,' Nicole said, when they had exhausted each other. 'I wish we were.' He kissed her. 'What are we going to do in Dunkirk?' she asked.

He didn't want to spoil an idyll, so decided against telling her he was required to put her on the first available ship.

'Wait for the regiment, I suppose. They'll probably be along by tonight. Actually, we should make a move.'

'It is so perfect here,' she sighed.

'It'll be better in Dunkirk,' he promised her. They got dressed and resumed their journey. They emerged from the wood and saw the rooftops of Ypres in front of them. 'There's a canal runs through Ypres,' Harry said. 'Let's hope those bridges are still intact.'

'If they're not, we'll wade across,' she said gaily. 'What I hope is that there is still some food in the town. I'm getting hungry again. And what I wouldn't give for a bottle of wine ...'

'Transport!' Harry shouted. 'I think we should ride this last bit.' Incredibly, there was an entire line of trucks, parked neatly by the road. 'Must be waiting by a bridge. Come on.'

He held her hand and hurried her forward, to where a group of MPs were standing in front of the trucks and cars which were, incredibly, empty. Nor were they at all close to any bridge. 'May I ask where you have come from, sir?' the sergeant asked.

'That wood,' Harry told him. 'We are all that's left of the medical unit from the South Midlands. Our truck was blown up. Now we'd like a lift with you.'

'You're welcome, sir,' the MP said. 'But we're on foot.'

'What about this lot?' Harry turned to the trucks, and saw to his consternation that several MPs were walking up and down with cans of petrol, pouring them over the vehicles.

'They're going up, sir,' the sergeant said. 'No room on the beaches. We're evacuating, you see, sir.'

'Evacuating? You mean leaving France?'

'That's right, sir. Haven't you heard? The Belgians have surrendered. There's no hope for it now. We'll be leaving in five minutes, sir.'

Harry was so dumbfounded he couldn't speak. 'Have you any water?' Nicole asked. 'We are so thirsty. Our canteen is empty.'

'Surely, Sister.' The sergeant gave her his canteen. 'Stand clear, now.'

The vehicles were all doused. The sergeant left them to light the rough torch made up by his men. Harry held Nicole's arm and took her to the shelter of the hedgerow. She gave him the canteen for a drink, then took a long swallow herself, while there was a tremendous whumpff from beyond the hedge, and flames shot skywards. The heat was tremendous, and Nicole cowered against Harry's bulk. 'All correct, sir,' the MP sergeant called. 'We'll be moving out in five minutes.'

'You won't believe this,' Nicole said. 'But I have to pee.'

'Well, you do it here,' Harry recommended. 'We'll wait for you.'

He crawled through the hedge, walked with the sergeant back to the other MPs, who were gazing at the burning vehicles. 'What a bleeding waste, eh, sir?' the sergeant asked. 'But that's war for you.'

'Stukas!' shouted one of the men.

'Must've been attracted by the flames,' the sergeant snapped. 'Take cover!'

Harry turned to look at the hedgerow, and heard the familiar scream of a plunging aircraft. He hurled himself to the ground, still staring at the hedge behind which Nicole was surely also sheltering. He heard the roar as the plane passed overhead, saw the bomb detach itself from its belly. The pilot had either overshot the burning vehicles or realized that they were already destroyed while at the same time automatically pressing the release lever. Even as Harry watched, the bomb plummeted into the hedge, and there was a huge explosion.

Part Three

The End of the Beginning

'Hobbes clearly proves, that every creature
Lives in a state of war by nature.'

Jonathan Swift
On Poetry

Chapter Nine

Voyage to the East

'Sit down, Harry,' Colonel Hartland said. Harry sank into the straight chair before the desk. Whenever he entered this office he felt like someone being interviewed for a job—because that was exactly what was happening, every time he entered this office. One day they would tell him whether or not he still had a job. Hartland was examining the sheet on his desk. 'Very satisfactory,' he said. 'Physically, you are as good as new. I know it seems to have taken a very long time, and there were times we wondered if you'd ever make it. But you have. Congratulations.'

'But I'm not as good as new, am I, sir?'

Hartland leaned back in his chair. 'I'm afraid that has got to be up to you, now, Harry. You know, over three hundred thousand men were lifted from those beaches outside Dunkirk. I'm not saying that a good number didn't need psychiatric treatment afterwards, but in most cases it was the trauma of having been defeated, of

255

having, in effect, been forced to run away. That is a condition which can most easily be remedied by a commanding officer who has the ability to restore morale, the will to fight, and win, the next time.' He leaned forward again. 'There were even those who did not want to leave the beaches, like yourself, who wanted to stay and fight it out to the death. But according to Sergeant Creese, you did not even wish to retreat to Dunkirk. Are you ready to tell me about the woman? It'll help, you know.'

The MP sergeant had told him there had been a woman, but this unhappy young man had refused to discuss her, throughout all the long six months he had been recovering from his quite serious wounds. Now that those physical wounds had been patched up, he had to be forced to talk. 'We were travelling companions, sir,' Harry said. 'We had become friends.'

'And you were cut up when she was killed. Very understandable. But this has been going on rather a long time. Six months. You say she was an Army nurse, whose name you can't remember? Not even now?'

'It was all a bit traumatic, sir.'

'Harry, I am going to be perfectly frank with you. You are lying. I think you know, and have known all along, what this woman's name was. And now I am

256

going to tell it to you: she was the Countess Nicole d'Aubert.' Harry's head came up. 'I have been speaking with Reverend Moore,' Hartland said. 'In fact, I asked him to come and see me.' Harry bit his lip. 'Your wife and son come to visit you every week,' Hartland went on. 'Does she know of this relationship?'

'No, sir.'

'Well, she won't learn of it from me, I can promise you that. But may I remark that every time Constance enters this hospital, there is not a man, or a woman, I suspect, who does not say to himself or herself, Brand must be the luckiest man on earth, to have so much to go home to.'

'I appreciate that, sir.'

'Well, it is not my business to condemn. According to Captain Moore, the Countess d'Aubert was a most lovely woman. That you fell for her was perhaps natural, especially as, I gather, circumstances were unusual, and that in addition to working together medically you were actually living in her house, and that, Captain Moore suggests, she rather gave you the come-on.' He paused, speculatively, but Harry did not rise to the bait. 'But,' he resumed, 'sadly, she is dead. So her death rather drove you round the bend for a while. Do you know, many of the VC winners have been men who have temporarily been driven round the bend by the exigencies of their circumstances. And you are to receive the MC, for your behaviour under fire on the beaches, even if it was inspired by grief and anger. But Harry, the Countess is dead. Nothing that you, or anyone else, can do, is going to alter that fact. You cannot spend the rest of your life looking over your shoulder. You have a beautiful and loving wife; a splendid son. You have a great career in front of you. All you have to do is stretch out your hand and grasp those things.'

Again he paused, and again Harry made no reply. Hartland drew a pad of paper towards him and began to write. 'I am discharging you from this hospital, with two recommendations. Firstly that you receive three months' recuperative leave, to be spent with your family.' He grinned. 'You'll be home for Christmas. And secondly, that at the end of that time you be returned to duty. In view of your wounds, you will not be assigned to a field unit. Unless you volunteer for one.'

'I would like to rejoin the South Midlands, sir.'

Hartland studied him for several seconds. 'I will note your request. But if at any time during your leave you should change your mind, you have the right to do so. That's all.'

258

Returned to duty, Harry thought, as he walked down the steps of the hospital to his waiting taxi, carrying his small suitcase. What duty?

He buttoned his greatcoat and looked up at the sky, dark with cloud, threatening to snow as it had snowed during the night. Yet even on this cold December day any action which might take place in or even close to Britain would happen up there. Here, deep in the security of the West Country, there was little evidence of the battle that had raged over London and the South-East during the autumn and indeed into the winter, but it had been a tremendous battle, fought by only a handful of men, on both sides, compared with the immense armies that had competed in France, the three hundred and thirty-odd thousand British and French troops evacuated from Dunkirk alone—but it was none the less the decisive encounter of the war. Had the RAF lost, then indeed there would be no duty to return to, for Britain might well have fallen by now. And he had joined up in the first place to defend England, home and beauty—and Louise's virginity, if she still possessed it, after serving in the ATS for nearly a year.

The driver made one or two abortive attempts to start a conversation, but as

Harry did not reply, he abandoned it, and drove into the station yard in silence. The train was not due for half an hour, so Harry sat on one of the hard wooden benches, gazing in front of him. The stationmaster emerged to look at him, then went away again; he was used to having exceedingly sombre young men leaving the military hospital and waiting for their train.

Forget the past, Harry thought. How easy it was for these pundits to issue recommendations. The odd thing was that a good deal of the past had already been forgotten, or never remembered at all. He did not remember being hit. But he had apparently been hit three times, while firing his commandeered machine-gun at the German aircraft wheeling overhead. None of the wounds had been immediately vital, but he had been very lucky to escape being permanently damaged, if not crippled. All he could remember was a sensation of numbness, before, apparently, at some time he had fainted from loss of blood. Sergeant Creese, it seemed, had had to carry him out to the waiting destroyer, wading shoulder deep through the water. At least Creese was going to get the VC for extreme gallantry under fire. As well, of course, as saving the life of an officer. He simply had to write to Creese.

To thank him for saving his life? Actually, the naval surgeons had done that, by stemming the flow of blood, removing the bullets, and setting the broken limbs. He wondered why they had bothered? But for them he might now have been chasing Nicole through some Elysium—if he could bring himself to believe in such things. But other things stood out with terrible clarity. Gregory, crumpled, dead, beside Henley in the water-filled cabin of the truck. The little girl kneeling by the side of the road, stretching out her hand to his. And Nicole.

But every time he thought of Nicole, of that delicious laugh and flowing auburn hair, of that velvet flesh and uninhibited sexuality, he wanted to weep, and a British officer simply could not sit on a public railway platform and weep. They'd probably send him straight back to hospital. But then, he dared not weep at home, either, because no one would understand.

'Harry? Oh, Harry. Welcome home!' Helen had of course visited her son in hospital, but she had not expected him back for Christmas, going on the last report from Hartland. Harry hugged her. 'We have the most tremendous news,' she told him. 'Your father is to get a KCB. And he's promoted major general. Seems he covered himself with glory in Norway.'

'That's tremendous. Will he be coming home?'

'He's actually home now. Today he's in London, though. We didn't know you were coming. He'd planned to come in and see you tomorrow.'

'I've three months' recuperation leave.' Harry looked around him. 'No bombs?'

'There was one a mile or so away. I suppose the Jerry got his navigation wrong. There's not much for them to aim at down here, but they have gone for Bristol several times, and we've seen one or two dogfights.'

'I must look out for them. Are Connie and Mark about?'

'They're in the conservatory. They'll be so delighted to see you.'

'Then let's delight them,' Harry said.

How odd, he thought, to have fathered a child, and never seen your wife visibly pregnant. Constance had her back to him, seated in a garden chair while she pushed the pram to and fro with her foot, and read a book. Thus he looked first of all at her hair, which she continued to wear long, but caught in a bow on the nape of her neck. Helen remained in the lounge doorway, and Constance did not hear his approach across the carpet, so that

262

he was standing above her for several seconds before she sensed his presence and raised her head. In that time he could look down at the breasts clearly delineated even beneath the woollen jumper, larger than he remembered because she was feeding, and then at the thighs, but not those splendid legs, because she was wearing trousers. But her belted stomach was as flat as he remembered it.

But then, how much did he remember? It was even odder that he had slept only three nights with his wife of a year, and ten times that with Nicole. But to think of Nicole, now, was criminal. 'Hi,' he said.

Constance leapt to her feet, turning as she did so. 'Harry!' She kicked the chair out of the way to be in his arms. He held her close and kissed her mouth and her nose, her eyes and her ears and her cheeks. 'Oh, Harry! Why didn't you let us know you were coming?'

'I didn't know I was coming, until this morning.'

She frowned. 'You don't have to go back?'

'I don't have to go anywhere, for three months.'

'Oh, Harry!' She kissed him some more.

'Baby's crying,' he said.

'He doesn't like being neglected.' She lifted the babe from the pram and held him out. Harry had held Mark in his arms in hospital, but this was different.

He hugged his son, and Helen deemed it time to emerge. 'If you knew how I have longed to see that picture,' she said.

'Me too,' Constance confessed.

'If ah ... you two would like to, ah ... chat,' Helen said. 'I'll look after Baby until it's time for his next feed.'

'Well ...' Constance glanced at Harry. 'That would be awfully kind of you, Mums.'

'Then off you go. You'll want to unpack, Harry,' Helen said, as meaningfully as she could; he could only unpack in his bedroom.

'Shall I carry your bag?' Constance asked, as they entered the house.

'I'm one hundred per cent fit again,' Harry assured her.

'I'm so happy about that.' She led the way up the stairs, opened the door.

'Same room?' Harry asked.

'Mums put a double bed in. I hope you don't mind. Or the way I'm cluttering the place up.' The room certainly looked different. Apart from the new bed, and the baby's crib beside it, there were new books, and feminine shoes under the chair, to match the feminine undergarments draped over it. 'I'm not the tidiest person in the world,' Constance confessed.

Harry closed the door, and at the sound of it she turned, sharply and nervously. Their meetings in the hospital ward had all been formal and asexual, apart from the obligatory kisses. 'How do you get along with Mums? And Dad?' he asked.

'They've been just perfect to me.'

'And yours?'

'They adore Mark. And when they get to know you better ... Isn't it odd,' she said. 'We've been married just on a year, and I feel more of a stranger to you than that first day at the Ritz.'

'Snap.' He moved towards her. She was a beautiful woman, and she was all his. She had to arouse some spark of desire in him. She simply had to. She didn't move, waited for him to come right up to her. He kissed her lips, without touching her. Then he did touch her, stroking her breast. She gave a little shudder. Because it was twelve months since a man had touched her there.

'Did I hurt you?'

'No,' she said. 'Would you like me to take it off?'

'Yes, please.' Perhaps that would get him going.

She took off her jumper, unbuttoned the shirt, draped it over a chair, then released the heavy brassière. 'It's for nursing,' she explained.

'Do you have any of the new ones?' he asked, gazing at the full breasts.

She blushed. 'Yes. I bought some after we were married. I know it's a sort of cheating but beggars can't be choosers.'

'You're not begging now,' he said.

She came against him, and after a moment's hesitation he held her breasts, one in each hand. 'Don't squeeze,' she warned. 'Or you'll get wet.' He released her, sat on the bed. She could tell that something was wrong, without having the least idea what it might be. 'There was a joke we used to share at school,' she ventured. 'Would you like to hear it?'

'Yes.'

'Well, it's a riddle. Why is a woman's milk better than a bottle?'

'Tell me why.'

'It's sweeter, it's healthier ... and it comes in such cute little containers.' She waited, but she knew his smile was forced. 'Would you like me to take anything else off?'

'Please.' That had to do it.

She took off her shoes and socks, unbuckled her belt, and slid her slacks down past her thighs, then let them go. She gazed at him with tremendous intensity as she did the same for her knickers. Her legs were as lovely as ever he remembered them, as were her thighs and what lay between. I

266

am the most miserable of men, he thought. She gave a little heave of the shoulders. 'I've nothing left to take off.'

Harry leapt off the bed, and stripped off his uniform as quickly as he could. Perhaps she would not notice his limpness, and when he held her naked in his arms ... he clutched her against him, kissed her mouth, felt himself stir, turned her so that they both fell across the bed. 'Oh, Harry,' she murmured. 'I have been so afraid of this moment. Of ...'

He kissed her mouth, savagely. He didn't want her to speak. But he made the mistake of closing his eyes, and immediately Nicole's face swam into his vision. He slid his mouth down from her face to her neck, then to her breasts, kissed the nipples and tasted the milk. He slipped lower to her stomach, while her legs came up, and then went down again; whatever she might not want, she was prepared to want anything, at this moment. He buried his face in the black curls of her groin. He had done this to her when they had first made love, and been powerfully affected. He had an idea she had enjoyed it too. But Nicole had also liked him to kiss between her legs.

He reared back from her, and then threw himself on her again. Now she spread her legs and brought them up. She wanted as much as he did, now. He panted. And sucked at her. He put his hands under her buttocks to raise her from the bed, while squeezing as hard as he could. She gave a little murmur of pain, but did not attempt to resist him. Then he rolled off her and lay on his back, panting.

She was panting as well. It was some seconds before she spoke. 'I know what you went through. Your wounds ...'

'I was hit in the leg, the arm, and the ribs,' he said. 'Not the balls.'

She sighed. 'You must give it time, Harry.' He didn't reply, and after a few more moments she sat up. She remained sitting for some seconds, not looking at him. Then she got off the bed and got dressed. 'I imagine Mums is getting pretty fed up with baby-sitting,' she said, and went downstairs.

'Harry!' George Brand clasped his son's hand. He had only managed to get to the hospital once, and that had been just after Harry had been taken in; he had been hardly conscious. 'By God, but it's good to see you looking so well.'

'It's good to be feeling so well again. I gather congratulations are in order.'

George pulled a face. 'I suppose the powers-that-be felt it was time. You've heard about Hector?'

'He's not dead?' Harry was genuinely alarmed; he was very fond of his cousin.

'No. But he's a prisoner. His lot retreated with the main French armies and tried to hold the line of the Loire. But they didn't have a chance.'

'Hell. How is Joss taking it?'

'Not terribly well. She's with her mother.'

'And the baby?'

'Oh, he's fine.'

'I'd love to be able to get up there and see them.'

George Brand offered his son some of his tobacco, and they filled their pipes together. 'I suspect you have more important things to do here,' George said. 'Other people seem to think so too.'

'You mean I'm confined to barracks.'

'That's what it indicates on your release paper. These barracks, anyway. I wonder if you'd care to tell me why?'

'Oh ...' Harry shrugged. 'Hartland seemed to feel that I still have a psychological problem.'

'And I would say he was right. I've spoken with Jimmy Dempster. He's invalided out, you know. Broke his spine on the beach. Lucky to be alive.'

'We all are, Dad. What's going to happen? We lost all our equipment, all our morale ...'

269

'Both of those are being replaced. And the fact that the Nazis have abandoned any idea of invading, at least until next year, is another plus factor. We are growing stronger every day, and the important thing is that we still have an army, which is desperate to have a return match. I was talking about you. Jimmy filled me in on a few points I hadn't been aware of. It's a rum old world. I mean, your battalion being stationed at Centot. Was Nicole as beautiful as her mother?'

'I never knew her mother, Dad. But if she was as beautiful as Nicole, then you were a lucky man.'

George considered this for some seconds. Then he said, 'I managed to get over Nicole's mother.'

'With respect, Dad, you didn't watch her die. Within an hour of having had sex with her.'

'Shit,' George commented.

'I seem to have a knack of getting myself up those kinds of creek, and losing the paddle,' Harry said.

George reached across and squeezed his hand. Harry was totally surprised; his father was not as a rule a physically demonstrative man. 'And Connie?' George asked.

'It's not very good.'

'We're very fond of her.'

'So am I, Dad, believe it or not. But ... there's no turn-on. At the moment.'

'Will there be?'

'I don't know.' Harry forced a grin. 'I never thought this would happen to me. Christ, I can go to the Windmill and get a hard-on. But put me alone with Connie ...'

'Could be guilt as much as memory. Does she know about Nicole?'

'God forbid!'

'I think it's something you should consider.'

'Did you ever tell Mother about your affair?'

'Yes. Eventually.'

'What was her reaction?'

'Somewhat stiff, at first. But she got over it.'

'That was, I assume, something like twenty years ago,' Harry pointed out.

'So? You have time on your side, too.'

'I was thinking more of changing social mores.'

'Adultery is actually less of a crime now than it used to be,' George pointed out in turn.

'But it is easier for a wife to obtain a divorce on those grounds.'

George knocked out his pipe. 'If you really can't make it with her, might that not be the best answer?' He held up his hand.

'Don't remind me; I am sounding like the ultimate sexist pig. And there's the boy to be considered. But there is nothing more soul-destroying than a loveless marriage, and I happen to believe that marriage, young marriage, is based upon a profound physical and therefore sexual attraction. If a man and a woman have such an attraction for each other, then they should want to go to bed together, or they aren't natural. That was ordained by nature for the procreation of the species, not by me. Obviously, one would hope that over the years a relationship builds up which negates the requirement for sex, but it has to have been there in the first place. You and Connie are very much in the first place.' He glanced at his son. 'Think about it. Seems to me that you have nothing to lose.'

Harry's entire mores was against telling Constance. One simply did not share one's conquests with other women, especially if the other woman happened to be your wife. On the other hand, as his affair with Nicole appeared to be pretty general knowledge in the Army, it seemed probable it would get back to her eventually—in which case it was essential he get there first. But he kept putting it off throughout his leave, his decision aided by the return of Louise in the middle of January for a week's leave. Louise had not been able to get to see him in hospital, and now she wanted to spend every possible moment with her beloved brother. She remained quite unaware that there was anything the matter with his marriage.

For the rest, he and Constance did everything a soldier and his wife are supposed to do when he is home on leave, with the one vital exception. They walked on the downs, trudging through the snow; they played bridge; they studied the news and gloried in Sir Richard O'Connor's brilliant offensive in North Africa which had driven the Italians out of Egypt and halfway across Libya, with enormous losses; they bathed Mark together ... and they slept together. But they seldom touched. Constance continued to put her faith in time. While Harry kept trying to make up his mind to tell her the truth, and putting it off again and again. Because he too had a certain amount of faith in time. He now knew how deeply he had been in love with Nicole, but the memory of even such a love had surely to fade, eventually.

He might never have told Constance, had he not received a letter from Peter Harris, when his leave had less than a week to go. *I have been sorting out the regimental papers,* Harris wrote—he had been promoted lieutenant colonel to replace Dempster—*and have come across Gregory's recommendation that you be returned to medical school to qualify as a doctor. This was endorsed by Colonel Dempster, and I am bound to say I think it is a step in the right direction for you. I have therefore forwarded the recommendation and I expect that you will be hearing from them in the near future. We shall of course miss you in the regiment, but hopefully you will be able to rejoin us as battalion MO in the not too distant future.*

Harry caught the next train to Salisbury, outside of which the battalion was training. What a feeling of nostalgia he experienced as he walked past some familiar faces—far too few—all of whom remembered him and came to attention. While outside the headquarters he came face to face with Price. 'Harry!' Price shook hands. 'Welcome back. With three pips ... well done!' Price himself now wore the crown of a major. 'But you're leaving us, pro tem, aren't you?'

'Not bloody likely,' Harry told him.

Price accompanied him into the outer office. 'I forwarded the recommendation myself. I'm the new adjutant.'

'Congratulations. You'll have to get it back.'

'You'll have to talk to the old man about that.'

'I intend to. May I go in?'

Price knocked on the door. 'Captain Brand to see you, sir.'

'Harry!' Harris came round his desk to shake hands. 'Good to see you. And looking so well. Dropped in to say goodbye?'

'No, sir. Dropped in to ask to rejoin.'

Harris raised his eyebrows, then returned behind his desk and sat down, gesturing Harry also to a seat. Price had discreetly withdrawn.

'Don't you want to be a doctor?'

'Not while there's any fighting to be done, sir.'

'Hm. Well, of course, we would be very pleased to have you back, Harry. But I do think it is something you should consider.'

'I have considered it, sir.'

'How are Connie, and the baby?'

Harry had to wonder just how much this man knew about his domestic affairs; he could have been informed by either Hartland or Dad himself. 'They are fine, sir. But they both know that I will be returning to duty as soon as my leave is up.'

'Yes. However, at medical school, you will be able to return home every weekend. Or, should you be sent to somewhere like Edinburgh, they'll be able to move up there to be near you.'

'Salisbury is closer to Lower Cheviston than any teaching hospital I know of, sir.'

'The battalion isn't staying in Salisbury, Harry. In fact, I must tell you, in the strictest confidence, that we are under orders for overseas duty.'

Harry did a quick reflection. The only places he knew of where any British army was actually facing an enemy was in either North or East Africa. East Africa! He'd be having another swipe at the Eyeties! 'May I ask where, sir?'

'No, you may not ask. And I'd like you to consider a couple of points. The first is that we were really badly shot up at Dunkirk. We brought back hardly two hundred men, and a lot of those, because of their experience, have been transferred to other units to assist in their training. This battalion is hardly more than a territorial one, at this moment. Oh, we are licking them into shape, but it is taking time and a good deal of hard work.'

'I'm not afraid of hard work, sir.'

'I never supposed you were, Harry. The point I am trying to make is, that if you have a dream of rushing back into action, forget it. This could be a long tour of duty. Certainly not less than a year, and a good deal of that year is going to be spent making these fellows battle hardy, before we will see any action. You have the opportunity to miss that, and rejoin us in some months' time. It's never a good idea to look a gift horse in the mouth.'

'I would like to accompany the battalion, sir.'

Harris gazed at him for several seconds. Then he leaned across the desk and shook hands. 'Welcome back, Harry. Oh, welcome back. You'll report for duty as soon as your leave is up. We won't be leaving for another couple of months, so you'll have time to get to know your men before we sail.'

Harry sat beside Constance in the garden; although it was only the end of March it was surprisingly warm, at least while the sun was out. She was still feeding Mark, and had her blouse and bra open. She made a most attractive sight. 'Did Colonel Harris tell you which hospital you'll be assigned to?' she asked.

'No. I'm not going to be assigned to any hospital.' She had been concentrating on Mark, who had powerful gums, so that she had to insert a finger to prevent him from hurting her. Now she raised her head. 'I've opted out of the medical deal,' Harry explained. 'And will have a company.'

She digested this, resuming her attentions to the baby. 'Does that mean you'll

277

be stationed in Salisbury?'

'No. We're being sent overseas.'

'Where?'

'I have no idea. They probably won't tell us until we're on the ship.'

She bit her lip. 'But you're looking forward to it.'

'We are fighting a war, darling.'

She sighed, gently removed Mark's mouth, and dried her teat. Then she lifted the baby and put him back into his pram. 'How long?'

'Before we actually go? I don't know. When we've gone, I'm afraid not less than a year.'

'Shit!' she remarked. Harry raised his eyebrows. He had never heard her swear before. 'Well,' she said. 'At least we've had three months. Sort of.'

'When I come back,' he said. 'Maybe we'll be able to make a go of it.'

'Do you really think so?' She refastened her brassière, buttoned her blouse. 'If we can't make it now ... with you going away ...' she looked down at him, willing him to touch her. He held her wrist, and pulled her on to his lap. She put her arms round his neck. 'Oh, Harry, I don't mind about the sex, really I don't. I just like being with you. But it seems to make you so unhappy ... Harry, you're leaving next week. If we were to try now ...'

She made to rise, and he held her more tightly. 'There's something you need to know.'

Her face became watchful. 'About you?'

'And others. Connie ... while I was in France, I fell in love.'

Now she frowned. 'You mean you had an affair? I don't really want to know about it.'

'I mean I fell in love.'

Constance released him and stood up. 'You fell in love,' she said, her voice cold. 'After marrying me.'

'No. It happened before I even knew I was going to have to marry you.'

She sat down in her own chair, face turned away. *Have* to marry me,' she muttered.

This was going to be far more traumatic than he had feared, Harry realized. 'I asked you to marry me, that night at the Ritz,' he reminded her. 'You turned me down. So ... I suppose I wanted to forget about you. And in France I met this woman, and I fell in love with her.'

'You fall in love very facilely,' Constance commented. 'There was that woman in Africa ...'

'How did you know about that, anyway?'

'Oh, Joss told me that you were on the rebound from an unhappy affair. That was before we had even met.'

'Well, maybe I was upset at the time. But ... things were different in France.'

'So who was this woman?'

'She was actually a French countess. She virtually owned the village where we were stationed before the Germans invaded.'

'A countess,' Constance said contemptuously. 'I suppose she was very beautiful.'

'As a matter of fact, she was. I don't know how much that had to do with it. There were ... factors drawing us together, and we just clicked.'

'You mean you had no difficulty getting it up with *her!*'

Harry refused to lose his temper; she had every right to be angry. 'Yes, I had no difficulty.'

She rounded on him. 'Then why did you marry me?'

'You asked me to, remember? And in any event, she was already married. We hadn't decided what to do about it, when she was blown up by a bomb. I held what was left of her in my arms, just after it happened.' He hadn't really been looking for sympathy; he just wanted to talk about it. In any event, he didn't get any sympathy; Constance's gaze remained stony. 'What I'm trying to say is,' he said, 'that, well ... it was a traumatic experience. It ... oh, hell, you may as well know the whole truth. We had made love only an hour before. We had lain naked together in a little wood, and we had *loved*. And then she was a heap of shattered flesh. I'm sorry. It's left me, well ... sexless.' He raised his head. She was staring at him. But there was still no softness. 'But I know,' he went on, 'that given time, it'll fade. It must. Perhaps another year, separated ...'

'And if it doesn't? You're asking me to wait a year for you to forget another woman? My husband?'

Harry sighed. 'Would you like a divorce?' he asked. 'I won't contest custody of Mark. He's your baby.'

'Thanks a bunch.' Constance got up, lifted Mark from the pram, and turned towards the house.

Chapter Ten

Heat and Passion

Next day Harry again reported to Salisbury, to be introduced to his company. As subalterns he had Lieutenants Simpson and Grace, neither of whom he had ever met before, but his CSM was his old friend Sergeant-Major Cutmore.

And to his delight, he would again have Pope under him; the batman was equally delighted to be able to resume his duties. The following day they were issued with tropical kit. 'Shorts?' Simpson asked. 'Do we really have to wear this stuff, sir?' He had rather spindly legs.

'Only when we get where we're going,' Harry assured him. 'So it is Africa, after all,' he remarked to Price.

'That bother you?' the adjutant asked.

'That pleases me very much,' Harry said. 'I have a personal score to settle with the Eyeties.' Who were again sitting pretty, as, reinforced by a German panzer division, they had just driven the British Eighth Army, weakened and distracted by its commitment to assist the Greeks—another campaign which had turned out a disaster —clear back to the Egyptian border. There were those who even spoke of the British position in the Middle East, the retention of Egypt and control over the Suez Canal, collapsing entirely.

'Well,' Price said. 'Keep your opinions to yourself, old boy. Even at home.'

Embarkation was not for another month, and after a week getting acquainted with his men, Harry was given a week-end pass. He did not have far to go, and arrived home just on dusk. Helen greeted him with a hug. 'Connie's gone.'

'Gone? Where?'

'Back to her parents. She took little Mark with her. Harry ... what happened?'

Harry sighed, and sat down, and his mother hastily poured him a large scotch. 'I was in love with somebody else, still am, I suppose ...'

'Oh, Harry! Not that dreadful woman in Ethiopia?'

'Good Lord, no. Someone I met in France.'

'Oh, *Harry!* What on earth is the matter with you?'

'I'm sorry, Mummy. That's the way it goes. I fell in love before I realized I would have to marry Connie.'

'But you didn't tell her.'

'Well, of course I didn't.'

'But you told her last week. Why?'

'Because we didn't have a marriage, Mother. I'm sorry. There it is. I offered her a divorce. She didn't say yes or no, then. Now I guess she's said yes.'

'What a mess. So now you'll want to marry this other woman. I suppose she's French?' Helen was not altogether a Francophile, after her own husband's experiences, and confession.

'This other woman is dead, Mother.'

'Oh, Harry! I am so terribly sorry. You never mentioned her.'

'To you, no. I did mention her to Connie.'

'Was she dead when you did so?'

'Yes. But that doesn't seem to have had too much effect.'

Helen considered for some moments. Then she asked, 'Will you go to see her?'

'No.'

'Not even to say goodbye to Mark?'

'I don't think I'm in the mood for that, right now, Mother. But I'd be grateful if you'd keep in touch with them, while I'm away.'

'Of course I shall. Mark is my grandson. How long will you be gone?'

'How long will the war last, Mother?'

After all the traumas of the past year, it was actually a relief to be at sea, with the battalion, able to concentrate one's mind entirely on the matter in hand. Being at sea had traumas of its own, in the shape of U-boats, but the troop convoy was well escorted, and this was trauma to which the average soldier was trained. Marital and sexual discord could be forgotten. Harry not only had no idea what the future of his relationship with Constance, and his son, might be, he was not even sure what he wanted it to be. He was going to fight, and how he wanted to do that! He had not been allowed to fight since Creese had carried him out to the destroyer off Dunkirk.

He had not yet heard whether or not Creese was going to get the recommended VC. His own investiture with the Military Cross had been put on hold, although he was now entitled to call himself Captain Harry Brand, MC. But only the war mattered now. It was apparently regarded as unsafe for the convoy to pass through the Mediterranean, because of the threat from the Italian Navy and Air Force, so they went the long way round, by the Cape of Good Hope. Once they were south of Gibraltar the weather became quite splendidly warm, and the threat from U-boats diminished with every nautical mile, so that the troops, having got over their seasickness, were left with nothing to do but sunbathe and gossip.

At least they had left England before the news of his separation from his wife had become public knowledge, Harry thought. But in any event all minds were concentrating on the task ahead, on life in the desert, on the fighting quality of the Eyeties. In this regard, Harry was in much demand for his experiences in Ethiopia, especially as there still was a campaign going on in that country, as the British and South Africans clawed it back for Haile Selassie. But he was also called upon for his reminiscences of the brief Flanders campaign, since he was one of the few surviving officers of the original battalion. Even more were his fellows fascinated by his account of the anti-VD campaign in Centot, although to his great relief Nicole's name only came into it in passing. But the new battalion MO, Cheetham, and his junior, Cooper, were intensely interested. 'Mind you,' Cheetham remarked, pessimistically. 'It'll be a different kind of VD where we're going.'

In all their discussions, Colonel Harris and Major Price presided with amused indifference. They know something we don't, Harry thought. They also had a lot on their minds, as Harry had understood before the battalion had even left England. As Harris had mentioned when he had first asked to rejoin, there was an awful amount of work to be done to turn what was essentially a territorial battalion into an efficient fighting force. The men were willing enough, and keen enough, but they were totally lacking in experience, and although they had been licked into pretty good parade ground shape before they had left England, they still had to come under fire, and the long, luxurious sea voyage, the first most of them had ever undertaken, saw them visibly softening. With champagne in the first-class accommodation, where the officers lived, at seven-and -six a bottle, and with most of the officers themselves as green as their men, this was a worrying development.

It was mid-December before they reached Simonstown, to be greeted with the news that Wavell had been replaced as Commander-in-Chief Middle East by Sir Claude Auchinleck, who had been commander in India. They had in fact, switched places, Wavell being sent to India in turn. 'Seems the powers-that-be consider Wavell to be tired out,' Harris told his officers.

'Auchinleck is a toughie,' Nelson, now also a captain, remarked.

'You knew that had happened while we were still at sea, didn't you, sir,' Harry guessed, as the convoy left Cape Town for the Mozambique Channel.

'As a matter of fact, no,' Harris said, and called a conference of his officers. 'I can now tell you,' he announced, 'that our next port of call will be Trincomalee.' He peered at them. 'That's in Ceylon. From Trincomalee, we will continue to Singapore, where we are to take up garrison duties for the next two years.'

'Singapore, sir?' Captain Davies asked. 'But ... we were going to North Africa.'

'I'm afraid we were never going to

287

North Africa, Davies,' Harris said. 'That was mere rumour, which I thought it best not to discourage.'

'But, sir, who are we going to fight, in Singapore?' Harry asked.

'We are not going to fight anyone, Brand. Our mission is to deter anyone from fighting *us*. And when I say we are disembarking in Singapore, we are actually going to move up into Malaya and take up garrison duties there. The fact is that since the surrender of France, the Japanese have bullied the Vichy French into allowing them to use French Indo-China both as a training ground for their troops and for the development of airfields. Now, we don't know what Tokyo has in mind. It seems incredible that they would take the risk of going to war with us, and of course we would have the support of the Dutch as well as all the resources of India, while they are engaged in such a life and death struggle with China. However, they started exerting pressure immediately following the fall of France, when we were somewhat beleaguered. They demanded the closing of the Burma Road by which we were supplying Chiang Kai-Shek. In the circumstances, we had no choice but to comply. However, now that we have won the Battle of Britain and are virtually secure from invasion, it is the

Government's intention to inform the Japs that we intend to reopen the Road. We don't know how they are going to react to this, and our presence is to help insure that they don't *overreact.*' One battalion? Harry thought. Harris might have been able to read his mind. 'There is of course already a sizeable British and Commonwealth Army in Malaya, something approaching a hundred thousand men, and should a crisis occur, Australia will certainly lend support. But as I say, hopefully that contingency will never arise. That's all.'

Malaya, for two years, Harry thought bitterly. Sitting on a tropical mudbank while the war is being fought, and no doubt won or lost, elsewhere. He almost put in for a transfer, but he was a Brand, and Brands by tradition went where they were sent. At least, he reflected, I am seeing the world. They didn't have much opportunity to see Ceylon, but they had to be impressed by the bustling efficiency of Singapore as well as the very real beauty of the place, apparent even as they sailed through the Dragon's Teeth, although they were taken aback by how small the island was, hardly bigger than the Isle of Wight. But looking north along the causeway which connected Singapore with the mainland of Malaya, which at this point was the Sultanate of Johore, they gazed at an enormous jungle. 'Fancy having to fight in that?' Grace remarked.

'That is the first thing we are going to have to learn to do,' Harry pointed out.

'The Japs will never dare attack us, sir,' suggested Grace. 'I mean, look at those guns.'

They were standing by the harbour, and certainly anyone attacking in the face of the great naval guns emplaced to look out over the Straits of Malacca would be asking for trouble. But although the actual naval base, described to them as one of the strongest in the world, was on the north side of the island, there were no guns facing across the Straits of Johore, he observed. No doubt they were protected in that direction by the jungle, he supposed. And, of course, by the Army.

They were allowed a month in Singapore itself, to become acclimatized before moving up-country. And quickly realized that they were part of a very heterogenous force indeed, in which Indian Army units comprised the main; the South Midlands were attached to the 11th British-Indian Division, helping to maintain the ratio—established after the Mutiny of 80 odd years earlier—of always having one British battalion to two Indian in every brigade. The Indian regiments had some British officers, sun-tanned men who had lived most of their service lives in the tropics and who regarded the white-skinned and heatstroke-malaria-dysentery-prone Tommies with contempt; as at Centot, the medical unit was the busiest in the battalion. But Harry quickly discovered a more important cause for being worried, a tremendous sense of *déjà-vu:* the people of Singapore, he observed, were no more happy to see the arrival of reinforcements from Britain than had the people of France been just over a year previously. No doubt, like the French, they considered their situation as a potential crisis, into which British arrogance had got them. This went, to their surprise, for the local British community as well, who regarded the influx of troops as an unwarranted intrusion upon their task of producing as much tin and rubber as possible for the war cause—and incidentally making as much money as possible for themselves.

Most disconcerting of all, the attitude of what-the-devil-are-you-lot-doing-here? was also that of their divisional commander, Lieutenant General Lewis Heath. Heath was a most distinguished soldier, and had just returned from taking part in the victorious East African campaign to assume field command of the Singapore

Army, but he was an Indian Army officer, and had been one all his life; there was no love lost between Indian Army officers and British regulars. To make matters worse, as Harry very soon discerned, there was even less love lost between Heath and the newly-appointed C-in-C Malaya, Lieutenant General Percival. Here was another distinguished soldier, but not only was he regular army, he also had no experience of tropical warfare—although he had served in Malaya already as chief-of-staff—and to compound the problem, he had, until his sudden appointment by the War Office in London, been in terms of length of service junior to Heath. It was difficult to envisage two such men working well together, if it came to a fight.

The battalion officers, however, were made most welcome. They were entertained at a reception held by the Governor, Sir Shenton Thomas, and entertained by the local dignitaries, which included the leaders of the resident Chinese society. Naturally they made Raffles Hotel their favourite off-duty rendezvous, but they were also inundated with invitations to cocktail parties and dances, with which Singapore, during the 'winter' months, and before the arrival of the monsoon, was filled. Harris insisted upon a certain amount of discretion in accepting these, reminding his men that they were here to prepare to fight and not to enjoy themselves, but he knew that it was important not to risk antagonizing the European community, while it was also necessary to keep the locals happy. It was while attending one of these functions, a cocktail party at the home of a Chinese millionaire, that Harry found himself gazing across the room at Marion Shafter.

For a moment he was too surprised to move, and just stood there staring. Nicole had entirely driven Marion from his mind, but there could be no doubting that it was she. She had allowed her straight yellow hair to grow, and it was past her shoulders, but there were the same boldly attractive features, the same voluptuous body, hardly restrained by the green cocktail sheath; if there was no *décolletage* to the dress, it was off the shoulder, and her breasts seemed to be fighting to get out. Then she half turned her head, and saw him. He had supposed she might be as embarrassed as he was, but instantly her face lit up with pleasure, and she excused herself from the people she was talking with and came towards him. 'Harry Brand! My God, but you're looking well.'

'So are you, Marion. But ... what are you doing here?'

'Well, you didn't expect us to stay in Ethiopia after the Eyeties took it over? Shafter decided to move on, and eventually we wound up here.'

'Shafter is here?'

She raised one eyebrow. 'Don't look so dashed. He's up-country. I prefer to stay in Singapore. The Malayan jungle is even worse than the Ethiopian desert.' Now he couldn't believe his ears, that she should so blatantly suggest a resumption of their relationship of their brief affair at their first meeting in five years.

'Why, Marion, I did not know you knew this officer?' His hostess, Thalian Tang, a petitely pretty Chinese woman.

'Captain Brand and I are old friends,' Marion assured her. 'In fact, the Captain is going to take me home, in due course. Aren't you, Harry?'

'Well ... ah ... I'm afraid I have no transport.'

Marion smiled. 'I do.'

The next hour passed in something of a daze, and Harry had a good deal too much to drink. Marion insisted on escorting him round the room, introducing him to various friends, who were mainly from the Chinese community—apparently Shafter did not consider the Chinese an inferior species. To his great relief she made no reference to Ethiopia, but merely said they were old friends from before the War. But Ethiopia had to be present in both their minds. He told himself that after the way she had treated him, again to become involved with her would be madness. But then he told himself that madness could only be a question if he again allowed himself to fall in love with her, and he was certainly not going to do that. Meanwhile, if she was again offering herself ... why not? She was a most exciting woman, and he was fancy-free, while it was so very long since he had had sex with anyone ... and there was an important point: Marion would surely prove whether or not he was truly impotent. And if he could make it with her, then he could surely make it with Connie—supposing he was ever going to be given the chance to do so again. 'It's past eight,' Marion said. 'I think we should be on our way. You don't have to tell anyone where you're going, do you?'

'I'm an off-duty soldier, not a truant schoolboy,' he reminded her.

'Of course.' She led him across the room to where Mr and Mrs Tang were saying goodbye to their guests, took their farewells, and then led him into the forecourt. 'Isn't it gorgeous? Just smell that jasmine. I think Singapore nights are the most glorious I've known anywhere.'

'And you've been everywhere,' he suggested, slapping a mosquito.

'Just about.' She unlocked her car, a small Austin, and he got in. 'Now,' she said, 'I think it's time you kissed me.' He was happy to do that, slowly and deeply, while his hands drifted up and down her sides and over her bodice, and her hands moved down to his crotch. How memory came surging back. But this time there were no bombs or bullets or knife-happy tribesmen to distract them. And he was hard as a rock. As she discovered. 'I don't think we want to hang about here,' she remarked, and started the engine. Reluctantly he let her go. 'So you joined the army after all,' she said.

'Well, when the shooting seemed about to start, I didn't have too much choice.'

She drove with great expertise, following what appeared to be a local custom of keeping her left hand firmly on the horn, which was very necessary as the brightly-lit streets were packed with other cars, people, bicycles, dogs and even chickens. It was impossible to believe there was a war on anywhere. 'Have you seen action?' she asked.

'Some.'

'And came through unscathed?'

'Not entirely. I spent six months in hospital after Dunkirk.'

'You were at Dunkirk? My, you have had a busy war. Would you believe that I have not heard a shot fired in anger since leaving Ethiopia?'

'Then you have been both wise and lucky.'

'And luckier still, to see you again.' She swung off the road and down a little driveway, to stop before a bungalow, set in delightfully secluded grounds. *'Voilà!'*

'This is yours?' Harry was astonished.

'Well, it's rented actually. It belongs to my friends the Tangs. They have been very generous to Shafter and me, since we came here.'

'I see,' Harry commented.

She glanced at him, as she got out of the car. 'Do you know, the phrase, I see, can be the most meaningful in the language? Aren't you coming in? You can't telephone for a taxi from there.'

Harry got out and followed her. 'I'm just surprised that you're still interested in me. After all, I shouldn't think I have Mr Tang's income, by a long shot.'

Marion unlocked the door. 'What you mean is, your white racist blood is boiling at the thought that I might have had sex with him.' She switched on the lights, walked into a very comfortably-furnished lounge. After a moment, Harry followed and closed the door. He was angry again,

297

as he had found it so easy to be angry with the memory of this woman. But he wanted her, too. Oh, how he wanted her! And he was going to have her, he knew.

'I'm afraid,' she said, bending over behind the bamboo bar, 'that I don't have any champagne on ice. I really hadn't expected to run into you tonight. Will scotch do?'

It was what he had been drinking at the party. 'That sounds ideal.' He moved behind her, and as she straightened with the bottle in her hand, slid his hands over her buttocks and then round in front to come up and hold her breasts.

'Why, Harry,' she murmured, turning her head so that he could nuzzle her cheek. 'You are interested, after all. Why don't you release the straps?' His hands slid round behind her shoulders to slide the straps down her arms, and allow the material to fall away from her breasts. Then he could cup the surprisingly cool flesh itself, while she poured two drinks. 'Mmmm,' she said, leaning back against him.

'Does Shafter know?' he said into her ear.

'I told you, we have an arrangement.' She turned in his arms, held his glass to his lips.

'But you always go back to him, is that it?'

'Being married to a husband with whom one has an arrangement,' she said, apparently very seriously, 'adds an extra dimension to life. I'm sorry I had to be a little bit abrupt when last we parted, but, shall I say, the circumstances were against our continuing our affair at that moment.'

'Too many Eyeties.'

'Oh, quite. But I can understand that you still bear a grudge. Would you like to beat me?'

'Oh, Marion!' He kissed her mouth, while still holding her breasts. No woman could ever replace Nicole, but this one was still eminently desirable.

'Still the English gentleman,' she remarked. 'Shafter beats me often. It's the only way he can get it up.'

'Now there's someone I'd like to beat,' Harry said.

'And I forbid you to. However,' she said, 'I think the least you can do is look at my scar. After all, you gave it to me.' She put down the drinks, came out from behind the bar, and knelt on a chair, pulling her skirt above her knees as she did so. 'Waiting on you, doctor.'

He stood behind her, pushed the skirt right up to her waist, gently eased down the knickers. She obligingly spread her legs, and he bent his head to kiss the still deep-coloured irregular mark on her flesh. 'Do you have to explain to your lovers how you got that?'

She giggled. 'I tell them it was a love bite. Why do you not give me another?' He nibbled the soft flesh. 'If you were to take my pants right off,' she said. 'You could fuck me like this. It's the way I like best.'

'As do the Chinese,' he said bitterly, but he was taking the knickers off, she raised her knees one at a time to assist him.

'You'd be surprised at the way the Chinese like it best,' she told him. 'I'll show you some of them. Later. Please, Harry, I'm randy as hell.' But so was he. All thoughts of impotence, or indeed, Nicole, were gone as he dropped his own pants and drawers and surged into her. 'Oh, Harry,' she said. 'Oh ... hold my breasts. Hug me against you. I want him in. Right, right in.'

He did his best to oblige, and as in Africa, they climaxed together, sliding down into the chair and then on to the floor. 'God Almighty,' he muttered into her neck. 'If you knew how that relieves me.'

'I can tell you needed it,' she agreed. 'How long have you been bereft?'

'It's a long story.'

300

'Tell me.'

'I need to go to the bathroom.' He pushed himself up. 'Where is it?'

'The door opposite the bedroom.'

'Right.' He went down the corridor, tried the door handle. To his surprise it was locked.

'Not that one!' she snapped, her voice suddenly high with alarm. 'The next one.' She was certainly a creature of moods. But he was too elated at the knowledge that he was not, after all, impotent, to care.

For the rest of his stay in Singapore, Harry saw Marion on every occasion he had a moment to spare. She was perfectly open about their relationship, at least amongst her Chinese friends, and he found himself playing bridge and tennis at the Tang's palatial estate, and being entertained like royalty. 'You seem, as usual, to have fallen on your feet, if that is the right portion of the anatomy,' Price commented. 'The old man wants to see you.' Harry raised his eyebrows. They were under orders to leave Singapore the following day, and he hoped Harris was not going to put some spoke in the way of his seeing Marion tonight, to say goodbye. 'You may go in,' Price invited.

Harry opened the door and stepped into the Colonel's office, found himself

301

facing not only Harris, but seated beside the desk and now rising to his feet, a man in the uniform of a colonial police officer. 'Ah, Harry!' Harris said. 'This is Superintendent Brierley. He heads the local Special Branch.'

'Pleased to make your acquaintance, Captain.' Brierley shook hands.

'What am I being charged with?' Harry smiled as he spoke.

'Sit down, Harry,' Harris said. 'I'm afraid it's not altogether a laughing matter.' Harry sat down. 'Superintendent?' Harris invited.

'I'm sorry to say, Captain,' the Superintendent said, 'that there is an unfortunately large element here in Singapore which is sympathetic to the aspirations of Japan. We have these subversives in all our colonies, whether they be oriented towards the Japanese, the Nazis, or most usually, the Communists.' Harry was beginning to feel uneasy. 'Amongst those individuals in Singapore who we deem it necessary to keep an eye on,' Brierley continued, 'is Mr Tang.'

'He is a Japanese sympathizer?'

'We think he is more than that. We think he is a Japanese agent.'

'But ... China is at war with Japan.'

'That is so, Captain. But there is a large fifth column in China. There is in

302

fact a puppet Chinese government, set up in those areas held by the Japanese in China. Now, we suspect that Mr Tang was actually set up in business here in Singapore by Japanese money. Certain it is that he pays regular visits to Tokyo.'

'And I have been seeing rather a lot of him,' Harry said thoughtfully. 'You don't have sufficient proof to arrest him?'

'We are not at war with Japan,' Brierley pointed out. 'We cannot arrest a man simply for having business dealings with a foreign country. Nor has he ever carried out any spying activities which could be called criminal. We are certain that he informs Japan of all social and economic changes here, and equally of all visible troop movements, such as the arrival of your battalion, but those too are not arrestable offences.'

'And you think I may have given him some information?'

'I know nothing to suggest that, Captain. I merely felt that you should be warned as to his activities.'

'Not that it is so important,' Harris put in, 'as we're leaving in the morning.'

'But I am sure you will be returning, at least on leave, from time to time,' Brierley said.

'Yes. Well ...' Harris looked at Harry.

'May I ask how you met the gentleman,

Captain?' Brierley asked.

'I was invited to a cocktail party at his house, soon after we arrived.'

'Several of my officers were,' Harris put in.

'But Captain Brand is the only one who has, shall I say, become a regular visitor.'

'Yes. Well ...' Harry flushed. 'At the party I met an old acquaintance, and it is she who has introduced me to the Tangs' circle.'

'May I inquire the name of this lady?'

'Marion Shafter.'

'Ah, yes, the missionary's wife.'

Harris raised his eyebrows. 'Wife? A missionary's wife?'

'I met the Shafters in Ethiopia, sir,' Harry explained. 'Before I ever joined the Army.'

Harris did not look altogether happy, so Harry turned back to the policeman. 'You know the Shafters, then, Inspector?'

'It is my business to know just about everyone in Singapore,' Brierley said.

'Then you regard Mrs Shafter also with suspicion?'

The policeman smiled. 'No, Captain. Mrs Shafter is, I'm afraid, one of those harmless creatures who flits from cocktail party to cocktail party, and, I may add, from man to man.'

'She rents her house from the Tangs.'

Harry could not be sure whether he was just making sure of Marion's innocence, or following one of the hundred and one thoughts which were rushing through his mind—such as a room in her bungalow kept locked, and her apparent acquaintance with the Italian officer in Ethiopia ... and the way she and Shafter had turned up at the field hospital, and the Ethiopian rallying point, just two days before it had been gas-bombed. She had been fairly aggravated about that. Because she and her husband had not yet had time to move on? But what on earth was he assuming?

Brierley continued to smile. 'We know about that. I suspect she is one of those people the Tangs regard as cover. Friends with a missionary and his wife, then obviously they have to be on our side. I should hate to think that you also are being used as cover, Captain.'

'I shall bear that in mind, Inspector.'

'That's all we ask.' Brierley shook hands with them both, saluted, and left.

'Stay a moment, Harry,' Harris invited. 'Sit.' Harry obeyed; he knew what was coming next. 'This woman, Mrs Shafter,' Harris said, somewhat hesitantly—he of course knew all about the Nicole business.

'Yes, sir. She and I were ... close friends in Ethiopia.'

'I really do not know what to say about

you, Harry. You have that lovely wife and son ...'

'I'm afraid my marriage is ended, sir.'

Harris frowned. 'You never told me this.'

'Well, sir ... Constance left me just before we embarked. I did not mention it because I suppose I was hoping it might blow over. But I have not heard from her since.'

'My dear fellow, she will only just have discovered where we have gone.'

'A letter written to me care of the battalion would surely have got here, sir.'

'Hm. I suppose so. I am most terribly sorry.'

'Thank you, sir. So am I.' And he was telling the truth.

'But this Shafter woman ...'

'She was a friend of mine before I ever met Constance, sir.'

'Yes, but still, a married woman ... what happens when her husband finds out? You must think of regimental honour.'

'Mr and Mrs Shafter have, shall I say, a modern marriage, sir. In any event, as we are going up-country tomorrow, I shall not be seeing her again, at least for a while.'

'Yes. Hm. Although as that police fellow pointed out, you will be returning to Singapore from time to time.'

'I shall promise to be most discreet, sir.

306

I trust you have no objection to my visiting Mrs Shafter to say goodbye.'

'My God,' Harris remarked. 'Modern youth. For God's sake *be* discreet, Harry.'

Harry wanted to visit Marion for more than merely to have a final fling. He was trying to make up his mind what to do, which depended on making up his mind if there was *anything* to do. As usual he took a taxi to within a block of Marion's bungalow, and walked the rest of the way. She saw him coming up the garden path, and opened the door as he reached it. He presumed she had servants, or at least a servant, but if she did the man or woman was never around when he called. 'You look hot and bothered.' She closed the door behind them. 'I've a bottle of bubbly in the fridge.'

'What are we celebrating?'

'Just celebrating.'

He kissed her, opened the champagne, poured. 'You mean you didn't know we leave tomorrow.'

'Leave? Oh, Harry! No, I didn't know.'

He sipped, and studied her. 'I think you did.'

She frowned at him. 'You are in a funny mood. Where are you going?'

'I have no idea. But you mean you don't know that, either?'

Marion sat on the settee, one leg draped across the other. 'I think there is something on your mind. Why do you not tell me?'

He sat beside her. 'Suppose I asked you what was in that room you keep locked.' He nodded at the corridor to the bathroom.

'If you asked me, I should tell you. There are various items of Shafter's in there. Things he has collected over the years and which are important to him. He always locks them up when he goes away.'

'Suppose I asked you to show them to me?'

Her gaze was cool. 'I should refuse, Harry. You have no right to poke into Shafter's business.' She smiled. 'Only into Shafter's wife.'

He glared at her, frustrated, afraid to put into words what he was thinking. 'Where is Shafter, exactly?'

'I really have no idea. Up-country somewhere. He moves from mission to mission. If you are going up-country, you may well meet him. If you do, give him my love.'

'What makes you think we are going up-country?'

'There is nowhere else *for* you to go, Harry. Unless you are leaving Malaya. Did you come here to make love, or not?'

Now he was definitely angry. 'I came here to say goodbye. So I shall say, goodbye.' He finished his drink, put down the glass. 'Thanks for the champagne.'

'There is three-quarters of a bottle left.'

'I am sure you'll find someone to drink it with.' He put on his cap and left. He was fuming, but it was entirely frustration. His instincts were telling him that there was something wrong with her, with what she was. But logic was telling him that even if she was helping the Tangs to send messages out of Singapore, and providing them with as much information as she could glean, there was not a lot he could do about it. Presumably he could denounce her, but he would need a lot of proof, and the worst that could happen to her would be that she was deported ... and there would be just the sort of scandal that Harris wished to avoid. While she still turned him on like mad. The best thing was clearly to forget her, at least until the next time he was in Singapore.

Next morning the battalion moved up-country, in trucks in preference to the railway which traversed the entire length of the country, first of all crossing the Causeway, and then following one of the very few roads which penetrated the jungle. 'At least it looks like easy country to defend,' Grace remarked.

'That's supposing the Japs stick to the roads,' Simpson countered.

'Well ... they have to, don't they, to move heavy stuff. And tanks. Don't they, sir?' Grace appealed to Harry.

'Tanks wouldn't do too well in that bush,' Harry agreed. But then, he was disturbed to note, neither would any of the men under his command. Granted that they were all green soldiers, and had been softened even further by the long, luxurious sea voyage, he and his fellow officers had done their best to lick them into shape during their month in Singapore. But the fact was, apart from the malaria and the dysentery, Singapore had been just too civilized, and equally, it was not the place they were going to have to fight. So while they had square-bashed and discussed tactics, which had included dispersion into the jungle and the creation of strong points in that impenetrable morass, no one had actually been into the jungle to find out what existing, much less fighting, in these circumstances was like.

The realities of this only became ap-parent as they drove north of Kuala

Lumpur. In the capital itself they were fêted, but Harris was under orders not to delay, and although he had to concede a march through the city with bayonets fixed and flags flying and the band playing, he got them on their way as soon as possible afterwards, to their required position along the Thai frontier, overlooking the Kra Peninsula, which there was talk of occupying in a pre-emptive strike if war with Japan came too close. 'Now,' he told his officers. 'Jungle exercises.'

Next morning there were some fifty men from B Company alone on sick parade. These varied from serious scratches or cuts from various pieces of razor-sharp leaf or branch, through the inevitable dysentery caused by drinking polluted water, again only a handful, to the very large number suffering from sheer fright, as they had been attacked, in their eyes, by a variety of monsters ranging from blood-sucking leeches to man-eating spiders. One or two even claimed to have had near brushes with tigers, although Harry could not imagine any self-respecting tiger wishing to get too close to platoons of men armed with at least one Bren gun. The whole was compounded by the unceasing rain, far heavier than anything they had previously known, the monsoon just having started.

However, this was something worth putting up with, they were told. 'No risk of the Japs making any move during the monsoon,' said the old India hand who had been given to them as a liaison officer. 'It just isn't on, in this weather. And the monsoon lasts until May,' he added.

Harry supposed that was reassuring in a purely strategic sense. But he wasn't at all sure his men were going to become any more ready to face an enemy after six months of this. It was the psychological factor which disturbed them. To men brought up in possibly the most civilized country in the world—in terms of nearness of towns, villages, good roads, hospitals and the absence of any dangerous creepy-crawlies—the concept that every tree, every bush, every leaf might contain something deadly or at least dangerous created a most unhealthy frame of mind. In vain did Harry stress that of all the creatures in the world man himself was the most dangerous and destructive, and that any animal, insect or reptile they encountered would only be acting on the defensive; if they believed him, they had to accept that if the jungle was already sheer hell, when every tree, every bush and every leaf might also conceal a Japanese soldier armed with a rifle and a bayonet it would become quite unacceptable. Nor was it possible to build morale by referring to British triumphs gained elsewhere; these were thin on the ground. True in May the Royal Navy had managed to sink the super-battleship *Bismarck*, but it was at the cost of the Navy's own most famous and best-loved ship, *Hood*, and the Germans had another monster waiting to come out, *Tirpitz*. In any event, by the time *Bismarck* went down, Greece had been lost as an ally, and with her, a large part of another British army, bombed and shelled out of the mainland and then out of the island of Crete, losing in the process all the gains made in North Africa. Now Auchinleck was apparently slowly rebuilding his strength, but whether he would actually be able to launch an offensive, no one knew.

To cap it all, in June, just before the battalion had sailed, the triumphant Germans had invaded Russia. This had initially been regarded as a good thing. No one might like the Russian regime, but equally no one could deny that Russia was one of the most powerful countries in the world, with an army counted in tens of millions. However, it seemed that men under arms did not necessarily constitute an efficient fighting force, and the Russians had been utterly demolished in a series of battles throughout the summer and autumn, losing millions of those millions and most of their equipment, so that the latest news put the Germans poised to capture Moscow. 'Would you say, sir, that Hitler has won this war?' Grace asked at the beginning of December.

'Shut up,' Harry said savagely, and went to battalion headquarters, to which he had been summoned.

'How are things, Harry?' Harris asked.

'I'm afraid they aren't good, sir,' Harry said. 'Morale is low. Every news bulletin from the West seems to be worse than the one before. My men are simply not getting over their fear of the jungle. And this bloody heat and rain ...' The December temperatures were higher than anything he had known, even in Ethiopia, and were accentuated by the humidity of the unceasing monsoon rain.

'I agree, it's pretty awful,' Harris said. 'How would you like some leave?'

'Me, sir?' Harry was astounded. 'There are others ...'

'Not quite in your category, Harry. It has to be a short pass, but we can spare you for a week. Say two days each way, you have three days in Singapore.'

'I don't understand, sir.'

'There's someone waiting to see you in Singapore, Harry. Your wife.'

Chapter Eleven

The Moment of Decision

For a moment Harry was too surprised to speak. As Harris could see. 'You had no idea she was coming out?'

'As I have told you, sir, I have not heard from my wife in very nearly a year. And I mean to say, how? There's a war on. One cannot just get up and go as one feels like it.'

'That depends upon who one knows in the right places,' Harris pointed out. 'I understand that Constance's father is now someone important in the Ministry of Transport, so I would imagine it's easier for her to travel than most. There's a despatch truck travelling south this afternoon. You have a seat on it. And Harry ... I would not visit Mrs Shafter on this occasion, if I were you.'

There could be no other reason for Constance to come to Singapore than in search of a reconciliation, Harry told himself ... But not even to write, just pack up her traps and leave, in the middle of a war ... although of course, so long as one kept a lookout for the odd Italian submarine operating in the Indian Ocean, Singapore was probably as safe a place as there was in the world at that moment.

Even so ... he had long known that Constance lived life entirely by her own agenda; her concessions to misfortune or other people's feelings were both begrudging and dismissive. But he objected to living in somebody else's chosen world. And if he wasn't careful, he was going to wind up a laughing stock.

On the other hand, he did so want a reconciliation!

The truck crossed the Causeway just after dawn on the second day, and as soon as they reached the city Harry went straight to Raffles; as he had been given leave by his CO there was no need to report to anyone. 'Captain Brand?' inquired the receptionist. 'Welcome, sir. Your wife is in your room. Shall I call and tell her you're coming up, sir?'

'I think she's expecting me,' Harry said, and took the lift. The corridor was deserted, save for the neat array of boots and shoes outside each door. He went to the number he had been given, hesitated before knocking. At this moment there was so much he wished could have been

316

left unsaid, or undone. But as it had all been said, and done, he had to take the situation from here. He knocked. 'Come in.' He drew a long breath, and opened the door. The room was in darkness, as the blinds had been drawn against the invariable bright morning sunshine, but he could tell it was a large room. It was also filled with Constance's scent.

'You're early,' Constance muttered from the bed. 'Put it down over there.'

Harry crossed the room and drew the blinds, to allow sunlight to flood in. 'Oh!' Constance grumbled. 'Don't do that.' She had thrown one arm across her eyes; she was wearing a nightdress. He went to the bed, and sat beside her. Immediately the arm was moved, and the sheet drawn to her throat while she blinked at him. 'Harry? What on earth ...?'

'You sent for me, remember?'

'Yes, but ... well, I didn't *send* for you. I wanted to see you.'

'A mere matter of travelling halfway round the world.'

'Well ... I've always wanted to see the East.'

'And having decided to damn the U-boats and anything else which might get in your way, you informed my colonel of your decision, but not me.'

She eased herself up the bed, still holding

the sheet to her throat. 'Did you come here to quarrel?'

'I came here to find out why you came here.'

'I should have thought that was obvious.' There was a knock on the door. 'I imagine that will definitely be my breakfast,' Constance said. 'Have you breakfasted?'

'Not seriously.'

'Well, then, you can have mine, and order another for me.'

Harry opened the door. The waiter raised his eyebrows at the sight of a uniformed officer, but made no comment, and set out the food, juice and coffee on the table. 'We'll have another of those,' Harry told him. He gave a little bow, and withdrew. 'You have this one,' Harry said. 'I can wait.'

'So can I. I don't like eating, anyway, until I've abluted and cleaned my teeth.' She got out of bed.

'I'm afraid I haven't cleaned my teeth this morning yet, either,' Harry said.

'Or shaved,' she observed: 'Eat.' She disappeared into the bathroom.

He was actually very hungry, and certainly for a Raffles breakfast. He was only halfway through when Constance returned. He reckoned she had showered on top of everything else, and looked as cool and *soignée* as he ever remembered her, but she had merely added a dressing-gown to her nightdress in the direction of getting dressed. 'You make me feel very guilty,' he remarked.

'You are very guilty,' she pointed out. 'But I imagine you are referring to the fact that you are eating and I am not. We could share that cup of coffee.'

'It has sugar in it.'

'I take sugar.' She sipped, gazing at him over the lip of the cup.

'How is Mark?' he asked.

'Very well, when last I saw him.'

'When was that?'

'Several weeks ago. And, before you start accusing me of abandoning our child, I will tell you that my decision to come here was endorsed by both of our families, and that Mark is being shared by Mummy and Mums. But we all felt that it is very important that he should have a father, as well as a mother and grandparents.'

'And I suppose it was Dad who told you where I could be found.'

'As a matter of fact, yes.'

There was another knock on the door, and a second breakfast appeared. 'How long have you got?' Constance asked, munching toast.

'Until Monday. How long have *you* got?'

'How long is a piece of string. Unless

319

you really do wish a divorce, I intend to remain here for at least the rest of the winter.'

'Remain where, exactly?'

'Here.'

'You've been able to find a flat?'

'Good lord, no. I meant right here.'

'My dear Connie, I can't afford to put you up at Raffles for an indefinite period.'

'You don't have to. Daddy is financing this trip.'

'Oh, for God's sake,' he got up and prowled the room.

'Does that offend your sense of manly pride?'

'Yes, it does.'

'Well, forget it. He can afford it. Let's say he's paying for our honeymoon. We never did have a honeymoon.' He stopped perambulating to look at her. 'Aren't you the least bit glad to see me?' she asked.

'Oh, Connie ...' he knelt beside her.

'You have to shave,' she reminded him. 'And clean your teeth. And you might as well have a shower while you're at it; I'm not going anywhere.'

She could be the most infuriating woman on earth. But also the most delightful. Quite apart from her very real beauty, which seemed to have deepened during the year since last he had seen her, she possessed a most attractive quality of total innocence in bed which contrasted so strongly with her aggressive confidence out of it. She had, at least so far as he knew, only had sex about half a dozen times in her life, and always by the same man—himself. Now her confidence dissipated into apprehension, as she remembered too well the catastrophe of a year ago. But she had travelled halfway round the world to overcome that hurdle, and by the time he returned to bed she was in it, and naked. Her eyes were shut, so he stood beside her, and said. 'Look at me.'

She opened them, tentatively, gazed at his face, and then lower. 'Oh, Harry!'

'The great healer.' He sat beside her to take her in his arms and kiss her, as deeply and almost savagely as he had ever kissed anyone, and then to explore her, inch by inch. He felt that he was again with a virgin, and he suspected she felt that way too. When he parted her legs to kiss her she gave a little murmur, but he presumed it was of anticipation. When he rolled her on her face she was bewildered, but relaxed as he kissed the backs of her thighs and then all the way down to her ankles and feet. 'Did anyone ever tell you that you have the best legs in the world?' he asked.

'I don't think so.' He gathered them and gently pulled them off the bed. 'What are you doing?' she asked, in some alarm, as she found herself kneeling on the floor, while her upper half was still on the bed.

'This is how I want to do it.'

'To ...' her head came up. 'Harry! Is that proper?'

'You're my wife,' he reminded her. 'And I love you.'

Harry supposed he was like a man who all his life had been banging his head against a wall, and suddenly discovered how pleasant it was to stop. Constance was his wife, and could be loved without any of the guilt or apprehension of the future that had always overlaid his relationships with Marion and even Nicole. Nothing on earth was legally or morally entitled to come between them, and the future stretched in front of them, an interminable vista of contented happiness. He knew he would never, could never, love Constance the way he had loved Nicole, but that love, by its very intensity, would have burned itself out. This steady glow would not do so.

It occurred to him that he had never enjoyed Singapore before; his month here earlier in the year had been a matter of frenetic training and equally frenetic bouts with Marion. He presumed Marion was still about, although he hoped they did not meet each other. For now he could explore the city and the island with his wife. On Saturday morning they behaved like utter tourists, strolled down Orchard Road and Elizabeth Walk, visited the Sri Mariamman Hindu Temple, walked out to Fullerton Road to look at the harbour, took a taxi ride into the 'interior'. Constance was amazed, as he had been when he had first come here, at how small it was, and she was equally confounded by the amount of space occupied by military installations and therefore barred to casual visitors; Harry deduced that there was a great deal more tension behind the scenes than was apparent even on the frontier. This tension was encapsulated by the presence, in Singapore Harbour, of two giant warships of the Royal Navy, *Prince of Wales*, one of the very newest battleships, famous for her part in the fight with *Bismarck* earlier in the year, forty-thousand tons of power armed with ten fourteen-inch guns, and *Repulse*, officially designated a battlecruiser because of her lighter armour, but, at thirty-eight thousand tons and with six fifteen-inch guns, hardly inferior in hitting power.

The two great symbols of British naval power had only just arrived and were *the*

323

sights of that weekend, and the entire waterfront was crammed with people staring at them, while rumour ran wildly from lip to lip, that they were on their way to Australia, or on their way to Hong Kong, or on their way to the American naval base of Pearl Harbour in Hawaii to join up with the American Pacific Fleet ... or that they were going to stay in Singapore, to form the nucleus of a British Far Eastern Fleet. 'Aren't they magnificent?' Constance asked. 'They make one proud to be British.'

They spent most of Sunday in bed, as he was due to begin his journey north the next morning. 'When will you be back?' she asked.

'God knows. This really has been compassionate leave.'

'Compassionate?'

'That's Army speaking. I suppose you could say it was, mend-a-marriage leave.'

'Are we mended, Harry?'

'I hope so. What are you going to do?'

'What do you want me to do?'

'I wish I knew. I want you to stay here, but I also want you to be with Mark. I want you to go home, yet I know you're safer here, and the thought of you risking those U-boats again ...' he sighed. 'I suppose you should go home. After all,

324

we've been here just on a year already, and our tour is for two years. This time next year we'll be packing up to come home.'

'And we'll be waiting for you. I know you're right. I don't suppose there is any chance you could be down here again for Christmas?'

'About a snowball's chance in hell, I should think.'

'I think Christmas in Singapore would be just wonderful, with the right company.' She sighed. 'I'll see about getting a passage, next week. Now don't let's talk about the future any more.'

He was up before dawn, to shave and shower and have an early breakfast before catching the truck going north. Constance didn't come down, but said goodbye in the bedroom. 'I love you, Harry,' she said.

'And I love you,' he assured her. Because he did. All his immature ghosts had been laid to rest. Now there was only the future to look forward to.

'Had a good weekend, sir?' asked the driver, a corporal.

'Yes,' Harry said. Well, he could see that.

They drove across the Causeway behind their headlights, swung on to the road leading north, and looked at each other at the odd sounds which were suddenly filling the morning. 'What the hell ... I beg your pardon, sir,' Corporal Bream said.

'Cut your engine and your lights,' Harry snapped.

Bream obeyed, and they both jumped down from the cab. Now the noise of the aircraft could be distinctly heard, as well as the crump of the bombs falling on Singapore; now too they could see the beams of the searchlights scouring the sky, and below them, the gleams of the first fires. 'Jesus Christ!' Bream remarked. 'The Nazis, sir?'

'No chance. Those are Japanese.' Harry bit his lip. If war had indeed broken out, then it was his duty to report to the battalion on the frontier just as quickly as possible. But he was two days away from the frontier, and the war was *here:* no one had ever doubted that a war between Japan and Great Britain would be mainly naval. And Constance was back there, perhaps injured ... perhaps ... but he could not allow himself to think that. 'Turn round and go back,' he said.

'Sir?'

'We need to find out exactly what's happened, Bream. It'll only mean a delay of an hour or two.'

'Yes, sir.' Bream turned the truck, with some difficulty, as the road was suddenly filled with vehicles, some trying to leave

Singapore, others trying to get into it. It took them an hour to regain the Causeway, where they found patrols of troops stopping every vehicle.

'Look, you must remember us, we just went out,' Harry told the MP sergeant.

'Right you are, sir. But we can't be too careful.'

The roads were even more clogged on the island. After another hour of staring at the distant fires—the bombers had long departed—Harry abandoned the truck. 'Get to GHQ and wait for me there,' he told Bream, and made his way into the city on foot.

It was a pretty ghastly journey. He had been in hospital in Somerset during most of the Battle of Britain, and in fact he had not been in London, or any of the heavily-bombed cities, at all, since the Blitz had begun. Nor did he suppose for a moment that the bombs dropped by a relatively few Japanese aircraft over a brief period could be considered more than a tiny percentage of those dropped on Britain. But the effects had none the less been horrendous. The city seemed consumed by a vast panic. It had in any event always reminded him of a huge anthill waiting to be disturbed. Now it had been disturbed. People, dogs, goats, chickens, were everywhere, moving aimlessly, shouting and screaming at each

327

other. Many people were still crouching in the drains—hardly better than open sewers—that ran beside the streets. The police were trying to restore order, but were having a difficult time of it. And that there had been cause for alarm was evidenced by the bomb craters in the streets and the smoke rising from burning buildings and warehouses on the waterfront. Both warships as well as their destroyers had steam up, but they appeared to be undamaged by the attack.

Harry was assailed with shouted comments and questions, mostly of the 'what are the Army going to do about this?' variety as he forced his way through the throng and finally reached the hotel. Here there was less pandemonium than on the streets, but everyone was obviously very shaken, and half-dressed guests were still crowding the foyer and gardens. There was no sign of Constance, so Harry went up to the room. 'Harry!' She was in his arms. 'My God, what's happening?'

'I'd say we're at war with Japan. Thank God you're all right. Listen, you simply have to get out now.'

'But I want to stay. To be near you.'

'Listen, dearest, those bombers are going to be back. And I have to get out to the battalion, and stay with them.'

'And fight with them.'

'Well, I shouldn't think it'll come to that. You'll be in far more danger here when the Japanese fleet turns up. Please go.'

She kissed him. 'I'll see what I can do. But Harry ... can you stay, just a few minutes?'

He shook his head. 'I'm virtually AWOL as it is. I'll try to let you know what's happening.'

The streets were less crowded by the time he got back out. It was quite late in the morning. He found Bream and the truck, waiting for him, and told the corporal to wait some more because he had something else to do before leaving Singapore. The police station was in a state of some turmoil, with special constables being sworn in and everyone clearly uncertain just what they had to do. It took Harry half an hour to gain admittance to Brierley's office, but the superintendent listened carefully to what he had to say. 'You had these suspicions when I interviewed you? But you didn't tell me of them.'

'I did raise Mrs Shafter's name, Superintendent. And you dismissed it.'

'It's quite an accusation. What do you think we'll find if we enter her bungalow and make her open that storeroom?'

'My guess would be a high-powered radio-transmitter.'

'You think she tipped off the Japanese about the arrival of those warships?'

'It would seem somebody did.'

'I think you should know, Captain, firstly, that there was never any attempt to conceal the fact that those ships were coming here, quite the contrary, in fact, and secondly, that we are receiving reports that the attack on Singapore was not an isolated incident. Seems there have been attacks on Hong Kong, in the Phillipines, and would you believe it, even on Hawaii, this morning. There is no land-based bomber in the world capable of flying from Japan to Hawaii and back, so it seems obvious they came from ships. And for ships out of Japan to have been within range of Hawaii means they had to have been at sea for some time. In other words, this attack must have been planned and got underway well over a week ago, that is before the battleships ever arrived in Singapore.' Harry was staggered by the immensity of the news. Such a concept must have been planned *months* ago, if not years. And it involved the USA, which had to be good news. Brierley stroked his chin. 'Tell me something, Captain,' he said. 'It's my impression that you and Mrs Shafter were lovers.'

330

'We had an affair, yes.'

'And now you want to turn her in? I hope this isn't just a case of a lover's tiff?' He caught the expression on Harry's face, and flushed. 'Forgive me. That was crude. But do you have any idea just what is involved if she is arrested for spying? There will be a great deal of unpleasantness; for her, there will be a great deal of publicity, no matter how much we may try to hush it up; and you may well be called upon to give evidence against her when the case comes to trial. Should it do so.'

'I understand that.'

'So what changed your mind about her? I simply have to know. Was it the arrival of your wife? No offence, old man, but if we do arrest the lady there is no chance your wife won't learn of your ... liaison.'

'I seem to have been incredibly foolish,' Harry agreed. 'But I knew something was wrong with the Shafters in Ethiopia. It seems certain they were passing information to the Italians. I don't know how. But they were hopping mad when we were gas-bombed while they were there. I mean, we were all pretty upset, but they took it personally. I believe that attack wasn't meant to happen until they had left us again, or until Bairan's men had gone on down-river—they were the ones supposed to be attacked.'

331

'But you did nothing about it then, either,' Brierley remarked.

'Look, Superintendent, I was just a kid. And let's face it, Marion Shafter is a pretty attractive woman. So she seduced me. I suppose it's her business to seduce men who can be of use to Shafter. I don't know what she had in mind for me; the Eyeties caught up with us before it could develop. But if they were pinpointing Ethiopian troop movements for the Eyeties, then she and her husband are responsible for the death of one of the finest men I have ever known. Okay, I went for her again when I arrived here. She made herself available, and my marriage was on the rocks. But I was suspicious of her almost from the start. Only, as you pointed out at the time, we weren't at war with the Japanese, and she wasn't the only one sending out information. Now we are at war.'

Brierley studied him for some seconds, then turned as there was a knock and an orderly entered the office. 'Just come in, sir,' the Malay said, and withdrew.

Brierley looked at the sheet of paper. 'Your outfit is up on the Thai border, right?'

'Right.' Harry frowned. 'Why?'

'Here is a report of Japanese landings at Khota Bharu. That's right on the easternmost side of the border.'

'Good God!' Harry leapt to his feet. 'I must get out there. What about Marion Shafter?'

'We'll take care of her. And her husband, if we can lay hands on him. Good hunting, Captain. Get one or two for me.'

The news that Malaya was actually being invaded had not yet been circulated— presumably it never would be circulated to the public to add to the panic, unless it became serious—and the sight of troops embarking at the railway station for transportation north was nothing new. Harry toyed with the idea of using the train, but decided that he would probably do better with the truck, where he would be his own boss. He and Bream got back across the Causeway without too much difficulty. But of course what was happening was known at GHQ, and they found themselves in the midst of a convoy of trucks also carrying reinforcements northwards. Quite a few of these were newly-arrived Australians, sun-tanned, powerful-looking and brash young men who declared their intention of 'knocking the Japanese right out of the ground.' Harry could only hope they could do that.

Owing to the congestion it was late afternoon when they reached Kuala Lumpur, and they decided to look for a billet for the night rather than press on in the darkness. But finding one was clearly going to be difficult; Kuala Lumpur was in an even greater state of panic than Singapore, and it had not even been bombed as yet. 'What a shitting awful mess,' remarked the major to whom he reported. 'What we need is to blast those fellows with aircraft. Where the hell is the RAF, do you suppose?'

'Defending Singapore, I would say. Is there any news of the battalion, sir?'

'The South Midlands? They've pulled back. Well, the Japs are moving behind them, see. And there are all those other landings ...'

'What other landings?'

'There are reports coming in of enemy landings all up and down the coast. Even on the west coast.'

'And you believe them? Landing on the west coast? That's not possible, sir.'

'Look, go and join your unit, Captain, and let me get on with my job.' Which appeared to be preparing to burn his files. Harry and Bream abandoned the idea of spending the night in the city, which was just as panic-stricken as had been Singapore. The difference was that here no one was making any effort to quell the panic, and a good many people were already leaving, streaming to the south

334

with as many of their belongings as they could carry. Shades of Belgium last year, Harry thought.

Having filled their petrol tank, they drove all night, a difficult business as it was too risky to use their headlamps. By dawn they could hear the rumble of gunfire, to their north-east. They were also now alone as regards soldiers, their erstwhile companions having dispersed to allotted positions. But there remained a huge number of civilians all around them, streaming towards Kuala Lumpur. 'What do you think we should do, sir?' Bream asked.

It was light enough to look at the map. 'If they've brought tanks and guns ashore, Corporal, they need roads,' Harry said. 'So they must be there and there and there.' He prodded the stiff paper. 'If you put your foot on it, we can get up *here*, before they reach it. If the battalion is retreating, that's the road they'll be coming down.'

'Yes, sir,' Bream said enthusiastically.

Progress continued to be slow, because of the people thronging the road, all making their way south. This was most definitely Belgium in 1940 all over again, save for the colour of the people, and the vegetation. Neither Bream nor Harry spoke either Cantonese or Malay, much less any of the hundred and one local dialects, but quite a few of the hurrying people spoke English, and shouted reports of Japanese soldiers being directly in front of them. But that was surely impossible, Harry reckoned; the nearest joining road capable of bearing tanks or guns was still a few dozen miles away. Then suddenly the road was empty, winding silently between the thickly-clustered trees. Bream instinctively touched the brake, and the truck slowed almost to a halt. 'What's your problem?' Harry asked.

'The quiet. I don't like it, sir. Not a bit.'

'Drive!' Harry commanded. Bream picked up speed, and then braked again, violently this time, sending the truck skidding to and fro across the road, but coming to a halt, while they gazed at the half-dozen men who had suddenly emerged from the jungle to their right, some hundred yards in front of them. They wore green uniforms, green steel helmets, and carried, amazingly, bicycles. 'Drive!' Harry yelled, at the same time picking up the corporal's rifle.

The truck surged forward as the Japanese realized there was an enemy bearing down on them. They scattered, but unslung their own rifles as they did so. 'Keep going!' Harry commanded, as he opened fire, emptying the entire magazine as rapidly as

336

he could work the bolt. Two of the Japanese fell, but the rest reached the safety of the bushes, leaving, however, their bicycles scattered in front of the truck. 'Don't stop,' Harry bawled, cramming another clip of ammunition into the magazine. As he did so the truck shuddered to the impact of bullets striking it, and swayed to and fro before bumping and crashing over the bicycles. Harry turned in his seat to empty another five rounds into the jungle where the Japanese had taken shelter, but as he did so the truck went careering off the road and down the steep embankment into the water-filled ditch, coming to rest on its side.

Harry was thrown to his left and had Bream thrown on top of him. Water filled the compartment, and he pushed the corporal off him and up as his head broke the surface. Then he realized Bream was dead, which was why they had crashed. He heard voices, and looked out of the window to see four of the Japanese on the road, shouting at each other as they pointed at the wreck, apparently unable to see him. But now two of them started to climb down the embankment, and they had fixed bayonets on their rifles.

There was no time to reload the rifle, and in any event they were very close. Harry drew his revolver, half fell out of the door into the waist-deep water, and began firing. He was an excellent shot with a pistol, and while his first round went wide, his second struck the man nearest to him, bringing him down with a gasp, and his third, as he aimed higher, hit the man behind in the forehead, virtually blowing the top of his head away. Then he had to hurl himself to one side as the remaining two Japanese fired into the truck. I have killed a man, he thought, as he crouched up to his neck in the muddy water. Or two, at least. More likely four. After more than two years of war!

And he was about to kill two more—or die himself. For the remaining Japanese were cautiously advancing; no doubt as he had not fired for several minutes they assumed he was dead. They were talking to each other, in a high-pitched chatter, as they reached the bodies of their comrades. Then they suddenly turned and both emptied their magazines once again into the truck. This time they struck the exposed petrol tank, and this went off with a tremendous whumpff of flame and smoke. Harry, on the far side, had to sink his head beneath the water to avoid the blast. When he emerged again, the Japanese were chattering even more loudly as they gazed at the fire, dissipating in a series of sparks as it reached the water.

They were certainly preoccupied. Harry drew a deep breath and stood up. He knew he had only three rounds left and every one had to count. Feeling like some Western desperado he levelled the revolver and shot the first man through the head. The second turned, bringing up his rifle, which was struck by Harry's fifth round, causing the soldier to stagger backwards and fall over against the embankment. Harry fired again, his last shot, into the man's chest, and he subsided down the bank into the water. But he wasn't dead, although the water around him was discoloured with blood, and almost immediately tried to push himself up. By then Harry had waded round the burning truck to seize the man's helmet and push it back down into the water and hold it there. The Japanese vainly tried to get his nostrils clear, but Harry was much the bigger and stronger man, and after only a few seconds the movement ceased. Six men! Harry thought. Just like that. Six men.

There was nothing to be salvaged from the burned-out truck; even Bream was an unrecognizable mess. Harry experienced a sickening sense of *déjà vu*. But at least there was no Nicole to be killed. As there had been no backup to the cyclists, he had to assume they were a patrol that had pushed well ahead of any main body. But equally they had come through the jungle, and if the Japanese could do that, he also had to assume that they were moving inland faster than he had thought possible. He no longer had a compass, but he could use the sun, and he decided to move north-west; that way, if he could keep going, he should reach the railway line. If he couldn't keep going, well ... he reloaded his revolver from the pouch of cartridges on his belt, then took one of the Japanese rifles and the strap of equipment which carried cartridges for it. This he slung over his shoulder, then set off, wading in the water—at least he was unlikely to die of thirst although probably of dysentery—and pausing every few minutes to listen. It was exhausting work, and occasionally startling, as when a twelve-foot-long python suddenly emerged from the bank beside him and slithered away at great speed. As his heart settled down he reminded himself of what he had said to his men, and realized that in this case the words were absolutely true: the python had been more afraid of him than he of the snake, and with good reason—he was on a killing high.

He heard gunfire in the distance, to the east, but did not deviate from his plan, while beginning to feel increasingly hungry. There was the odd berry which

340

looked quite attractive, but he decided against that kind of risk. It was past noon, and the sun was hovering above the trees, causing the jungle to steam, when he heard noise from directly in front of him. He reckoned there were a good number of men out there, and ... as he paused to listen, he realized they were speaking English. A few minutes later he was standing before Colonel Harris.

Harris looked exhausted, as well as being unshaven and generally filthy—but that went for the entire battalion. Not that Harry, soaking wet and mud-stained, was much better. The colonel listened to his report with a grim expression, then nodded. 'They're penetrating very fast. And they're using the jungle, as well. But we have orders to hold them, here.' The battalion was certainly digging in, around the main road leading south, setting up their machine-guns and preparing to fight.

'I thought the moment war broke out we were going to occupy the Kra Peninsula,' Harry commented.

'That was always a non-starter,' Harris said. 'It would have meant violating Thai neutrality, and we don't do that sort of thing, do we? Even when we know they're backing the Japanese. What we *are* required to do, is stop the enemy from cutting the railway. And that is what we are going to do. By the way, how was Singapore?'

'Singapore was great, up till Monday morning, sir.'

'And Connie?'

'All's well that ends well, sir.'

Harris sighed. 'Unfortunately, this hasn't ended yet, Harry. It's only just begun.'

Harry was disconcerted at his commanding officer's evident loss of morale. 'Came at us out of the dark and the trees, sir,' Pope explained, laying out dry clothing for his captain. 'Bit of a panic. The Colonel wasn't happy about it.'

Neither were the men, Harry decided, and he joined his company. Simpson had them in good order, but they were looking decidedly shaken. 'Was it like this in France, sir?' Grace asked.

No, Harry thought, it was not like this in France: there was no bloody jungle. But he felt it would be a mistake to say that. 'Very like this,' he agreed.

'And we got licked there too,' someone muttered.

Simpson turned, aggressively, to discover who had spoken, but Harry shook his head. 'We're not going to get licked this time,' he said loudly. 'The Japanese are men, like us. No better. I have just killed six of them.'

He hated boasting, but this time it was necessary. The word passed rapidly down the ranks. He wondered if they believed him. And he was soon proved wrong. The men were just having their evening meal when they heard firing, and it came from the south ... and south-west! 'Holy Jesus Christ,' Simpson said, scrambling to his feet. 'They must've landed on the west coast after all.'

'That's not possible,' Harry snapped, and went in search of orders. Harris had already sent a patrol south, and they came back an hour later, thoroughly shaken, to say that a Japanese force was astride the road.

'How the hell did they do that?' Price demanded. 'We're covering the only lateral road.'

'They went through the bush,' Harry said.

Everyone looked at Harris, and then at the radio-operator, who was trying to get through to Kuala Lumpur. When he did manage to get orders, they were predictable. 'Pull out. Fall back on the capital.'

'How the hell do we do that?' Nelson asked.

Harris sighed, and then squared his

343

shoulders. 'Through the bush, gentlemen. Like the Japanese.' He attempted a grin. 'In the dark.'

Harry supposed that was the longest night he ever endured, and it was only the first of many. But the first was the worst. They followed their compasses and whispered words of command, but they may have well have shouted, as they floundered through the bush, seeing imagined pythons and cobras behind every bush, almost hoping they *would* run into the Japanese so that they could fight a human enemy. By dawn they had reached their new position, and again set up a perimeter, but to Harry's consternation, of the eighty-seven men who had composed the company when he had rejoined them, only eighty-four were present. 'We've seen no enemy,' he pointed out to CSM Cutmore.

'I kept telling them all to keep up, sir,' the sergeant-major said.

'You mean they could be lying back there, just fallen out in the dark?' Simpson was aghast.

'We'll have to send back and look for them,' Grace said.

Harry went off for a word with Price. 'No one leaves his position,' Price said. 'We can't have half the battalion wandering around that bush looking for stragglers and getting lost themselves. You're not the only company to have lost men. If they're alive, they'll come in. If they're not, we can't help them.'

Morale-wise, that directive went down like a lead balloon, but of course it was the only sensible decision to take, and in fact two of Harry's stragglers did come in later that day, scared stiff by the experience of being lost. That still left one man missing, but it was not quite as great a catastrophe as Harry had feared was going to be the case, and over the next couple of days, as they held their position without being attacked, a sense of stability began to creep back into the battalion.

This was abruptly ended when they were told that both *Prince of Wales* and *Repulse* had been sunk.

Apparently, the great ships had steamed north to prevent further Japanese landings, but they had lacked the air cover which a carrier would have provided, and had been attacked by a Japanese air flotilla soon after dawn on the Wednesday morning. The result had provided disturbing proof that even the largest and most heavily-armed warships in the world, and moving at full speed—the American battleships sunk at Pearl Harbor had been stationary—were

345

helpless against determined air attack where they could not provide air cover of their own.

For the troops on the ground this was crushing news. The British Army had had in its illustrious history some pretty dicey moments; historically morale rested to a large extent upon the claim that however often defeated, it had always won the last, and therefore decisive, battle. But the Navy had *never* been defeated! Until today.

The defenders of Malaya continued their retreat, constantly setting up supposed strongpoints and being forced to abandon them as the Japanese infiltrated behind them. Harry supposed it was a masterly campaign by the Japanese, as they made steady progress while seldom having to fight anything resembling a pitched battle. For the British, and their Australian and Indian allies, it was a nightmare, as the terrors of the jungle became multiplied by the supposition that together with the pythons and the cobras there was also a Japanese marksman behind every tree.

What made matters worse was a growing feeling of being let down by the other chaps. Both the Australians and the Indians could not help but look with consternation at the unbroken series of British military disasters since this war had begun. Both the British and the Indians considered that the Australians would rather drink beer than fight. And both the British and the Australians wondered, often aloud, why the Indians weren't as at home in the jungle as the Japanese appeared to be. Ever backwards. This was Belgium multiplied a hundred times. On Friday 19 December Penang Island was abandoned. This was a nasty business as all sorts of rumours promptly circulated that the proportion of those evacuated, especially as regards women and children, was directly related to the colour of their skins. This latest disaster did not directly affect the South Midlands but on Christmas Day there came the news that Hong Kong had fallen amidst horrifying tales of rape and massacre. Harry could only pray that Connie had got out of Singapore; there was no opportunity to get any news of her.

In the New Year there at least seemed a glimmer of hope, as the various Allied nations engaged in South-East Asia accepted a unified command, called ABDA —American-British-Dutch-Australian—with Wavell as C-in-C. But this positive step came too late to help the defenders of the peninsula; only two days later the much-rumoured nightmare came true, as the Japanese, having occupied Penang and obtained thereby an unexpected bonus in the form of a large number of undestroyed boats, actually did land on the west coast, and on Sunday 11 January, Kuala Lumpur fell. Now the retreat became headlong. The troops, and most of their commanders, had only one desire—to reach the comparative safety of Singapore, even if they were told the island was being bombed on a virtually round-the-clock basis. Anything would be better than the jungle.

With the end in sight, however, a good deal of morale and discipline was magically restored. The various units awaited their orders to cross the causeway with some patience. The South Midlands had by now been reduced to little more than two-thirds of their original strength. Of the two-hundred odd casualties, only a couple of dozen had fallen in battle. An equal number had just gone missing, but the great majority were malaria or dysentery cases who had had to be left behind as prisoners of war. In view of the news from Hong Kong, their chances did not seem very high. On 30 January 1942, the last British troops, the Argylls, preceded by their two surviving pipers, crossed the Causeway, which was then blown up by the Royal Engineers.

Chapter Twelve

The End of the Beginning

'First South Midlands,' remarked the staff officer, looking over the ragged collection of men in front of him with a somewhat disdainful air. 'You are allotted Sector Seven B, Colonel. The eastern end of the Strait. You will defend it and act as a mobile reserve to the forces covering the Causeway.'

'My men need at least two days' rest and recuperation,' Harris protested.

'I'm sorry, Colonel. There is no time for that. We must expect the Japanese to attack the island as soon as they have regrouped. It is essential that we stop them getting across the water.'

Harris nodded, wearily, and the major saluted and withdrew. Harris looked at his officers. 'You heard the man, gentlemen. We will move to our position and dig in.'

'Will we be able to replace any of our MGs, sir?' Nelson asked. They had lost a great deal of their equipment in the hurried retreat, and had crossed the Causeway without a single truck left. 'We're not going to do too much stopping with just rifles.'

'We shall see what can be done. Major Price, you'll go into Singapore City with a requisition list. Now, company dispositions.'

Harry rejoined his men, who were on the right of the battalion. They at least still possessed one machine-gun, which was promptly set up. 'Bit low on both food and ammo, sir,' Simpson said.

'Both are on their way from the city,' Harry assured him, and summoned Pope. 'Obviously I can't leave here,' he told the batman. 'But you can. I'm giving you a twelve-hour pass. I want to know when Mrs Brand got away, and on which ship.'

'Yes, sir,' Pope said.

Harry then settled down to making his men as happy as possible, a considerable task; there were only sixty-three of them left, and thus every man was mourning a lost comrade. Their position, on the right of 18 Division, was as far removed from the Causeway, which was the narrowest and therefore most vulnerable stretch of the Straits of Johore, as it was possible to be and remain on the north side of the island. It therefore seemed possible that, unless the Japanese attacked immediately, it *would* be possible to have at least a little rest, if there seemed little chance of any recuperation—at least in the accepted military sense. Harry immediately organized a three-watch rota, which meant that every man had eight hours off to four on. 'Now we wait,' he told his men. 'At least, there's no chance of the Japanese getting behind *this* position.'

It was none the less eerie, for even at this widest part the Straits were only about two thousand yards across, and thus they had to continue to stare at the forest they so thoroughly hated. They could also hear a good deal of noise coming across the water, even if it was difficult to interpret it. Morale remained very low. It was not merely that they had been utterly routed in the battle for Malaya, it was the feeling that they were isolated, if not forgotten; certainly written off save for how long they could hold Singapore. No one supposed it could be held forever, without massive reinforcements.

There was also a feeling of total exposure. Japanese planes roamed the skies at will, having shot down all but a single squadron of Hurricanes. They were usually on bombing raids, but they also used their time in the air over the island to observe the various troop dispositions and movements being carried out in plain view beneath them. The troops almost began to wish for an assault to be mounted, so that they could hurl it back.

Food and ammunition trucks arrived that afternoon, and the men were able to have their first hot meal in several days. That did wonders. Harry was having a cup of tea with Simpson and Grace when there was a discreet cough, and he looked up at Pope, standing a few feet away. 'A word, sir?' the batman requested. Harry got up at once, and went to him. 'Back here, sir.'

Pope retreated into the trees, and Harry followed him, frowning ... and gazed at Constance. She wore trousers and a loose blouse, sandals and a Chinese straw hat, and looked somewhat travelworn—she had just walked a dozen miles. 'We had a bit of trouble getting through the MPs,' she explained.

'What in the name of God ...' but he took her in his arms.

'Oh, Harry,' she said. 'I have been so worried.'

'*You* have been worried. What the hell are you still doing here? Hasn't there been an evacuation?'

'There was one ship, about ten days ago. But you had to queue to get papers and tickets, and I hate queues. So I decided to wait. And thank God I did. The ship was torpedoed and went down. There were only a few survivors.'

'Jesus!' He hugged her, and looked round, but Pope had beaten a discreet

352

retreat. 'Where are you staying?'

'Oh, I'm still at Raffles. It's actually very comfortable, and the food is still good. There's an air of Götterdämmerung about the place, but I suppose that's to be expected. Harry, will you be able to get in?'

'Not a chance.'

'Well, then ...' she licked her lips.

'You, Connie? On the grass in the open air?'

'Actually, it's something I've always wanted to experience.'

'I'll probably be cashiered,' he said. But after nearly a month, he really didn't care.

He sent her back into the city that night, again with Pope as an escort, and with instructions to stay put. After what had happened to the refugee ship, he didn't know if he could insist upon her taking another, even if one was available. But the thought of Connie a prisoner of the Japanese, after what had happened in Hong Kong ...

Next morning he was summoned to battalion HQ, situated only just behind their position. He assumed that Harris had learned about Connie's visit—it was certainly common knowledge to the company—but instead found his old friend Brierley waiting for him. 'We have your lady under arrest,' Brierley told him. 'She's in Changi, spitting blood. No news of Shafter himself, I'm afraid. The point is that while we did find a radio-transmitter in her bungalow, as she denies it was ever used to communicate with the Japanese, we need supportive evidence to proceed, before a magistrate, and Colonel Harris says you can't be spared.'

'Definitely not,' Harris said.

'So I have to ask you to make a written deposition of your charges against her,' Brierley went on. 'That will serve for committal. When the case actually comes to the Supreme Court, you will *have* to appear in person to give evidence, but presumably this business will by then have been sorted out.'

This business, Harry thought; a bloody Japanese takeover of Singapore. 'You mean, in the midst of all this, the due process of law is still grinding its way forward?' he asked in amazement.

'Isn't that what we're fighting for, old man? You're not suggesting that because the enemy is at our gate, as it were, we should just take Mrs Shafter out and shoot her, before she's been convicted?'

'Is that what will happen to her, when she is convicted?'

'No. If she's convicted she will be hanged.'

Harry swallowed, and sat down to make his statement.

The next few days were uncanny in their quiet. The various sounds continued from across the water, suggesting that the Japanese were still bringing up heavy equipment, but only the occasional rifle shot broke the silence along the Strait. Harry encouraged his men to shoot at anything looking like a Japanese moving in the bush across the water, but there were few of these.

On the morning of Thursday 5 February, the battalion was visited by General Wavell himself, accompanied by Generals Heath and Percival, as well as the Brigadier, as part of an inspection of the entire defensive position. Harris assembled his officers to meet the great men, and then Wavell addressed them. 'You should know,' he told them, 'that yesterday the Japanese called upon this garrison to surrender. This demand I refused. We will defend Singapore to the last man and the last round. This is for two reasons, apart from the honour of the British Army. The first is that every day we, and our Dutch and Australian and American allies, delay the Japanese attempt to overrun South-East Asia, with its enormous reservoirs of tin and rubber and above all, oil not to

355

mention its rice crops—we give our people the time to prepare and launch a massive counter-attack, which will bring the enemy expansion to a halt and ensure his ultimate defeat. The other is more personal. I can tell you that huge reinforcements are being rushed to our aid, and once they get here we shall take the offensive and drive the Japs out of Malaya. We have only to hold on until those forces arrive.

'Now, I know you received a bloody nose on the peninsula. We all did. We were taken by surprise, by a well-equipped and daring enemy who had been well-trained in jungle warfare. Many of our people, your people in particular, had not received such training. Now they have learned by experience. And now, too, the Japanese cannot use their insidious infiltration tactics. They will have to come at us across the water, where we can see them, and then it will be man to man, and I have no doubt who are the better men. God save the King.'

Harry found himself watching the two subordinate generals. Heath and Percival did not look at each other, nor would they look at any of the men Wavell was addressing. They know it's all a load of codswallop, he thought. We're done. Two days later the Japanese started bombarding the island.

They had clearly concentrated a considerable force of artillery, and the noise was tremendous. As usual, it was galling not to be able to reply adequately. The Army had no heavy guns, and only a few of the huge naval guns could be swung sufficiently to aim north, with the result that their firing was haphazard rather than targetted. The troops crouched in their slit trenches and kept their heads down; Harry was far more worried when the guns aimed over their heads, at Singapore itself, he had visions of Raffles crumbling into dust, with Connie inside it.

His emotions were a huge conflicting jumble. To have her come halfway across the world for a reconciliation was the most compellingly romantic thing he could think of. To think that the year and more of frustration and unhappiness was behind them, that they had only the future to look forward to, was exhilarating. But getting to that future now seemed an immense task, and having her virtually in the firing-line had to bring back memories of Nicole, only now it was Connie he was seeing, a crumpled mass of blood and bones. He slept uneasily, awoke when the bombardment stopped, sat up, looking right and left in disbelief. Simpson had been on duty, and now he knelt beside his

357

captain. 'I think they're trying to cross,' he whispered. 'Listen.'

Harry listened, while he rubbed sleep from his eyes and scratched his unshaven chin. There was definitely small arms fire from the west. 'What do we do?' Grace asked, also waking up.

'Stand to. But quietly.' He checked the rounds in his revolver, but also armed himself with a rifle and bayonet, as did Pope. Harris and Price arrived. By then the sun was up and the firing had increased. 'Do we know what's happening, sir?' Harry asked.

'No, we don't. But I imagine it's a probing attack designed to see if we draw in our people from other positions, such as this one. So we stand firm.'

The senior officers went off again, and the firing grew in intensity. The men took off their steel helmets as the heat increased, and became restless. Harry spent the entire morning walking from post to post, reassuring and calming nerves. From one of these tours he was summoned by a panting Simpson. 'Orders from HQ, sir. We must evacuate and pull back to the reservoirs. The Japs are across in strength. They've dispersed the Australian 22 Brigade and captured Tengah Airfield.'

'Jesus Christ!' That meant half the island had fallen in one attack. It was Malaya all over again. He had to face his men. 'All right, chaps, we're going to pull out and retire to the reservoirs. Smartly, now.'

Morale had observably collapsed. The men muttered as they collected their weapons and began to move out. Some did not even pick up their guns and had to be sworn at by CSM Cutmore. They retreated through native villages and small plantations, from time to time uncertain where even the rest of the battalion were, but regained contact as they reached the several reservoirs situated to the north-east of the city. Here they dug in again, and here Harris visited them again. 'There is to be no further retreat,' he told them. 'Without water, Singapore cannot hold out. Therefore we hold this line, or we die. I know I can rely on you. Thank you.' If he was hoping for some response such as a cheer, he didn't get it. The men regarded him in stony silence. 'Will they fight?' he asked Harry as they retired to be alone together.

'They'll fight,' Harry promised him. 'Is there news from Singapore?'

'Sounds pretty grim in there. I hope to God Connie has the sense to stay in the hotel.'

'But there's no chance of her getting out?'

'Harry, I don't think there's a chance of

any of us getting out.'

'But ... these massive reinforcements Wavell was talking about ...'

'I think that was morale boosting. Anyway, he's gone.'

'Gone?'

'Of course he wanted to stay, Harry. But he's been ordered out. His command is all South-East Asia, including India. We're just an outpost. But the fact that he's been ordered out means that London has written us off: they can't afford to lose a commanding general.'

'So, who *is* in command?' Harry asked.

'Why, Percival, of course.'

'With the same orders? Last man and last round?'

'Of course.'

There was no possibility of sleeping. The entire battalion stood to throughout the night, hearing the rumble of guns to the west, only a few miles away, and hearing too the crashing of the bombs being showered on the city behind them. Belgium all over again, Harry thought. Only this time there was no navy waiting to take them off. And he was one of the very few men in the battalion who had survived Dunkirk. The men were growing more and more agitated, as they listened to the firing gradually creeping round behind them.

360

The officers did the best they could to keep their spirits up, but Harry's mind was in Singapore, and the coming catastrophe. The unthinkable was going to happen. If Singapore was to be defended to the last man and the last round, then it would fall to a general assault, and thus there would be a sack, when every woman in the city would be at the mercy of every soldier in the attacking army. He found himself sweating with apprehension at the thought of what Connie might have to undergo.

The Japanese attacked the following morning. It was just before dawn, and the battalion were sleeping on their rifles, save for the sentries, when a voice called, 'Hi, Tommy-boy, you there?'

There was a ripple as the soldiers were awakened, and the click of rifle bolts. 'No firing,' Harry snapped. 'Pass the word, Sergeant-major. No firing. They're trying to discover where we are, and how many.'

'Tommy-boy! ' called the voice. 'You no there? Maybe you run away, eh? You no fight Japanese.'

'Will they come, sir?' Simpson asked.

'They'll come,' Harry said. And wondered if he hated them. Actually, he didn't, as soldiers. He hated them as men who might soon be raping Connie. He wanted to kill, with a desperate urgency.

'Tommy-boy!' called the voice. 'You run away, eh? You run away from Germans, eh? How you fight Japanese?'

A shot rang out; someone's nerve had cracked. 'Shit!' Harry commented. Almost in the same instant a mortar shell plummeted out of the darkness, landing close to where the rifle had been fired, exploding in a huge gush of sound and cries of pain. 'Open fire!' Harry shouted, and the company went into action. So did the entire battalion, a fusilade of rifle and machine-gun fire rolling up and down the ranks.

The firing died, and there was silence, save for the moans of distress. 'Where are the bastards, sir?' Pope inquired.

'They're there, Corporal,' Harry assured him. It was almost light, although gloomy because of the low cloud and drizzling rain. Now the jungle in front of them seemed to explode as a dozen mortars hurled their shells towards the British lines. 'Eyes front!' Harry bawled, well knowing that most of his men had instinctively ducked; he had nearly done so himself. He knew the assault would follow the barrage, and there they were, little men in those green uniforms he remembered so well from the road outside Kuala Lumpur, charging behind their fixed bayonets.

'Fire at will!' he shouted, and stood up.

362

Pope handed him the rifle and bayonet, and stood beside him. The Japanese swarmed over the perimeter, losing a good many men, but driving onwards with an utter carelessness of life or injury. The South Midlands returned fire and stood up to meet them, bayonet to bayonet, but they still lacked experience and were at least as appalled by the casualties they were inflicting as by those they were suffering. 'Stand fast!' Harry bellowed, emptying his rifle magazine into a knot of green-clad bodies. But some of them still came on, bayonets gleaming in the first sunlight. He dropped his rifle and drew his revolver, emptying that in turn, and had the satisfaction of seeing the bodies in front of him disappear. Then he heard a groan, and looked down to see Pope on his hands and knees, blood pouring down his shirt.

Harry knelt beside him, and heard feet pounding up to him. He looked up at an out-of-breath battalion runner. 'Orders to pull out, sir.'

'To do what?' Harry looked at his men, who were actually cheering, as the Japanese attack faded away. 'We're holding them.'

'You may be, sir, but the battalion has been forced back. You must come out, sir, or you'll be cut off.'

Harry looked at CSM Cutmore, who had just come up with a casualty report.

'Lieutenant Simpson is dead, sir. And Lieutenant Grace is wounded.'

'Send the wounded back, Sergeant-major. Then pull the men out.'

'We can hold them, sir.'

'Not on our own, Sergeant-major. Prepare to withdraw.' He knelt beside Pope again. But Pope was dead.

The Japanese were watching, and as the South Midlands began their withdrawal, they attacked again. Harry had remained to oversee the sending out of the wounded, and to watch his men falling back, when there was a huge shout and the little green-clad men flooded the position. Then it was desperate hand-to-hand fighting such as Harry had never experienced before; indeed, he longed to have a sword, which he felt would have been more useful than a rifle and bayonet. The Japanese officers carried swords, with which they did frightful execution at close quarters. Harry had reloaded his revolver and shot one man at close range and then had his life saved from a bayonet thrust by CSM Cutmore, who threw himself on the weapon and died. Harry shot that man as well, but now there was nothing for it than run or die; his command had entirely disintegrated.

He ran back a few steps, turned, his

revolver thrust forward, and saw the wave of green-clad infantry, having paused to shoot or bayonet anyone showing the least sign of life, resuming their advance. He was seen and several shots were sent in his direction. He knew he was hit but it didn't seem very serious, as he stumbled down some steeply sloping ground, tripped and rolled several feet, losing his tin hat in the process, and ending up kneeling in the shelter of a clump of bushes. He saw Japanese advancing past him, on the higher ground; they had not seen him. Painfully he began crawling through the bushes towards the sound of firing. The Japanese were being checked as they closed in on the city itself, and now were forced back by a counter-attack. Harry found himself in the midst of a company of Indian soldiers, bayonets red with blood. 'You're wounded, old man,' said the English officer. 'Stretcher-bearers!'

Harry had been hit in the thigh, but the bullet had not severed an artery, and the stretcher-bearers bound him up and gave him an anti-tetanus shot. 'Makes it easy when you're wearing shorts, sir,' one of them said.

They also insisted on carrying him away from the firing-line, although he wanted to be allowed to walk. But the pain was severe as the shock wore off, and he was in agony by the time they deposited him before Harris, which was where he had insisted upon being taken in preference to the hospital. 'Harry?' The colonel had reconstituted what remained of his headquarters in a clump of trees on the outskirts of the city itself. He had also lost his helmet and was mud-stained but unhurt, at least physically. 'My God, I thought you were dead. Price is dead. So are Moore and Nelson.'

'How many do we muster, sir?'

'Something under three hundred. I have lost my command, Harry.' He looked close to tears.

'Not yet, sir. I'll just go and find my company ...'

'Harry, you're wounded. You're going to hospital. That's an order. Anyway, you don't have a company any more. What's left of it I've given to Nelson. You are relieved of duty.'

The stretcher-bearers lifted him again. Harry allowed them to carry him a few hundred yards then said, 'Halt.' The stretcher-bearers laid him on the ground and looked at him inquiringly. They were now in the suburbs, and in the midst of a huge, howling, milling mass of people and animals; it was like the day war had broken out only quadrupled. Above their heads smoke billowed and blackened the morning sky, in the distance there were sundry explosions, while from the north the firing was continuous. The people had nowhere to hide as the sounds of catastrophe closed in on them, and any police who might have tried to control the mob were conspicuous by their absence. 'Listen,' Harry said. 'I'm sure you fellows have more important things to do than cart me about. I'll get off here.'

'You can't go far on that leg, sir,' said the corporal.

'Do I have far to go?'

'Ain't you in pain, sir?' the private asked.

'I've been in pain before.'

'Well, sir ...' the corporal opened his haversack and took out a small bottle and a hypodermic syringe. 'Morphine, just in case it gets too much.'

'Thanks.' Harry placed the drug in his haversack, and the two men helped him up.

'You sure about this, sir?' the corporal asked, as Harry staggered about a bit, testing out his leg, watched now by a curious crowd as he nearly tripped over a mongrel which tried to lick his calf. 'I wouldn't trust these people not to cut your throat. They've gone right off us.'

Harry drew his revolver, with the utmost

deliberation, checked the chambers, and reloaded. Then he replaced it in his holster, but left the flap unfastened. 'I'll be all right. Right?' He grinned at the people nearest to him, and they stepped back.

'Good luck, sir,' said the corporal.

By gritting his teeth against the pain Harry was able to use his left leg, and proceeded at a hobble, pausing every few yards to hang on to a lamppost or lean against a wall while he caught his breath. He attracted a good deal of attention as he staggered along, but the people were surprisingly friendly, in contrast to the medical orderlies' dire predictions, and several offered to help him. They also changed characteristics as he neared the Padang. This was a more prosperous part of the city, and he was surrounded by whites and upper-class Chinese and Malays. Here again he was offered help, as well as food and drink, while they plied him with questions. 'We're holding them,' he said, hoping that he was telling the truth. 'I'll be back out there as soon as I have this wound tended.'

Amazingly, Raffles was relatively un-damaged. Most of the glass was shattered and lay in crunching splinters under his feet, and there were one or two cracks in the walls, but at least it was not on fire, and happily the wind was northeast and blowing the smoke from the burning warehouses on the front away from the hotel. There was even a clerk on the desk, although he wasn't wearing uniform and was chain-smoking cigarettes, something the management would not have tolerated under normal circumstances. 'Captain Brand,' Harry said. 'Is my wife upstairs?'

The clerk looked at the row of pigeon holes. 'Her key is not here, sir.' Harry nodded and went to the lift. 'They are not working, sir. There is no electricity.'

'Damn.' The stairs looked like a mountain, but he dragged himself up the three floors. From time to time he passed people, who looked at him curiously, but few spoke. Harry wondered what they were thinking of it all. Presumably they were residents of the city, people who had lived here, perhaps for years, in all the splendour of British colonial rule, protected and enhanced by the might of the Empire, as signified by the Royal Navy, in the main, but also by the soldiers stationed here, victors in the Great War, upholders of the greatest empire in history. Now that empire was crumbling before their eyes, at least here in South-East Asia, and before the onslaught of little yellow men whose mission was the total destruction of white supremacy. And there was nothing they could do, either about it, or to escape it.

He banged on the door. 'Come in,' she said. He opened the door, and fell into the room, exhausted, getting his hands in front to break his fall. Constance had been seated by the window; she was again wearing trousers. Now she got up and came towards him. 'My God,' she said. 'What are you doing here?'

Harry pushed himself up and sat against the wall. 'You wouldn't have a drink?'

'Scotch.' She went to the table by the bed and poured some into a toothmug. Exhausted and in pain as he was, he could not help but be aware there was not a great deal of warmth in her greeting. Oh, shit, he thought. She knelt beside him to give him the mug, wrinkled her nose as she surveyed him and smelt him, and then frowned at the blood on his stained bandage. 'Are you hurt?'

'A little.' He drank, deeply. Nothing had ever tasted so good.

'Then you should be in hospital.'

'I chose to be with you. It might not be for very long.'

She gazed at him for several seconds, then she said, 'Wouldn't you rather be down at Changi Gaol?'

'Look, don't start that.' He held out the

mug. 'That tasted like two.'

She got up, refilled it, surveying the bottle as she did so; it was almost empty. 'I was at Changi, yesterday,' she said. 'I was asked to go there, by your friend Mrs Shafter.'

'That bitch,' he growled.

'A bitch of whom you seem to have been very fond.'

'Look, I was the one who turned her in.'

'I think she knows that, so she wanted me to get the whole picture. Ethiopia, that idyllic month here, your plans to get together again, which were spoiled by my unexpected appearance.'

Harry sucked whisky into his system. 'She told you all that? Then she's a liar.'

'Is she, Harry?'

'Look, we had an affair in Ethiopia. An affair! A one-day stand. I fell for her. Hell, I was a kid. You knew that, because Joss told you. She got us together because she, the family, wanted to make me forget her. Well, you succeeded.'

'You mean you got her out of your system by seducing me, and getting me pregnant, whereupon you went off to France and fell in love with your countess, before I messed up all your plans.' Harry bit his lip. But she was speaking the absolute truth. 'And having

371

done the right thing and married me, you get as far away from me as possible and take up with this woman again. So you then worked out she was some kind of spy and turned her in. Bully for you. But I'm still the one left on the outside. I'm sorry, Harry, but it's not my scene. I've had it up to here.'

He was too tired and in too much pain to attempt to present a defence. 'What are you going to do about it?' he asked. 'In the present circumstances.'

She gave a bitter smile. 'The ultimate irony, that I should chase you halfway round the world and wind up in a Japanese prison camp.'

He realized that she had no idea what might be involved in that, or more importantly, before that. 'Would it do any good for me to say that I love you, and only you?'

'As of this moment.' She waved her hands. 'I'm sorry, Harry, I need to think about it. About the whole situation.'

Again, he realized, she had no idea how imminent was the catastrophe looming over both of them. 'What would you like me to do?'

'I think you should go to the hospital and have your wound properly looked after. Then ... perhaps you could come back here, this evening.'

'Let's hope we're all still here, this evening,' he said. He hobbled down the stairs to where the crowds of people still milled about the hotel grounds, staring at the clouds of smoke from the burning buildings and installations which blotted out the sky, and listening to the sound of gunfire, punctuated by explosions, so continuous as to appear almost normal. Several policemen were in the grounds, trying to maintain order. Harry hobbled to a white inspector. 'I need to get to the hospital,' he said. 'Can you give me directions?'

'I wouldn't go to the hospital, Captain. It's been overrun by the Japanese. I believe all the wounded have been murdered. As well as the nursing staff.'

'Shit!' Harry commented.

'There is a First Aid Station by the dock. I'll have one of my men take you down.'

The First Aid Station was a crowded, unhappy place, but there were several nurses and a couple of doctors, and one of the nurses took off Harry's bandage to look at his wound. 'Not too bad,' she said. 'You've had anti-tetanus?'

'Yes,' Harry said.

'Well ...' she bound it up again with a fresh bandage. 'You should rest. While you can.'

373

'Were you at the hospital?'

'Today is my day off.'

'Do you know what happened?'

She raised her head. She was grey-haired and about his mother's age, he estimated, not particularly good-looking, but by no means unattractive, with her crisp features and matronly figure. 'Yes,' she said. 'And I imagine the same thing is going to happen here, soon enough, if that fool Percival doesn't stop fighting.' She gave a grimace. 'You're not going to stand too much chance, Captain, in a Japanese prison camp with that leg. Here.' She gave him a little square bottle. 'That'll hurt like hell, but it should fight off the scepticaemia.'

Harry grinned. 'That's not iodine?'

'I'm afraid it is. What's so funny?'

'I'll tell you, sister. Next time we meet.'

Harry felt much fitter now that his wound had been re-dressed, but the analgesic tablets the nurse had given him made him drowsy, and he sat on a low wall to wait for the effect to wear off. He blinked at the harbour, which was a mass of sunken ships and shattered installations, yet amazingly at the yacht club most of the pontoons seemed undamaged, and the various small craft bobbed at their moorings. They made an attractive sight, and he felt he could sit

374

there forever, just staring at them, when he was aroused by a tap on the shoulder. 'Brand, isn't it?' He looked up at a vaguely familiar face, wearing a major's crowns on his shoulder straps. 'Barnett. We met in Kuala Lumpur.'

'Sir!' Harry struggled to his feet.

'Pretty grim show. The boss has called a meeting of all senior officers available. Aren't you coming?'

'I'm not a senior officer, sir.'

'Be my guest. These could be the last words of command you'll ever hear from a British officer.'

The command room was crowded. General Percival had always come across to Harry, on the very few occasions he had met him, as a reserved, calm figure. Tonight he clearly showed signs of stress. Seated beside him, Heath looked even more stressed; the antagonisms between the two men were now clearly visible. Percival waited for everyone to find a seat, or stop shuffling their feet at the back, and then stood up. 'I want you all to understand our situation,' he said. 'We have over eighty thousand men still under arms in this fortress, and we are maintaining our lines in the vicinity of Bukit Timah. However, we are bound to consider the civilian situation. I am informed by His Excellency that there have been, up to now, some thirty-five thousand civilian casualties. This is unacceptable. In addition, since the Japanese have captured most of our reservoirs, we have only sufficient water for another twenty-four hours. After that time, Sir Shenton Thomas is afraid that all civilization in Singapore may break down, and that we may well have to contend with a racial conflict within the city as well as one without.'

He obviously hasn't been into the city recently, Harry thought; civilization had broken down several days ago, but there had been no sign of any racial war. 'In all these circumstances, and notwithstanding the messages of encouragement I have received from General Wavell, and indeed from the Prime Minister,' Percival went on, 'I have come to the conclusion that to prolong the struggle can only cost lives, without serving any useful purpose as regards the winning of the war. I therefore intend to send out a white flag to General Yamashita at dawn on Sunday.' He paused, and looked over the tense faces in front of him. 'I, we, all of us, will of course be bound by the terms of the surrender. I will do my utmost to obtain adequate terms, but I cannot be hopeful about this. The best I can anticipate is that I will manage to avoid any risk of a massacre such as took place in Hong Kong. Now, regular officers who still command units will of course remain with those units. It is their duty to do so. You will inform your men of my decision and give them my thanks for their enormous efforts. However, I am aware that there are some officers who no longer have units to command. In that case, it is possible that you may wish to consider your positions prior to our surrender, remembering that you have just twenty-four hours in which to act; once we have surrendered, you must abide by the terms of that surrender. Should any of you wish to undertake independent action, it must be a private matter, and confided to no one. No senior officer can admit to having condoned such an action, and I should warn you that any officer attempting independent action, and failing, is liable to be shot by the Japanese.'

Another pause, while he looked over their faces. 'I wish to thank you all for everything you have done. I only regret that your efforts have not been rewarded with success. Thank you.'

'What was all that about?' Harry asked Barnett, as they left the building into a late afternoon rain squall. The teeming water did nothing to diminish the sound of the guns, but it slightly lessened the uproar in the city, while the low clouds deepened the intense gloom of the smoke-filled sky.

'He was inviting those of us who feel like it to try to escape,' Barnett said. 'And at the same time warning us that to attempt it would be virtual suicide. Well,' he glanced at Harry's leg, 'I don't suppose you have much option.'

'Are you going to risk it?'

Barnett shook his head. 'I think a Japanese prison camp offers a better prospect of getting home. One day. Good luck, old man.'

So that is quite definitely that, Harry thought. He didn't think the chances of surviving a Japanese prison camp in a war which did not look as if it was going to have a successful ending were very good, especially for a wounded man. Even with his bottle of iodine!

As for Connie ... but he could at least have a civilized goodbye. He hobbled along to the hotel. The crowds there too had diminished and quietened, driven to shelter by the rain. And no doubt the news of the impending surrender was beginning to filter through. There was no one on the desk at all, now, and the interior of the hotel was a vast, dark cavern. As before, he dragged himself up the steps, praying that she would still be there. He didn't suppose she had anywhere to go.

This time the bedroom door was locked. 'Who is it?' she asked.

'Harry.'

The latch was released, and she stepped back to allow him in; he saw that she was carrying a small revolver. 'One can't be too careful,' she remarked. Harry lurched across the room and collapsed in a chair. Constance carefully locked the door again. 'My God but you look a mess.' Water was dribbling from his clothes on to the floor. 'I'm afraid there's no more scotch.' She sat on the bed, placed the revolver on the table. 'What are your plans?'

He shrugged. 'Stay here with you, as long as possible.'

'Just like that?'

He sat up. 'Darling, the time for fun and games is over. Percival is surrendering on Sunday. We have just thirty-six hours left, before, well ...'

'At least you'll get proper attention.'

'You think so? The wounded at the hospital were bayoneted in their beds. The nurses were raped. Percival is hoping to avoid anything like that by a formal surrender, but ... they surrendered in Hong Kong, too.'

'You think they'll rape us?'

'There's certainly a chance of that.'

She walked up and down the room. 'So

have you come to tell me to use the last bullet?'

'I can't tell you to do anything, Connie. I don't have that right, any more.'

She stopped in front of him. 'What are you going to do?'

He shrugged. 'There's not a lot I can do. I came here to say goodbye.'

She knelt in front of him. 'Is there no hope at all?'

'If one was fit, maybe. Percival has given any officer who does not have a command the right to escape before the surrender, if he can.'

'Escape where?'

'Well, I suppose, across the strait to Sumatra is the only practical plan. It's only twenty-five miles.'

'Can't we do that?'

'We?'

'You and I, Harry.'

'It's virtual suicide, you know. If we're spotted by the Japs ... anyway, I don't know anything about handling boats.'

'I do,' Constance said.

'This last summer I've done a lot of sailing,' she explained. 'The family moved down to Wales to avoid the bombs, and there was a yacht club where we were. I know I could sail a boat to Sumatra.'

'And the risk?'

'If we die, well, at least we die together.'

'I thought ...'

'Don't think,' she recommended. 'When the chips are so far down, well ... you're my husband.'

It was already dark. They left the hotel, made their way through the people who were thronging the streets, shouting and wailing, whispering and weeping, to the yacht club. Here there were more people, but no one questioned their right to be there, or attempted to stop them when they wandered on to one of the pontoons. There were people in some of the boats as well, preparing to put to sea, or arguing about it. Again no one took any notice of the wounded officer and the woman. 'Take your pick,' Harry muttered.

'I already have. That one,' Constance said. She was pointing at a double-ended Bermuda-rigged prahu, twenty-four feet long with a little shelter cabin amidships.

'How do we get her out?'

'There's enough wind, and it's offshore. No problem.'

'We've no food or water,' he reminded her.

'If Sumatra is only twenty-five miles away, we'll be there in about eight hours,' she told him.

He was amazed at her expertise. Because of his wound he was not sufficiently mobile to do more than watch in awe as she bent on the sails, cast off the mooring warps, and pushed the craft away from the pontoon. As it began to drift across the harbour she heaved on the halliard, and the mainsail went up the mast. 'Hang on to that rope,' she commanded. 'It's called a sheet. Keep it fairly tight.'

Harry obeyed, and the sail began to fill.

'Hey!' someone shouted from the pontoon, but that was now fifty yards away, and fading into the gloom, although the burning city behind it made a lurid backdrop. Constance set the foresail, then came aft and sat beside him, taking the tiller. 'You can make that fast now,' she said. 'The wind is just right.'

'Did I ever tell you that you're a marvel?' he asked.

'No,' she said.

Constance had apparently even learned to navigate, and sailing due west, they made the Sumatran coast before dawn. When it was clear they were within a mile of the land—they could see the mountains looming out of the darkness—she handed the sails and let them drift to negate the risk of hitting any rocks, but at first light

382

they were under way, lowering the sails again as they coasted into the beach; Constance dropped the anchor when they were about twenty feet off shore. Now it was light they could explore the cabin, and found to their delight not only a primus stove with fuel, but also a tin of coffee and one of biscuits. There was even just sufficient water in the tank to enable them to boil a kettle and have breakfast. 'However,' she pointed out. 'One cannot live off coffee and biscuits.' She helped him over the side and they waded to the beach.

Apart from being exhausted, they were both somewhat subdued, as they had spent much of the night looking back at the glare of the fires rising above the city, and listened to the artillery still firing from around Bukit Timah. But now the noise had died, and the only evidence of what they had left behind them were the distant smoke clouds merging with the rain clouds moving in from the north. Weary as she was, Constance hunted about and located a little stream rushing down to the sea. She helped Harry over, and they lay on their bellies together to slake their thirst. 'Now,' she said 'Food.'

'Chance would be a fine thing.'

'It's all about us,' she pointed upwards. He raised his head and gazed at the coconut clusters hanging from the palms. 'You reckon you can climb that?'

'No,' she agreed. 'Didn't you tell me you're a crack shot with a revolver?' He glanced at her, and then up and down the beach. 'There doesn't seem to be anyone around,' she pointed out. He drew his revolver. 'You aim at the stalk holding that big bunch,' she suggested.

'And then?'

From her waistband she took a foot-long knife. 'Found it in the seat locker.'

'You're sure I never told you that you were a marvel?' he asked.

'What I'd like you to do is prove you're my equal,' she retorted.

He held the revolver in both hands, squeezed the trigger. The bunch of coconuts swayed as the bullet cut through part of the strand holding them to the tree. Harry fired again, and the fruit came plummeting down. Two of them actually split open when they struck the ground, and Harry and Constance knelt shoulder to shoulder as they lapped at the milk before tearing the husks open to get at the soft but so nourishing white fruit inside. Then they could hack at the others at their leisure.

Apparently no one had heard the shots. It was evening before a fisherman approached through the trees, and stared at the anchored yacht and the white people on the beach. Harry pointed his revolver at him, and he went away again. They left immediately. They had seen no planes over the Straits of Malacca all day; the Japanese were too concerned with occupying Singapore.

During the night they made a good fifty miles, although the wind was fitful, and put in to Sungaikabung the following morning. Now they were some seventy miles from Singapore, with no means of knowing what was happening there. 'I think we're going to make it,' Constance said.

It took them eleven nights to work their way up the Sumatran coast. They stuck to their plan of sailing from dusk to dawn, keeping well offshore to avoid rocks, and putting in with the first light. They encountered various locals, who were happy to sell them food, even if the language barrier prevented much exchange of news—what there was was all bad. However, they saw no Japanese activity, although some planes flew high over Sumatra during the day. But those could have been the RAF; they could not tell.

Harry guessed the Japanese had better things to do further south. He had originally toyed with the idea of trying to make Batavia, but rejected it. He had guessed that would be the way the Japanese would take, and after what he had seen in

Malaya he had little faith in the ability of the scratch army of Dutch, British, Americans and Australians to withstand the enemy for very long. He wondered how his erstwhile comrades were getting on.

By the eleventh day, Harry's leg had all but healed, thanks to liberal doses of the iodine supplied by the nurse in Singapore. He could not help but smile even as he suffered exquisite agony whenever Constance applied the antiseptic; how the wheel does turn, he thought. And then wondered what had happened to Marion. But if his suspicions about her were correct, she was no doubt being fêted.

They had even made love, lying on the beach, with the sea to wash in when they felt like it. 'You know what?' Constance remarked. 'I reckon this is the honeymoon we never had. Can you imagine what it would have cost us to come to a place like this, if there'd been no war?'

By the eleventh day, too, he had learned how to handle the prahu; Constance willingly allowed him to do more and more. She knew it was good for him, psychologically, and she loved to see him assert himself. That evening they sat on the beach at Sabang, the island off the northernmost tip of Sumatra, and studied the small scale chart of the Bay of Bengal, which they had found in the cabin. There was a town, and even an airstrip, on Sabang, but they decided against visiting either of those; they had had enough of fear and panic, and they were unwilling to risk an encounter with an over-zealous official who might refuse them permission to continue their escape. By now they had every confidence in themselves. But ... 'This is the big one,' Harry said. 'It's about a hundred and thirty miles of open sea between here and Great Nicobar. That will take us about a day and a half.'

'You're the skipper,' she reminded him.

'Trouble is, once we go, we go. There's no possibility of taking shelter during the day if Japanese planes come along and get inquisitive.'

'On the other hand, we can't stay here,' she pointed out.

'Well,' he said. They had now got the business of living off the land, and the sea, down to a fine art. In addition to the always available coconuts, they had come across an abandoned banana plantation—'Best concentrated food in the world,' Constance said—and they had also used, successfully, the fishing tackle they had found in the cabin, cooking their catches on the primus stove. 'I suppose we could honeymoon for the rest of our lives. Or until the war is over.'

'No,' she said. 'The Japanese will come eventually. And what about Mark?'

Constance loaded the yacht with food and filled every container she could find with fresh water, while Harry studied the sky, wishing he had paid more attention to weather lore in the past. There were scattered clouds to the west overhead, and some heavier stuff in the east. That was probably rain gathering over the mountains of Malaya. He had no idea if it would come out to sea, or whether it would be dangerous if it did. He didn't see why it should be; the prahu was a well-found boat. On the other hand, it was still the monsoon season, when storms were always likely.

They put out at dusk, and sailed steadily just west of north, using the yacht's compass. It was 28 February 1942, and a bright night; the sea was no more than slightly choppy in the fresh breeze. And the breeze was propelling them on. At dawn the sun rose out of a red and angry sky, and the mountains of Sumatra were blue blotches behind them. Harry could only hope that the weather would not break for another twenty-four hours.

Constance did not appear to notice the clouds. She sat in the bow and fluffed out her hair. 'This'll be our first daytime trip.

I think I'll sunbathe.' They breakfasted, then she stripped and lay on one of the thwarts, legs dangling over the side. Sailing in the Indian ocean, in daytime and away from the shelter of the islands, was a new experience for both of them. Presumably there had been marine life all around them in the Straits, but they had not seen it. Now they were besieged by flying fish, and surrounded by dolphins. They even saw the sharper, more sinister fin of a shark, but it kept its distance.

Harry watched the clouds, which rose slowly. There was going to be rain, at least, in the not too distant future. But with every hour they were getting nearer their goal.

It was just after lunch that they saw the planes, three of them, high in the eastern sky. 'Now's the time for our survival drill,' Harry said.

They had rehearsed this several times during the past week, tied the ropes round their waists, and went over the side. 'I just hope that shark isn't still around,' Constance said.

They allowed the prahu to tow them along while they watched the planes, did not go beneath the hull until the aircraft started to wheel out of the sky. They were indeed Japanese, and they swooped low over the little boat. But as Harry had calculated, they saw no reason to waste either bombs or bullets on such a derelict target. After a few passes they flew away again, south towards Sumatra. 'Whee!' Constance panted, as she climbed back on board. 'I was scared. Tell me about Nicobar, Harry?'

'It belongs to India. It's a penal settlement, I think. There'll be English officials there. From Nicobar we'll get to the Andamans, and from the Andamans we'll get to India. We're just about there, Connie.'

'Then I'll get on with my tan,' she said, and looked up. 'Bother!' Clouds were obliterating the sun.

Harry calculated they had done about half the journey. There were only sixty-odd miles to go. But at four knots, which was the best he could coax out of the prahu, that meant fifteen hours. Soon there came a steady drizzle, which increased into a downpour. The wind dropped completely. 'Not much point in getting dressed,' Constance remarked, as the huge drops bounced off her skin. 'There's going to be a lot of it.'

The clouds were ominously black, and covered the whole sky now, thinning only far to the west. And still there was no wind. 'Put the rope on again,' he said.

'Whatever for?'

'Because I think we're going to need to be strapped in, very shortly. I *would* get dressed, if I were you, or you'll get rope burn. Tie the rope tightly round your waist and make sure it's secured to the thwart.'

She looked up at the sky. 'Is it going to be bad?'

'I don't know. I've never been in a real storm at sea. We don't want to take any chances.'

She tied on the rope, made it fast to the thwart, and then came aft to sit with him, beside the tiller, while they had a meal and drank some water. Rain was now filling the bottom of the boat, and as soon as they had finished eating he gave the helm to Constance and started baling. Then he realized that the drops were hitting the side of his face, and that the sail was filling as the prahu began to race through the water. 'Whee!' Constance shouted. 'I never knew this thing could travel so fast.'

'Neither did I,' Harry muttered. 'Can you hold her?'

'No problem,' she assured him, although the muscles were standing out in her arms and shoulders.

The wind increased dramatically; water came slopping over the gunwales, and Harry went on baling with all his strength.

Although it was early afternoon, it was as dark as midnight. Then the gloom was split by a sizzling bolt of lightning, accompanied by an enormous explosion of thunder directly above their heads. The first flash was followed by others, in such rapid succession that the day became a kaleidoscope of dark and light. The thunder was continuous, and so loud it almost blotted out thought. Constance was panting, and Harry abandoned baling to take the helm. The wind was now tearing at the little craft, threatening to roll it over, and the seas were already more than six feet from trough to crest. Harry instinctively turned the prahu away from the storm, running to the west. But she was going too fast, threatening to turn stern over bow. Constance was now in the bottom of the boat, baling with all her strength, and he dared not leave the tiller. He pulled out the knife, nowadays stowed in his belt, and slashed the sheets controlling the sail. Instantly it flew away from the mast, hung horizontally for a few minutes, and then disappeared altogether. Minutes later the foresail tore away.

Without the sails the prahu was more manageable, for a while. But the seas were getting bigger all the time, huge walls of dark blue topped with foaming white crests. Harry could hear the roaring behind him as they came up, and wrestled with the tiller to keep the prahu directly in front of them. Despite the rain and the cold, sweat poured down his face and chest. Never had he known such a physical ordeal combined with such physical danger, and such physical fear, too. Not even his single-handed fight with the six Japanese on the road north of Kuala Lumpur, or the sight of the green-clad men charging his position outside the reservoir, had been more than child's play besides facing the full strength of an angry ocean.

Yet at the same time he experienced a kind of exultation, that he was still alive, that he was doing battle with the greatest elemental force in nature, and holding his own. And that he was battling with Constance at his side, or at least at his feet, working tirelessly to keep the boat afloat, looking up every so often to give him a quick smile.

Then he heard the greatest roar of all, and looked over his shoulder at some twenty feet of solid water, rising high above the little boat, its curling crest about to overbalance and come down directly on them. 'Hold on!' he shouted unnecessarily: they were both holding on for dear life.

The wave surged on, and picked up the prahu. Harry lost control of the helm, and then had a sensation of flying through the air. He was brought up with a jerk as the rope round his waist tightened, then pitched forward again as it parted. Instinctively he threw out his arms and clutched at the mast, hugging his body against the wood, hearing it snap just above his head, but holding on with all his strength. He was engulfed in raging water; the prahu had turned upside down. Rivers of pain ran up and down his arms and filled his lungs as well; water pressed against his face. Then he was in the air again, briefly, before the boat was rolled over again. This happened several times; he lost track of how often.

For hours, his body was belaboured by wind and rain as he continued to cling to his stump of a mast. He never knew for how long the storm raged, only gradually became aware that there was less noise, that the turmoil had subsided. Slowly, fearfully, he released the mast and sat up. The waves were still high, but they were not breaking, and though the wind was fresh, it was also warm. The thunder and lightning had departed, and there was even a trace of starlight visible high above him.

And the prahu still floated, waterlogged and mastless. He had survived.

He crawled aft. 'Connie! Connie, where are you?'

But like the jerrycans of water, the carefully-stowed fruit, their revolvers and the compass and charts, Constance had disappeared.

For several seconds Harry was too numbed even to think. Then he hurled himself aft, splashing through knee-deep water. 'Connie!' he yelled. 'Connie! Oh, my God, my darling! Where are you?' He burst into tears as there was no response. Then he saw the rope.

It trailed over the stern. Desperately he grabbed it. There was weight on the end. He pulled it in, hand over hand, peering into the darkness. Constance came up to the side, and a last pull on the rope, which was secured under her armpits, brought her up to and over the gunwale. 'Connie!' he said, dropping to his knees beside her, praying for a movement. 'Wake up, Connie, please. I do love you so.'

'I love you too,' she muttered.

Constance had been in the water for several hours, and could not stop shivering. Harry held her in his arms for the rest of the night, up to their thighs in water, praying for light. When it finally came, and the sun rose out of a clear sky, it rapidly became very hot. But now they were faced with a new, and insurmountable problem.

They were clinging to a waterlogged hulk, with no food or water, and now that the wind had dropped, no means of moving. 'Are we going to die, Harry?' she asked.

'I'm afraid it doesn't look too good,' he admitted.

'Do you know,' she said. 'I don't care any more. We know that Mark will be looked after. And we found each other before the end. That's all that matters.' She gave a little sigh. 'I would have liked to see him again, though. Just once.'

'Yes,' Harry said.

They were too thirsty, and exhausted, to talk much more. Harry toyed with the idea of having them drink salt water, but everything he had ever read seemed to suggest that was a quick way to thirst-madness; it would be better to hope for a rain shower—they might be able to get something from that.

But there seemed little hope of rain, as the sun rose higher into a cloudless sky. At least Constance was no longer shivering. Instead she was lying so still, half in and half out of the water that he touched her every so often to make sure she was alive, and was invariably rewarded with a wan smile.

But they were going to die. He could not see any possible outcome. He felt bitter about that. They had been married only just over a year, and they had done so little in that time, with each other. They had never been to a dance together, except on the night they had met. They had never gone on holiday together. They had never bought a house, or a car, together.

But they had created a son, together, who would carry on the Brand name. And who would never know where and how his parents had died. They would just have disappeared off the face of the earth.

But they would have done so together.

He reached out his hand to touch her again, and she raised her head, but instead of smiling at him her face became contorted with terror.

Harry twisted his head, and looked at a huge area of disturbed water, out of which there was emerging the conning tower of a submarine. 'Oh, Jesus,' he muttered. But even a Japanese prison camp promised a chance of survival, and there was none on the hulk of the prahu. He pushed himself up and waved his arms, gazed almost in disbelief at the officer who had appeared on the tower and was now climbing down the ladder to the deck, followed by several seamen—they were wearing white shorts.

'Captain Harry Brand, First Battalion South Midlands Light Infantry? And Mrs Brand?' Lieutenant Commander Bull scratched his head as he looked at the two half-naked and exhausted people standing before the desk in his tiny cabin; the submarine had already submerged again, having found more than anyone on board had expected from its inspection of the drifting derelict. 'Where the devil did you spring from, Captain?'

'Singapore, via Sumatra,' Harry told him.

'Good grief. Well, we have some hot food for you, and then we'll see about some clothes ...'

'And a bath,' Constance said. 'I so want a bath.'

'I think we can manage a shower, Mrs Brand.'

'May I ask where you are taking us?'

'We are currently based in Trincomalee. Does that suit you?'

'Anywhere I can get back into uniform suits me, Commander.'

'You don't have a battalion any more, Captain. You do know that? Singapore fell a fortnight ago.'

'I still have a war to fight, Commander. And a lot of comrades to avenge.'

Bull looked at Constance.

'When you've been right down at the bottom, Commander,' Constance said. 'In every possible sense. The only way left is up. We intend to do that, together.'

This Large Print Book for the Partially sighted, who cannot read normal print, is published under the auspices of

THE ULVERSCROFT FOUNDATION

THE ULVERSCROFT FOUNDATION

. . . we hope that you have enjoyed this Large Print Book. Please think for a moment about those people who have worse eyesight problems than you . . . and are unable to even read or enjoy Large Print, without great difficulty.

You can help them by sending a donation, large or small to:

**The Ulverscroft Foundation,
1, The Green, Bradgate Road,
Anstey, Leicestershire, LE7 7FU,
England.**
or request a copy of our brochure for more details.

The Foundation will use all your help to assist those people who are handicapped by various sight problems and need special attention.

Thank you very much for your help.